STORM
WARRIOR

STORM WARRIOR

DANI HARPER

Text copyright © 2013 Dani Harper
All rights reserved.
Printed in the United States of America.

Published by Montlake Romance
PO Box 400818
Las Vegas, NV 89140

ISBN-13: 9781477805947
ISBN-10: 147780594X
Library of Congress Control Number: 2013931717

For my hero, my Rhys, Ronald Joe Silvester

"Some day you will be old
enough to start reading fairy
tales again."

—*C. S. Lewis*

PROLOGUE

~7∿

Black Mountains, Wales
AD 92

The howling of dogs in the distance told him his Roman keep-
ers had found his trail again. Rhys spat out a curse, along
with some blood, and forced himself to keep going.

The site of Isca Silurum, the fort that housed the Second
Augusta Legion, was a broad, flat plain in a bend of the River
Usk. It was less than a day's easy march southward to the ocean,
but Rhys had headed north and west to the interior. North and
west toward his tribal lands. North and west to the hills, to the
rough and rocky terrain that might discourage the many search
parties and their savage dogs.

So far, the rugged ground had only slowed them down. After
three days, it had become obvious—the Romans were determined not to let their favorite gladiator go.

He was determined to remain free.

The landscape was beginning to look familiar as he left the
southern lands behind him, lands that belonged to another tribe
overrun by the Romans. After three decades of war, the remaining sons of their once-proud leaders had been rounded up and
sent to Rome, not as prisoners but as students. Education and
assimilation were devastatingly effective at controlling a conquered people. Rhys knew that the young men would return

to their homes every bit as Roman as their overlords. For all he knew, the same thing was happening in his own tribe and clan, perhaps in his own village. If there was anything, anyone, left of it. Like all the Celtic tribes in this part of the country, his clan had struggled for decades to repel the Roman invaders. The tribes had defended their borders ferociously, held the armored aggressors back for a full generation, but the Romans were relentless. The armored troops had withdrawn for a few years in order to quell a huge Celtic uprising east in Brethon. But when the Romans had finished slaughtering the warrior queen, Boudicca, and her thousands, they had returned to Rhys's land with a vengeance. He hadn't been old enough to hold a bow when the Romans targeted the spiritual heart of his people by falling upon the great sacred island of Ynys Môn and slaying all the druids there. He had barely reached his full height when his father and older brothers were killed in a fierce battle to defend their village hill fort.

Sadly, their deaths had not purchased their people's freedom. All the Celtic tribes fought with courage and skill, but they were no match for the organized and disciplined troops of the empire. It wasn't long before the Romans declared victory and levied taxes.

Not all the Celts were conquered, however.

In the past, they'd learned the art of war not only from hunting but from conducting secret raids on other tribes. It was a game of sorts that benefited all. One tribe would steal six fine cattle. The other tribe would retaliate by taking four strong horses. Each tribe gained new blood for their herds at the same time that they practiced the art of stealth. It helped keep them all in fighting trim. In telling the stories of his raids, Rhys's father had impressed upon him the importance of surprise: *always do the unexpected.*

An older and battle-hardened Rhys used those tactics as he began to lead raids on Roman patrols, using stealth and strategy to pick them off in the dense forests and misted hills. When he was growing up, archery had been used in hunting rather than battle, but it was well suited to the style of fighting he and his followers practiced now. Silent and effective, bows could deal death at a distance and strike terror into the hearts of the survivors. And while the Romans were looking in the direction the arrows had come from, a second party could easily emerge from the opposite shadows and cut them down to the last man with sword and dagger. It wasn't long before spooked soldiers had given Rhys a nickname, whispered over campfires with many backward glances into the darkness: the Bringer of Death.

The patrols had dwindled for a time, even stopped for a while. Then one day a scruffy-looking unit had wandered into Rhys's territory. Unshaven, they looked lazy and lax. Older men these, some with unsoldierlike bellies. Laughing and talking foolishly like troops on leave, not a unit on patrol. They even fell out of the disciplined march from time to time, drinking from wineskins that were not army issue. It wasn't all that surprising—Rome seldom sent its best and brightest to the far-flung frontier once a land had been subjugated. Yet, the patrol hadn't fallen into any of the tribe's traps, appearing instead to blunder around them as if by pure chance.

Rhys had thought about that many times since. It should have warned him that all was not as it seemed. It should have warned him…

The patrol had meandered off the path and was lolling on a riverbank when Rhys and his followers launched their ambush. No sooner had they broken cover than they found themselves facing Roman swords, looking into the sharp eyes of not only seasoned but elite soldiers. The undisciplined foolishness had been a clever facade.

But Rhys and his men were seasoned too. The battle was fierce; the riverbank was soon slippery with blood as Romans and Celts alike met blades. No one prevailed. They were evenly matched it seemed, until suddenly the sound of many horses, galloping hard, could be heard over the fight.

The Romans had timed their trap well. The elite unit had held the Celts' attention long enough for a mounted patrol to catch up to them. Rhys yelled out for his followers to retreat just before a weighted net was thrown over him. A blow to the head silenced him, and he spiraled into darkness.

He'd awakened a prisoner, chained by the neck to four of his men, the only survivors of the battle. On the long march south to Isca Silurum, two had died from their wounds. Once at the Roman fort, two more had been used as targets during a training exercise. Rhys had expected to be next, but the Romans had other plans for the Bringer of Death.

The newly built amphitheater just outside the fort walls needed fodder for its bloody spectacles. Intending to make an example of him, his captors had thrown him into the sandy arena with a wild boar. Pain-maddened from a number of oozing flesh wounds, the massive creature bellowed its fury and shook its scythe-like tusks at Rhys. Someone in the stands tossed him a broken sword, barely the length of a dagger, which caused much laughter. The laughter faded when Rhys nimbly dodged and feinted, staying one step ahead of the charging animal. The crowd had expected the Celt to die and quickly. Yet, it wasn't long before the boar squealed horribly and thrashed on the ground with its throat cut.

Still gripping the handle of the sword, Rhys had stood quietly and watched the boar's blood soaking into the sand, certain that his own blood would soon follow. Instead, he had been relegated to a cell and brought out again the next day. And the next. The Bringer of Death proved true to his name. For two years, against all comers, against man and beast alike, Rhys had been forced to fight for his life. The 5,500 soldiers stationed at Isca Silurum wagered their pay on him, alternately cheering him and cursing him according to their wins and losses.

These men were the same ones who chased him now. He should have known the Romans wouldn't easily give up their main source of entertainment here on the frontier. Plus, the legion leaders were no doubt glad to have a task to assign to their bored soldiers, all of whom were likely betting on which man would find the gladiator first. Ironically, Rhys's escape was simply providing one more amusement for his captors.

Not that his escape had been easy. He'd broken the jailer's neck and garroted two guards, but the second had managed to stab Rhys before dying. The wound was just under his ribs, and pain had sawed at him with every step since. He'd suffered worse, but the loss of blood was starting to tell. He was tiring fast, and sometimes he was dizzy. He pressed the heel of his hand to the bundle of dry moss that he'd bound to the wound and willed himself to go on.

The dogs howled again, closer this time. These were no game hounds but big war dogs, accustomed to hunting men. Accustomed to *killing* men. Rhys had used every clever trick he could think of to stay a scant step ahead, to buy time so he could reach the hill country.

Always do the unexpected. His father's words came back to him as he sought to throw the dogs and their handlers off the trail once and for all.

Rhys doubled back and headed for a steep hillside, angling his way downwind of the Roman hunters until he reached a shallow noisy creek. He could cover the rest of the distance by traveling up the center of the wide stream. The noise of the tumbling water would cover any splashing. He touched his fingertips to his collarbone, to the blue hound tattoo that marked him, and breathed a prayer to the gods.

The water was cold enough to make him gasp, but it cleared his head, as did the jarring pain in his side. He jogged doggedly through the creek, sucking air through gritted teeth, one hand clamped tight against the wound. The bleeding was worse now, but he dared not slow down.

Shivering, Rhys left the stream at the base of the hill and considered. If he could climb its sheer slope, the dogs would be unable to follow. If he couldn't, he'd fall to his death. *Still free*, he thought; he'd still be free. As long as he could see the sacred blue of the sky as he died...By all the gods, anything would be better than returning to the dark, windowless cell of the arena.

His breath hitched in his lungs as he began the ascent, pain knifing through his injury until his entire left side throbbed savagely. The hillside appeared taller and steeper by the minute, and it seemed to take forever before he was even above the trees. He felt exposed on the rock face, although he knew the hunters' eyes would be searching the ground for his trail. Even if they did look up, the forest branches would likely shield him from their sight.

Nothing would shield him if he fell. Rhys had to stop more and more frequently, clinging to handholds with eyes closed until dizziness passed. It was early summer, and he was sweating from exertion, but he felt as cold as if it were winter. There was a strange tinny taste in his mouth. He knew that if he looked down, the rocks would be smeared with his blood.

Finally, he gained a high, narrow ledge that was supporting three late-blossoming rowan bushes and rested his elbows on it, gasping for air like a fish. The pain had become a live thing that raged in the cage of his body and shook his very bones. Rhys grasped the base of one of the bushes, seeking to steady himself, hoping that by resting a few moments he could somehow find enough strength to continue. Knowing that he had little left. He was spent, bled out like a deer with an arrow in it. His vision was narrowing. Behind the blooming rowans, he could see no rock face, only darkness.

Gaping darkness...

By all the gods, there was a cave! He fought to drag his body onto the ledge. Agony reared up like an angry bear, slashing and biting at him. Still he struggled on, teeth clamped against the scream that threatened to rip from his throat. Just as it seemed certain that he would black out and tumble to the ground below, he managed to heave his broad-shouldered frame securely onto the rocky shelf, with the thick trunks of the sturdy bushes between him and the open air. Lungs heaving and heart threatening to smash through his chest, Rhys reverently touched his collarbone just as his eyes rolled back in his head.

The full moon was high in the heavens when he awoke at last. The pain awoke too, chewing at his side the way a hungry wolf tears at a carcass. It drove the grogginess from his mind, and he lay blinking on his back. It was good to see the sky, he thought. Good to see the dark, deep blue, an ocean upon which the stars could sail...He wondered if his father and brothers were up there, his sister. The members of his tribe who had stood against the Roman invaders. All dead, all slain...

The Romans. Immediately, he listened for the sounds of dogs, of hunters, but there was nothing but the whir of insects, the calls of night birds, and the barely audible squeak of bats. His pursuers had likely camped for the night, but he could see neither fire-glow nor smoke from the forest below. Rhys rolled to his good side, although his wound screamed at him just the same. He stared out from between the glistening flower clusters of the rowan bushes with his teeth chattering uncontrollably. Tiny white petals had snowed down around him as he slept, but they did nothing to stave the chill from his body. With a strange kind of detachment, he knew he would die if he remained on the ledge—was likely dying anyway.

It would be easier to die.

Yet, the gods had decreed that one must struggle to live, and so Rhys once more forced himself to move. His head swam and his stomach lurched until he thought he might vomit from the pain. He didn't have the strength left to stand, but he needed shelter. If he could just get warm, it might be safe to rest for a while…On all fours, he made his way inside the dark cave, reaching out a hand from time to time to feel his way along the wall. The stone was dry, and as he struggled farther into the darkness, the floor of the cave became a soft mix of sand and dead leaves. Rhys inhaled carefully, trying to draw a scent from his surroundings, alert for any sign that the cave was the den of a predator. He smelled nothing but his own sweat and blood. He moved on, inches at a time, desperate to get deeper into the cave before his ebbing strength gave out entirely.

Without warning, the blackness of the cave's interior gave way to gray. At first, he thought he'd gotten turned around and was somehow facing the entrance again, but a glance over his shoulder showed the rowan bushes against the starry bright sky behind him as they should be. Ahead of him, though, there was light where there should have been none. Light, faint but growing steadily, was coming from *inside* the cave.

Mere heartbeats later, Rhys found himself nearly blinded by an uncanny brilliance, a white light that shamed the full moon. He squinted into the light and, for a brief, wild moment, considered flinging himself off the ledge or perhaps calling out to the Romans who were hunting him. But pain, exhaustion, and blood loss combined to betray him. One thought remained as he passed out, a phrase every child in his village had heard often, a warning that every elder delivered in harsh whispers...

Beware the Tylwyth Teg.

ONE

~⁊⌑~

Caerleon, Wales
Twenty-First Century

The dog was back.

Dr. Morgan Edwards tried to focus her attention on the tour guide as he related the history of the ancient Roman amphitheater. The enormous arena, capable of seating nearly six thousand, had been built outside the walls of Isca Silurum, a legionary fort. Legend held that, in another time, this part of Wales had been a favored base for King Arthur himself.

Morgan had been born and raised in America. Fascinated by her grandmother's country, she was usually keen to learn all she could about it. Yet, her attention kept returning to the huge black mastiff that sat silently by a square-cut stone. He surveyed her with the great, sad eyes of his massive breed, a breed more ancient than the ruins around it.

I'll bet you eat a lot, fella.

Morgan had treated only three mastiffs in her busy veterinary practice. Her clients by and large appeared to prefer beagles and dachshunds, Labs and poodles. Her clinic in Spokane Valley, Washington, saw a few Great Danes and Saint Bernards as well, but the great black dog would dwarf even those big breeds. She knew that mastiffs had been used by the Romans for war—their fearful size making them lethal weapons. They had been used in the arena as well, perhaps right where she was standing. The thought made her shiver, or maybe it was the strangeness of having seen the mastiff on every day of her trip, at every stop. While the dog never came close, he never failed to make an appearance. At first, she'd thought there were an awful lot of the monstrous dogs in this small country. That is, until she'd spotted the distinctive metal collar around his muscled neck. It was wide and ornate, almost like a broad silver torque. Perhaps it was a replica of some ancient design. Maybe the animal was part of the tour, a living prop?

She grabbed the flowery sleeve of her traveling buddy, a tall white-haired woman named Gwen, whom she'd met at the beginning of the tour. "He's here again."

The older woman looked over her glasses with bright eyes, spotting the animal at once, even as she clutched her travel bag to her chest. "How fascinating! I wonder what kind of energy such a creature would have. Probably negative, don't you think?"

"Energy?"

"I'm sure it's a *grim*, you know, just like the ones in my books. A *barghest*. What the Welsh call a *gwyllgi*, though goodness knows I'm not pronouncing it right. A messenger from the faery realm."

"A messenger of what?"

"Why, whoever sees a grim is usually dead in a month and almost always by violent means."

"Great. So, it's the canine version of the Grim Reaper?"

"Not quite. A grim only heralds death, it doesn't collect souls. At least that's how the old stories go, but I've never read of a grim being out in broad daylight, have you? Are its eyes glowing red?" Gwen frowned as she strained to see.

Morgan hid a smile. As a child, her *nainie*—the Welsh word for grandma—had told her stories about the grim, but she hadn't thought of it in connection with the flesh and blood animal that sat not thirty yards away. Gwen loved all things supernatural, however, and *of course* she would think of the dog in paranormal terms first. *To each his own.* Morgan chose to humor her friend, dutifully shading her pale-blue eyes and squinting. The dog's baleful eyes seemed amber, almost golden. "Nope, not even bloodshot," she reported.

"Well, it's probably just an ordinary dog then, but I suppose we shouldn't take chances. I don't want it heralding my demise or yours." Gwen laughed, a pretty sound that reminded Morgan of delicate glass wind chimes, and turned to follow the group that was now shuffling its way to the bus. Morgan looked back at the dog. She'd always had a deep affinity for animals, a connection to them, and although the mastiff was intimidating, she sensed a great sadness radiating from him.

She'd taken only a few steps toward the animal when the bus driver sounded the high-pitched horn, signaling it was time to leave. *Crap.* "Do you need help? Are you lost?" she called out to the dog. She'd often been teased for talking to animals as if they were people, but she felt strongly that animals understood intent if not words—although many understood words better than their owners gave them credit for. "If you could just tell me what you want, I'd love to help you." The dog blinked suddenly, rapidly, but otherwise didn't move. His expression remained mournful, his tail unmoving. To Morgan's practiced eye, the animal didn't appear neglected. His black coat was as glossy as a raven's wing, and although he was lean, she could see no ribs in the broad, muscled body, no evidence of hunger. What did the dog want? Why was he following the tour bus? And why had the other tourists failed to take notice of the unusual canine? They should have been talking about it, quizzing the staff, and taking photographs. Instead, no one seemed to pay the dog any mind except Morgan and Gwen.

The horn sounded a second time, and reluctantly she obeyed. After she took her seat beside Gwen, she looked out the window, but the dog was nowhere to be seen. There were only the rolling green hills and the silent ruins.

～

Wales had plenty of large modern motels, but this tour featured smaller historic lodgings. Part of the tour group was booked into the Three Salmon Inn, and the rest, including Morgan and Gwen, in the smaller Cross Keys Hotel. Morgan thought the centuries-old building was charming and comfortable, but to Gwen it was downright exciting.

"They have a ghost here, you know. Some say it's a serving girl, and others say it's a monk."

Morgan's eyebrows went up as she perused the menu in the hotel dining room. "Isn't there a big difference between the two?"

"Well, a mysterious figure in a long gown could be either one, now couldn't it? It says in the pamphlet that's all that anyone has seen of it. I wish *I* could see it."

"You'd really like to see a ghost, wouldn't you? Most people would run the other way."

"Most people would rather not have proof that other worlds exist," said Gwen. "But I prefer to be open to all possibilities."

"My grandmother used to say something very similar."

Gwen smiled as if the remark pleased her immensely. "I think the roast beef sounds good, don't you?"

"Hmm? Oh, yes. I like those little Yorkshire puddings that come with it. Although I've never understood why they call them puddings—they're much more like a crispy little bun."

The waiter collected their menus and their orders, and Gwen pulled a book from her handbag. "Look what I found in the gift shop here."

Morgan took the proffered book—*A Field Guide to the Ghosts of Wales*—and thumbed through it. The older woman had collected several paranormal writings along the tour and probably had enough to fill a suitcase by now. Morgan had never met anyone who was so enthralled by supernatural topics. Well, there *was* her veterinary partner Jay...He seemed to be enthralled with anything that was strange or unusual. She was certain she'd never get a word in edgewise if Jay and Gwen should ever meet.

"Every single castle, hotel, pub, and crossroads we've seen so far has allegedly been haunted," Morgan said. "I'm starting to wonder if the locals make up ghost stories on purpose to attract tourists."

Gwen laughed heartily, her voice like a cheerful cadence of bells. "Well, now, child, they've certainly attracted me!" Still chuckling, she took the book back and began reading a passage aloud.

Morgan didn't have to wonder what her Welsh grandmother would have said. Nainie Jones had been certain of the existence of spirits, just as she had firmly believed in the Tylwyth Teg, the Fair Ones. As a child, Morgan had listened for hours to her grandma's faery stories, hanging on every word. Believing. But by the time Morgan reached her early teens, her belief had naturally faded. More than that, she'd discovered the fascinating world of science and already knew she wanted a career in veterinary medicine. She still loved to hear Nainie's stories, of course, but had mentally filed them with Santa Claus and the Easter Bunny. Her grandmother had sensed the change.

"Some people don't believe because they're afraid to, or they believe and hope they're never proved right. There are many things all around us that are old and powerful," Nainie had explained one day. "Magics and mysterious realms, strange peoples not of this world. They're not to be feared but to be respected, and it's long been a gift in our family to know them. If you keep your heart and your mind open, one day *a leap of knowing* will come to you too." Nainie had pulled the shiny silver necklace from inside her dress and looped the long, cool chain around her granddaughter's neck. She pointed to the carved medallion with the smooth, polished stones surrounding it. "This has been in our family for generations, and it's time it came to you. Keep it with you until your heart calls for it, my darling one. It'll help you to have faith, and it'll show you truth when you need it most."

Morgan had had no idea what Nainie was talking about. It felt like another faery tale. *A leap of knowing*—what on earth was that? It sounded like her grandmother was talking about her uncanny ability to sense the future. After all, Nainie had always known who was at the door before they had a chance to knock, what was in the mail before the postman brought it, and sometimes what was going to happen to a friend or relative several days in advance. But Morgan didn't have a psychic bone in her body, as far as she could tell.

Her grandmother wouldn't explain further, just assured her that she would learn for herself in due time. Morgan was pleased with the necklace, however, and solemnly promised Nainie she would take good care of it. Later, alone in her room, Morgan promised herself to someday visit Wales and see the land that had sparked all the wonderful old stories. Years had passed before she could finally manage the trip, but she wasn't disappointed. The tiny country was beautiful, rich with quaint charm and friendly people, and she felt comfortingly close to her beloved grandmother at every turn.

I guess that's what I was really looking for. Morgan deeply missed the woman who had raised her. As Gwen finished reading the tale of the Cross Keys ghost, Morgan smiled at her. "You know, I've always wanted to visit Wales, but it's been extra nice to meet you on the tour and travel together. I hope it doesn't offend you if I say it's a little bit like having Nainie along."

"What a lovely thing to say, dear," said Gwen. "How could I be offended when it's obvious you loved her very much?"

"I guess I talk about her a lot, don't I?"

"Not the way you think. You point out places and things she's spoken of. Why don't you tell me more? You said that you lived with her."

"My parents died in a boating accident when I was five, and so I went to live with my grandmother in Spokane…" They were all the family each other had left, but it had been enough. Nainie Jones had a generous spirit and had loved Morgan with a marvelous blend of humor and patience. And Morgan had felt her grandmother's pride in her at every turn, from the first time she walked to kindergarten by herself to the day she left for veterinary college on a full scholarship.

"Nainie told me such wonderful stories, and she taught me through them too. If I did something wrong, she always had a story that would show me why I shouldn't do that again." Morgan laughed. "It usually worked, at least when I was younger. When you're sixteen, it's tough to be afraid of the Fair Ones stealing you away!"

Gwen's eyes twinkled. "At that age, I imagine not being asked to dance would be far more terrifying than the faery folk."

"I didn't know what *terrifying* was until Nainie died." Morgan had been in her third year of veterinary school when it had happened. "It was so unexpected. She'd always seemed so healthy, so full of life. But she passed away in her sleep. The doctor said it was her heart."

"I'm so sorry, dear. You must have been devastated."

"I was." It had been a terrible blow, bringing back all the pain and loss she'd felt as a little girl when her parents didn't come home. And *fear*...This time, she was totally and completely alone in the world.

Study was therapy and so was work, and Morgan had thrown herself ever deeper into both. Within a few years of graduation, she had built up a thriving veterinary practice and had brought in two partners to help handle the volume of clients. The extra hands meant she could finally take a break, and it was long overdue. Morgan passed over the bright flyers advertising exotic destinations and told the travel agent to book her a trip to Wales.

"So here I am," Morgan finished. "I can't help but wonder if Nainie would be pleased if she knew I was here."

Gwen's bright eyes looked far away for a moment. "I think those who have gone on are very happy to know that they are still cherished." Then her gaze turned mischievous. "And I'm certain your grandmother would have enjoyed it thoroughly when you asked the shopkeeper for a purple cat yesterday."

Morgan put her hands to her face. "Omigod, that was *so* embarrassing! I grew up hearing Nainie speak the language, but I never quite got the hang of the pronunciation myself. You're right; she sure would have laughed at that one." In fact, Morgan could almost hear the rich, deep chuckle that had seemed so huge for such a little woman. No one had a laugh quite like that, although Morgan had heard snippets and echoes of it on her trip, especially in a family pub the night before last. It was said that the Welsh laughed with their entire bodies, and it certainly seemed to be true.

Gwen looked over her shoulder, then back at Morgan. "You know, dear, I'm not really up to date on what girls consider handsome these days. Tell me, do you think that silver-haired fellow at the bar is good looking?"

"Mmm, not bad at all. But the one standing by the door has a much better butt."

It was a game they'd played almost every night of the tour, and it set the tone for the rest of the evening. The two women talked and giggled like high school girls throughout the meal, even more so when Gwen ordered chocolate cheesecake for each of them.

"This is so decadent!" Morgan laughed, picking off a decorative curl of shaved chocolate and popping it into her mouth.

"Not at all. One must take their pleasures where they can find them. Besides, I heard one of the ladies on the bus say that calories consumed while vacationing don't count."

"I sure hope not, or I'm going to have to pay an extra baggage fee on the plane just for all the pounds I'm gaining."

A woman with a seeing-eye dog passed their table, and the black Lab reminded Morgan of the strange dog that had been following the bus. A sudden impulse had her flagging the waiter. "Do you have a bone left over from that lovely roast?" she asked him. "It's for a pet."

"Of course. I'll be glad to wrap that up for you, miss."

As he disappeared, Gwen leaned over. "My goodness. Is that for what I think it is?"

"I can't help it," Morgan said and laughed. "I'm a veterinarian, so I have a compulsion to look after animals. And if I wasn't a vet, I'd *still* be worrying that the dog was hungry. Or lonely. Or something. I thought I'd get the bone just in case." In case she ever got close enough to the huge black mastiff to offer it.

~

The hotel room was plunged into blackness when Gwen switched off her reading lamp. "Oh my. Is that too dark for you, dear?"

"No, it's just fine, thanks. I sleep better when it's like this." In fact, it was almost *country* dark—obviously, there were no streetlights on this side of the building. Morgan was pleasantly reminded of the old farmstead she had moved to just outside of Spokane Valley. There, the dark was peaceful. She seldom even turned on the yard light, preferring the stars and the moon at most.

"You're a brave girl. Aren't you even a teeny bit frightened to have that great black beast following you everywhere? Why, it gives me the shivers to know that it's a harbinger of death."

Morgan imagined Gwen had the same kind of shivers that many people did—there was a certain deliciousness to such fear and an eagerness for more. It was human nature to be fascinated by mysterious things, especially scary things. "I'm sure he's not following me; he's just following the bus."

As a vet, Morgan had observed that pets could develop just as many neuroses and odd behaviors as their owners. In her own practice, there was an Alsatian that insisted on following the family's kids to school and waiting for them outside the fenced grounds—even though the school was four miles away and the children were driven there. The dog's behavior was understandable on some level, but the urge persisted even if it was a weekend and the children were at home. Unless tied up, the dog would make the journey, every single day.

The mastiff must have a similar compulsion. Why he chose to follow the tour bus around, Morgan couldn't imagine. Maybe the bigger the dog, the bigger the object of its obsession. She'd already checked with the bus driver, but the man was new and had never seen the animal before. The young tour guide was no help either. Thank goodness there were just a handful of miles between towns in this very tiny country. Still, she fell asleep wishing she could do something for the enormous canine.

The dream began with a scent. The smell of cool, damp earth and rain and the faint whiff of horses. She was naked, lying on furs and facing the open door of a tent made of skins. The breeze was slight but enough to make her shiver and cause her nipples to harden. Her ass was warm, however. In fact, her entire backside was heated, pressed tightly against a very large, very male body. Not a stranger, although in the whimsical reality of dreams, she didn't know who he was. She wasn't afraid, although she could feel the rock-hard muscles of his arms, his chest. He was a powerful man, yet every instinct told her that she knew him as well as she knew herself—she could feel the bond between them more powerfully than even his touch. As if on cue, his large hand, calloused and work-hardened, slid over her hip and traveled gently upward. Her skin tingled deliciously beneath the rough palm, and she shivered again, not from cold but from pleasure as his hand rubbed over her breasts, fondling and squeezing.

His hot breath tickled the back of her neck as he applied soft open-mouthed kisses and measured bites. His broad fingers tugged softly at her nipples until she felt an answering tug deep in her core. She writhed, impatient for more. His hand slid between her legs where she was already slick. He teased at her clit then stroked her deeply until she gasped. *Now, now, now...*She ground her ass into his groin, feeling his erection thick and hot, wanting it inside her, filling her, claiming her…

Suddenly, a deafening crash overwhelmed all her senses. It filled the entire world, echoed and re-echoed, and Morgan sat bolt upright, clutching her ears. Where the hell was she? Lightning strobed away the darkness, and she recognized the hotel room.

Her head was ringing as she sat there, waiting for her heart rate to slow down. Although whether it was hammering from fright or arousal, she couldn't say. A cold blast of wind made her look up to see rain slanting inside the open window. *Oh crap.* Morgan got up, slipping a little on the wet hardwood floor as she reached for the window frame. Nothing happened. She struggled for several minutes to work the old sash window loose. It jerked and slid only an inch at a time, as she tried to remember if the classic advice to stay away from windows during thunderstorms was true. Finally, the casement was closed, and the storm, which must have been passing directly overhead when it awakened her, moved off toward the north.

Relieved, she was straightening the twisted and wet curtains when another flash of lightning made her stop dead and stare. A familiar creature, blacker than the night, sat at the edge of the parking lot. Looking up at her.

TWO

⚯

The electricity's out.

Morgan simultaneously jumped and yelped at Gwen's voice.

"Did I frighten you, dear? I'm so sorry."

"No, no, it's okay. The storm's made me jumpy, that's all." Morgan could hear the clicking as Gwen pulled at the lamp chain several times to no effect.

"I was just saying the electricity is out. Perhaps, I should go downstairs to see if they've a torch we can have."

"That's okay, I can go. I'm already up."

"That's very sweet of you, thank you. But mind you be careful on the staircase and promise to tell me all about it if you see any ghosts. It's just the kind of night for it."

Morgan dressed quickly in the darkness. She suspected her sweater was inside out and one of her bra straps felt twisted around, but such things didn't matter under her jacket. She promised Gwen to ask about some milk for her and left the room. She was thankful to see a scattering of emergency lights in the hallway and along the sweeping stairs. Gwen's ghosts didn't worry Morgan—she was much more concerned about breaking her neck.

The lobby that had seemed so quaint and charming a few hours ago looked different in the dark. With its antique furniture and heavy woodwork, it resembled a scene from an old movie. A horror movie, maybe something with Boris Karloff or Bela Lugosi. All it needed were cobwebs. Morgan's ringing of the countertop bell brought no response, but she wasn't surprised, considering it was the middle of the night. She hadn't been overly optimistic about finding a flashlight—what Gwen called a torch. On impulse, she borrowed an umbrella that someone had left by the door and headed outside.

The storm had moved fast. Lightning now flickered in the hills, and thunder growled faintly after it. The rain hadn't diminished, however. Morgan gripped the umbrella with both hands and turned it against the wind, hoping it wouldn't blow inside out. She'd have a hard time explaining to its owner what she'd been doing. She wasn't sure she could explain it to herself. She just had this burning need to make sure the dog was all right.

Rain blew under the umbrella and soaked her until she finally gave up on it altogether and folded it under her arm. She walked around the building slowly, using a hand to feel her way along the walls. The entire town was dark, its quaint streetlights useless. There were candles lit in the windows of the pub across the road, but there were no other signs of life as she rounded the corner to the back. Suddenly she caught sight of the dog. He was right where she had seen him from the window, still sitting in the mostly empty parking lot. And still staring at her.

Morgan hurried under the back-door awning. It didn't offer a lot of protection from the sideways rain, but it was something. "Come here, boy. C'mon, it's too miserable to be out here. Come inside with me like a good boy, c'mon." She crouched and waggled her fingers, then drew the tinfoil packet from her pocket and unwrapped the roast bone she'd saved. "Look what I brought for you." She waved it, hoping the animal would catch the scent. While she might have imagined the dog's surprise, there was no denying the dog wasn't moving. As still as a concrete statue, he stared at her as always.

"All right, then, bud, I'll come to you." She was already soaked to the skin, so a little more rain couldn't hurt. Experience told her that making eye contact with a strange dog communicated challenge or threat, and so she kept her eyes averted. She stopped five or six yards away and gently tossed the bone at his feet. Then she turned sideways and just stood there, waiting. Ordinarily that was a clear canine invitation to investigate. But the dog didn't come over to sniff her as she had hoped. Nor did she hear any sounds to indicate that he was checking out the bone. She turned her head and was amazed to find the animal was gone! The roast bone lay untouched on the wet pavement.

"Damn it," she muttered in frustration. Leaving the bone, she hurried back to the hotel and fumbled in her soggy pocket with cold, numb fingers for a key card. Which was worse, Morgan wondered, that she was being followed by a disappearing dog or that she'd been dumb enough to go out in such weather to try to help it? *I could have been struck by lightning, for heaven's sake.* And just what would she have done with the dog if she'd managed to coax him inside? The canine outweighed most humans. It would be like wedging a wet pony into her cozy hotel room. At least she had an understanding roommate. Gwen would no doubt have welcomed a chance to test the dog's energy or some such thing.

Morgan replaced the umbrella in the lobby, then decided to leave her soggy shoes by the radiator there. She peeled off her socks and hung them on the radiator as well—they wouldn't catch fire, would they?—then made her way down the hall barefoot, guided by the strange yellowish glow of the emergency lights. The hotel had a quaint cooler that offered slices of pie and cake, squares of cheese, and biscuits. Luckily, there was a pint of milk left, and she dropped the last of her pocket change into the cigar box next to the cooler. At least her roommate would have her sleep aid. Morgan wondered idly if any of the foods could help her resume dreaming. *Cake before bed will give you nightmares,* Nainie Jones used to say. Wasn't there anything that would give you incredibly sexy fantasies? Morgan would like nothing better than to continue the amazing dream she'd been having. Well, one thing could be better—if she really *did* have a lover she felt so deeply connected with.

At this point, no lover had appeared in her life at all. She had had plenty of dates and boyfriends, but no relationships that were truly serious, nothing that coaxed the embers of her heart into flame—or whatever was supposed to happen. *It's probably my own fault.* Morgan had never really looked for love, always supposing that she'd find someone *later.* Later, after graduation, after college, after she got through her practicum, after she set up her clinic, after she had more time…To be honest, she'd nursed a small hope that she'd meet someone special while she was on vacation. And wasn't that just narrowing things down for the universe? *Don't bother me with love until three weeks in such and such a year when I'm finally on holiday.*

She laughed at herself even as she carefully watched her feet on the stairs—and she didn't see the monstrous dog sitting above her on the landing until she was nearly eye level with it! She yelped and gripped the railing, nearly losing both the milk and her footing. But in the seconds it took her to recover and look again, the creature had vanished.

"Okay, now this is just crazy." Morgan looked down the hall. There was no place for such a big animal to hide. The emergency lights were sparse and faint, but she wouldn't miss seeing a black dog against a yellow wall. "I'm obviously overtired," she muttered. She'd been thinking way too much about the dog lately—small wonder that she thought she saw him for an instant. The fact that she hadn't been thinking about the dog *at all* in the moments before she saw him notwithstanding. It was just a strange night, and she needed to go back to bed.

Gwen was delighted with the milk. Morgan was just grateful that her bare feet and wet clothes wouldn't be noticed in the dark. She toweled off her hair in the bathroom and hoped her clothes would be dry by morning. Her flannel sleep shirt felt like bliss. The bed did too; although, it had been a whole lot warmer in her dream.

She fell asleep thinking about the sexy stranger, but she dreamed of the dog instead. She was back in America, back in the Spokane Valley. Going about her daily tasks. Working at the clinic, shopping, banking, picking up the mail. And everywhere she went, the enormous black creature was at her side. His broad back was level with her waist, and she could rest her hand there as she walked. She could feel the warmth from the dog, the texture of his fur. More than that, she felt as if he belonged there, had always been there.

When morning came, she was surprised to find that she missed him.

～

Kindness was in the woman's voice; concern warmed her pale-blue eyes. For *him*. Most people in his country either pretended not to see him or made a hasty departure. They knew what he was about, what his dark purpose was, and they feared him.

Not Morgan Edwards. She didn't seem to be aware of the significance of his presence or perhaps didn't care. Instead, she had noticed him, watched him, even worried about him. She'd ventured out in a storm to make sure he was all right, not knowing he was unaffected by the rain. Offered him food, not knowing he didn't eat. And finally, she had invited him inside.

Inside. He'd long forgotten what that was like. To be warm and comfortable, if he was able to feel such things, but also to be welcome. Wanted. Curiosity, in itself a novelty, compelled him to accept the woman's invitation, if only for a moment. He'd watched her with interest, admired the fearless efficiency in the way she moved. She'd been startled when she came face-to-face with him—but she hadn't screamed. He'd been startled too. Morgan Edwards was pretty by human standards and almost as finely featured as the fae themselves. Yet, while their hair was fine and icy white, hers was thick and glossy, its waves the color of a newly hulled chestnut. He didn't breathe, yet her scent had filled his nostrils, crept into his lungs to nestle by his unbeating heart and warm it. It shouldn't be possible.

He'd vanished then, returned to the elements outside, to the cold and familiar darkness. Yet a faint spark had been fanned to life inside him, some emotion he could not name. Emotion was a stranger, must be a stranger, and yet he felt something. Because of Morgan Edwards.

But the woman was marked, and he must not interfere. He was forbidden to interfere. *Destiny ruled over life and death*, the Tylwyth Teg had said, before charging him with his terrible task. *What destiny has decreed, you will herald. It cannot be altered or defied.* Yet, for the first time in centuries, he considered that perhaps the Fair Ones were wrong.

THREE

~~~

Spokane Valley, Washington, USA

B arely home a week, Morgan found herself on the run from morning to night, and this day was no exception. She'd had four surgeries that morning and several appointments and walk-ins in the afternoon. Most were for dogs and cats, but a snake, a chinchilla, and a tree frog came through the door as well. She'd spent an hour after the clinic closed poring through books and searching the Internet for the nutritional needs of pink-toed tarantulas, thanks to a frantic phone call from twelve-year-old Ryan White about his beloved Ozzie. The pictures creeped her out, but in the end Morgan was able to call Ryan back with some suggestions for Ozzie's diet.

Exhaustion dragged at her as she switched off the lights. The three animal health techs—Cindy, Melinda, and Russell—were working out wonderfully. As assistants, they had made a huge difference in the last few months, but the clinic was busier than ever. Maybe it was time to bring on a fourth vet. Jay was on call tonight, and Grady was already heading out to a local riding stable for a foaling. Morgan was just grateful it wasn't her turn as she locked the doors behind her. The clinic was located in an industrial park on the edge of town, and most people had gone home by now. It was blissfully quiet. She paused outside her car door to breathe in the cooling air, rich with the scents of late summer fields—

The attack came out of nowhere. She was grabbed by the shirtfront and pushed backward over the hood of her car. Morgan found herself face-to-face with a rough-looking man with a scraggly goatee. His bloodshot blue eyes were set in a pallid face marked with open sores, and he was holding a knife to her throat.

"I'll cut you, bitch. Understand? Where's your fuckin' purse?"

"In the car. It's in the car—in the trunk," she breathed, afraid to move.

"Why the hell's it in there? You lyin' to me?"

She held her hands up. "No. No. I don't need it in the clinic; it's in the way there. I lock it in the trunk where it's safe."

He snorted at that. Still holding the front of her shirt, he yanked her to her feet but didn't let go. "Open it," he said, waving the knife. Morgan fumbled for her keys with shaking fingers, then scrabbled through them for the right one, and somehow managed to get it into the keyhole. The sores on the man's face were a clue, but her brain felt paralyzed. Suddenly she knew. *Meth.* The guy was a meth user and probably needed cash for a cheap hit. He might not hurt her if she could pay him off...unless he had a big drug debt. She unlocked the trunk and tried to step back.

"Naw-aw," he said, giving her a hard shake. "Get it for me, bitch."

She must have tossed her purse a little too hard this morning—she'd been in such a hurry. It was way at the back of the trunk, and she'd have to crawl halfway inside to get it. Every instinct she had warned her not to do so. "Look, there's some cash in my purse, and I can write you a check." She tried to sound reasonable, tried to keep her voice level, calm. "You can take the car too. I'm locked out of the clinic, and I'd have a long walk to town from here, so you'd get away, no problem."

"Shut up and get the fuckin' purse." He brought the knife close again, and she nodded quickly. He shoved her back as he finally released her shirt.

In one movement, Morgan threw the keys at his face, spun, and took off running with everything she had. She ran straight for the road that linked the industrial park with the highway leading into town. She'd hoped her assailant would focus on the purse, maybe the car, but instead, he was right on her heels.

*Omigod, omigod, omigod...*She hadn't done any sprinting since high school, but fear gave her adrenaline. Still, she could hear the man close behind her, yelling, swearing. Morgan ran for her life, praying that someone would drive by and see her, but there wasn't a car in sight. She ran on and on, her lungs beginning to burn. Suddenly, she slid on a chunk of gravel and went down hard. The man was on her in a split second, the knife a gleaming arc—

It didn't connect. With a blood-curdling roar, a massive black shape crashed into her assailant, knocking him away from her. Morgan scrambled to get to her feet as the pair grappled—the man screaming shrilly and stabbing at the dark fury that was trying to get at his throat.

It was a dog—*the* dog—but...but...

The red splatter on the pavement slapped her astonished brain back into reality. One of the man's arms was already torn and useless. In another few seconds, the animal would surely kill him, and so she had to make a fast decision. It went against all common sense and reason, it contradicted all her training, and it was terribly dangerous, perhaps even deadly. But in her heart,

Morgan Edwards believed she had to interrupt the dog's attack. She forced herself to approach the savage animal and slapped his muscled flank as hard as she could. "No!" She threw every bit of authority she could muster into her voice. "Stop it. Stop it now. Get off him." She reached over the broad back with a courage she didn't know she had, closed her hands over the ornate metal collar, and pulled it with all her strength.

For a moment, nothing happened. She half expected the mastiff to turn on her, and there would be nothing she could do about it. This close, the creature seemed big enough to bite her in half. Then the massive dog yielded and began to back away from the man. Morgan kept both hands on the wide, heavy collar, focusing all her attention on the dog, watching for signals in his body language, knowing he might decide to attack her at any moment. "That-a-boy. Good dog, good boy. Come away from him. That's the way."

She didn't see the wildly swinging knife until it was buried hilt deep in the dog's side. A horrible gurgling bellow rang in her ears, and the animal spun toward his assailant, nearly yanking Morgan off her feet.

The man crab-scuttled backward, torn and bloody with his ruined arm tucked tight against his chest. He was wild-eyed and gibbered incoherently as the big dog snarled and snapped at him. "Stay with me, buddy," she whispered. Morgan knew she couldn't hold the creature back if he lunged, but she held on just the same.

Surprisingly, the dog didn't move. The man did, however. He staggered to his feet and tried to walk backward, then turned and ran unsteadily toward the highway. Morgan's hands were cramped from gripping the collar, but she waited until the man was gone before letting go.

The dog seemed to have been waiting too. As soon as his enemy was out of sight, the great creature sank to the pavement with a deep moan.

~

Morgan peeled off the bloodied green scrubs and threw them into the clinic laundry basket. She put her jeans and T-shirt on reluctantly—at three in the morning, they felt like cardboard. She was dead tired, and all she really wanted was to crawl into bed. Any bed. If she had to stay up much longer, the table in the staff room was going to look really appealing.

Still, it was a privilege to *be* tired. She thanked her lucky stars, Jesus, Buddha, her guardian angel, karma, the universe— anyone and anything that might be responsible for sending the big dog to save her. And for sending Jay Browning to help her save the dog. As the youngest member of her practice, he didn't look like a veterinarian, not with the long ponytail, the crystals and charms around his neck, and the T-shirts that promoted UFO conventions. But his unorthodox appearance—and interests—couldn't hide the fact that he was clever, capable, and talented. He had been driving back to the clinic to finish up a pharmaceutical order. Instead, he'd found Morgan kneeling over the massive canine in the middle of the road, tearing up her cotton jacket to make pressure bandages. Jay had called the police on his cell, then pitched in.

They'd applied the bandages to reduce the bleeding, then carefully rolled the dog onto a tarp. By then, no less than three patrol cars had arrived. Two teams went in search of the attacker. The remaining two officers ended up interviewing Morgan while helping the vets heft the dog into the back of Jay's pickup. At the clinic, it again took all four of them to muscle the unconscious animal onto a stainless steel table.

The senior partner took his hat off and fanned himself with it, his face red with exertion. "That's not a dog; that's an Angus cow."

The younger officer lifted the dog's eyelid. "He doesn't look good. Are you sure he isn't dead?"

"He's alive," Morgan said. "And I plan to keep him that way."

She sounded more confident than she felt. Transporting him had used up many precious minutes. By the time she was ready to operate, the dog's gums were pale and his pulse thready—he'd lost a great deal of blood. Luckily Jay was a perfect partner for this dance. He ran the gas and started an IV, laid out instruments and sutures for her as she operated on the worst of the dog's injuries. The angle of the knife had caused it to nick other organs, including the heart, before coming to rest in a lung. It took every ounce of skill Morgan had, but she was determined and the dog was strong.

By the time she sutured the last of his wounds, she knew the dog would live.

She would live too because of the dog's heroism. Morgan had no illusions about what would have happened to her otherwise. But as much as she tried, she couldn't come up with a plausible explanation as to how or why the dog was there. The unusual collar proved to her that the animal was no look-alike. It was unmistakably the same black mastiff that had been following her throughout her trip to Wales.

No way was she going to reveal that detail to the police, however. It sounded crazy, even to her. Jay, however, would likely believe her. *Maybe I'll tell him later.*

Jay chose that moment to come bouncing into the room, charms and ponytail bobbing. He bounced everywhere it seemed, even at ungodly hours of the morning. His wife always seemed high energy too. Maybe it was that organic food that Jay was always bringing for lunch...Whatever it was, Morgan wished she had some. "This guy's way too big for any of the recovery kennels," he said. "What do you think about putting him on a blanket and some foam in your office? We can close the door, and then he won't be in the way in the morning. He's going to be dozy for quite a while, so I don't think he'll make much of a mess in there."

"That'll work just fine. I can sleep on the couch and keep an eye on him." She rubbed both hands over her face and through her hair.

"Why don't you let me do that, Morgan?"

"It's okay, really. I'm way too tired to drive all the way to my place, and besides, you have a wife to go home to."

"Are you kidding? Starr would kill me if I let you sleep here alone after being attacked tonight. I'll call her again, and then I'll take the couch in the waiting room."

Morgan wanted to say no, it wasn't necessary. But she knew, deep down, she was running on the last dregs of her adrenaline. Once it wore off, it would be a toss-up to see which would claim her first: exhaustion or the cold fear that swam just beneath the surface. "Thanks for that and for showing up tonight too. I don't know what I would have done without you."

"Well, it would have been a helluva lot harder to get the dog into the clinic for one thing. When I drove up, it looked as if you were leaning over a moose calf, not a dog. He's humongous. And that collar's really something—straight out of *The Lord of the Rings* or something. Where did he come from?"

"I have no idea," she said honestly, as her heart made a decision she hoped her brain could live with. "But if no one claims him, I'm keeping him."

~

Morgan was certain she'd be too tired to dream, but no sooner had she closed her eyes than she found herself in a forest clearing by a fallen tree. Stars pinwheeled high above, and a group of horses milled about just within the trees. She could smell them, hear them as they stamped and snorted, making the sounds of animals settling for the night. She was far from settled. Instead she stood, naked, waiting, anticipating. Then she felt him standing behind her. He hadn't made a sound, but she was as aware of this man's presence as she was of her own.

She quivered as he nuzzled the back of her neck, planting kisses there. His broad, rough palms skimmed lightly over her shoulders and down her arms to her wrists and back up to her shoulders to begin again. Down and up, barely touching her, down and up. It sensitized her skin until every part of her body was yearning to be touched. His strong hands glissed the length of her back, their power leashed. He traced intricate circles and symbols there with the same maddeningly gentle touch, as a soft, warm breeze flowed sensuously around her legs, her face, her breasts.

Gradually his hands circled lower, grazing softly over her bottom, round and round, back and forth until she wanted to scream from the sheer tension. She could barely stand still. Her breasts were tight, her insides clenching until she could feel the moisture collecting between her legs. *Touch me, damn it, please!* Suddenly he gave her just what she'd been craving—he cupped her buttocks and squeezed them hard, kneaded them with his broad hands. It electrified her. The pleasure jolted her body, prickling her already hard nipples and tingling her through her clit.

He pressed lightly on her upper back, bending her until she had to place her hands on the fallen tree. His other hand slid between her legs, and she parted them readily. She was aching to be rubbed and rubbed hard, but again, the broad fingers barely brushed over her tight wool and swollen lips. She tried to rub herself on his hand, but it eluded her, softly stroking her inner thighs instead until she trembled all over, nearly frantic with arousal and need.

Without warning, he knelt behind her and began pressing soft, moist kisses to her buttocks. She was wriggling now, wanting more, but he threw a powerful arm around her hips and held her in place. Slowly, painstakingly, he kissed his way over every inch of her bottom, interspersing the kisses with light nips that were immediately laved with his tongue. Bliss shot through her like a hot current through copper wire. Her last coherent thought was to marvel that everything within her was so intricately connected that to be touched in one place was to be touched everywhere…

Then two strong fingers slipped inside her, and all thought vanished as she gasped aloud. She slid down them, praying he wouldn't pull them away, and nearly cheered when he thrust them deeper. She could feel her own rush of moisture, feel him alternately crook and splay his fingers as she rode them faster, harder. Gradually he added part of a third. *Yes, oh, yes, omigod, yes…just like that, don't stop, oh, don't stop…*The pleasure ramped up, even as her legs began to get rubbery, and his thickly muscled arm was holding her up as much as it held her to him. *Faster,* *harder.* He rubbed his thumb over her wet clit and triggered an avalanche. She screamed out as the orgasm thundered down on her, overwhelming her senses until she tumbled bonelessly into her lover's lap.

She looked up into his face just before she was jarred awake by the frantic peal of the alarm clock.

FOUR

~7\\~

The X-ray lab was dark, cool, and fairly quiet, a welcome respite from the busy clinic. Too bad the developer fumes had such a pungent odor to them, Morgan thought. The exhaust fan was on full blast, but still her eyes stung a little. She swished the film frames in the vertical tank of developing fluid as she watched the glowing numbers on the timer click down to zero. Quickly, she dunked the frames in the rinse tank, turned the timer on again, and leaned on the counter. Two weeks, her supplier had said. Just two more weeks until her shiny, new digital radiography equipment would be set up and installed. Two weeks until somebody finally hauled off the last of the antiquated equipment and chemicals she'd inherited when she bought the practice. Two weeks and her clinic would be fully in the twenty-first century. *Only a couple of decades late.*

The satisfaction of achieving such a major goal and the prospect of never having to develop X-ray film again weren't enough, however, to keep Morgan's thoughts from straying to what had clearly been the hottest dream of her life. Not only had she had an intense orgasm, but she'd actually gotten off in her sleep!

She'd awakened with her underwear damp, her body quivering and still clenching with little aftershocks of pleasure. Just thinking about it made certain parts of her body tingle anew.

Blissful gratification aside, what intrigued her more was the glance she'd gotten of her dream lover. She didn't recognize his face, and it wasn't a face that any woman would forget. Handsome but not in a pretty way. He could have been a cowboy or a Viking or a sea captain—the strong features were definitely on the rugged side. Dark hair, nearly black, long enough to shadow a strange bluish symbol on his collarbone, a creature of some sort. What she remembered most, however, were his eyes. They were the color of ale and old gold. And they had looked at her with incredible tenderness, perhaps even love—

Somebody banged on the door, making her jump. "You in there, Morgan?" It was Jay.

"Yup, I'm here." She knew he wouldn't open the door, not with the red warning light on. "Finishing up the X-rays on that ferret."

"I just got off the phone with the cops. They found the guy. They've got him locked up right now, waiting for you to ID him."

"Really?" Relief washed over her, and suddenly she felt shaky all over. She was glad the younger vet couldn't see her. "That's great news, Jay, thanks."

"Thought you'd want to know. I put the officer's number on your desk. If you want someone to go with you, Grady and I are both available."

"Thanks." She was grateful for such good friends who were willing to back her up, but she wanted to do this by herself. She was hoping the process would be similar to what she'd seen on TV, where she could point the man out of a lineup from behind one-way glass. Maybe even by watching video footage in another room completely. However it was done, it would be satisfying to say, "That's him," and know her attacker was in jail.

And if the black dog hadn't intervened, her attacker would have been her *killer*—and likely never caught. It was fitting that she'd named the big canine on the clinic records with a Welsh word she'd borrowed from some of her grandmother's stories. *Rhyswr*. Hero.

~

He was surprised to awaken. He'd expected to be dead; he *should* be dead. But then the last time he'd thought that, the Tylwyth Teg had stepped in.

They wouldn't have saved him this time.

He'd disobeyed the Fair Ones, using the powers they themselves had given him. He'd abandoned the land he was bound to, traveled the high winds in the guise of dark mist, crossed the cold seas, all on his own errand. He'd saved Morgan Edwards, a mortal marked for death, planning to forfeit his immortality and trade his life for hers.

Yet, she had turned around and saved *him*. It shouldn't be possible. He breathed when he had not breathed for centuries. It hurt to breathe, but that was even more of a miracle. He couldn't remember the last time he'd felt anything. Not only did he live, he was mortal.

Morgan called him Rhyswr. She'd whispered the Welsh word to him many times as she'd tended him. He knew what it meant although he didn't feel like a hero. Rhyswr. Still, there was something strangely familiar about it. Long-forgotten memories began to rise to the surface of his mind, fragmented images, thoughts. Rhyswr, Rhyswr...

Rhys! He was *Rhys*! He hadn't heard his own name spoken since before the Romans captured him, hadn't remembered it since the Tylwyth Teg changed him. Even fettered by this bestial form, he felt a rush of freedom course through him like strong drink. He felt something else too. A deep stirring in his heart for this woman who had given him so much.

Rhys made a decision. He had not known freedom or choice in nearly two thousand years. This one time, he would both choose to serve and choose *whom* he would serve. Wherever Morgan Edwards went, he would follow her. He would be her protector to the end of his days.

～

The big mastiff slept most of the time but was healing well. Morgan often snatched a few minutes throughout the day to sit with the dog, while she fingered the heavy metal collar around his muscled neck. Not only were there no tags or nameplate, she could find no fasteners, no buckles or clasps. It was like nothing she'd ever seen, and she'd been unable to remove it. Thick silver coils and links interlocked in an intricate Celtic design. An inset to the left of the throat framed a silvery creature inlaid with blue stones. It was definitely a canine, perhaps a hunting dog of some sort. The collar itself seemed more like a chain mail torque from a museum than any kind of pet restraint. It was as mysterious as the animal that wore it.

"Where did you come from, Rhyswr?" she asked the sleeping dog. "Where are your owners? They've got to be missing you." The mastiff must belong to American tourists, she had decided. It would certainly explain why the dog was following her bus, and more importantly, it was the only possible explanation for how the animal had gotten to the United States. However, she had been the sole American on her particular tour. Had the dog become separated from an earlier group? It was easy to picture frantic owners searching, backtracking, and finally finding their oversize pet in time to take it home. But what were the chances that his home was right here in Spokane Valley?

The coincidences were almost beyond belief, but Morgan had been right that her partner Jay would believe her. He'd whistled at the strange story yet immediately begun coming up with ideas for locating the owners.

Morgan had already contacted the travel agency, the tour company, even the British consulate. She'd left many messages for the older woman who had been her tour buddy too. Wouldn't Gwen be amazed to know that the so-called grim had apparently followed Morgan home? So far, however, her calls hadn't been returned. Perhaps her new friend was busy traveling somewhere else.

With Jay's help, Morgan managed to phone or e-mail every veterinarian, animal shelter, kennel club, groomer, and pet shop in the northwestern United States. Jay found a pair of mastiff breeders in the state that Morgan hadn't known about, although calls to them revealed that their dogs were all brindle, not black. In fact, they insisted that mastiffs were *never* black. The breeders were happy to pass the information on to their association, however. There were ads running in two different Spokane newspapers and one in a tristate publication. Jay had even placed an ad in a couple of paranormal e-newsletters and several online forums that Morgan had never heard of. A week had gone by, then two, and still no one seemed to be missing a giant black dog with an expensive collar. It made no sense at all.

"Well, Rhyswr, that's it," she told the dog as she snapped her cell phone shut. She was sitting on the floor and decided she had little hope of getting up. It wasn't just that the oversize city yellow pages weighed heavily in her lap—the dog was dozing with his massive head resting on her leg. He might as well have been a pony. "I don't think there's anyone left on the planet I can contact." Morgan stroked the dog's velvety ears, worked her fingers into the thick glossy fur of his neck, and smiled as he nudged his head back in a clear signal for her to continue. "I'm really sorry that your owners have been so careless with you. But you're welcome to come and live with me. What do you think about that?"

The dog thumped his tail without opening his golden eyes.

"I'll take that as a yes. I know you're still stiff and sore, but it's time to get you out of my office. It's starting to smell kind of doggy in here, you know? You'll like my place. I've got some land and a whole lot of trees, just right for a big fella like you." His tail thumped again and she smiled. "Somehow I can't picture you in my car, even if I open the sunroof, so I've got the keys to the clinic van. If that doesn't work, well, I guess there's always the livestock trailer."

≈

Transporting the dog proved to be easier than she expected. She'd been afraid that the step up into the van would be difficult for the injured animal, but she'd forgotten how tall he was. Although his wound made him slow, Rhyswr walked into the van almost effortlessly and sat calmly with his nose at her shoulder as she drove to her home in a rural area north of the city limits. When she'd bought the run-down farm two years ago, she'd wondered if she was making a mistake. The commute would be long, and while the sprawling old house was in much better shape than the barns and outbuildings, it had still required a great deal of upgrading. But the farm had rapidly become her sanctuary. And for a king-size canine, it would be heaven on earth.

Morgan pulled into the long, winding driveway and was soon standing in the grass with her new four-legged roommate. She'd looped a leash around the heavy metal collar, but it wasn't necessary. The mastiff looked to her for his cues, moved when she moved, his great head level with her waist. "Well, Rhyswr, this is the place," she said as she unlocked the front door. "But I'm sure not going to carry you over the threshold." She stepped inside and held the door open. Here, the dog hesitated. He lowered his head and peered inside, uncertain.

"Come on, boy, it's okay. You can come in," Morgan coaxed. "You belong here. This is your new home. Come on home, Rhyswr."

The great animal chuffed and stepped forward. But as the dog cleared the doorway, the air was filled with a bell-like clanging that made Morgan cringe and cover her ears. When the metallic tones finally died away, the silvery collar lay on the floor. "Omigod, all I did was tie a leash around it!" Kneeling, she tried to pick it up and was surprised to find that many of the finely woven coils had shattered. She was staring at the broken links in her hands when an enormous wet pink washcloth blocked her vision. "Hey!"

His tail wagging furiously, the huge black creature was almost puppylike in his sudden desire to wash her face with his tongue. "Stop that. Yuck! No licking, *no licking*!" It was a challenge for Morgan to regain her footing—not just because the dog was so big and kept knocking her off-balance but because she was laughing so hard. Finally, she braced herself against a wall and gripped the dog's wrinkly muzzle with both hands. She didn't have a hope of holding those giant jaws closed, but at least only her fingers were getting wet. Finally, the dog got the message and settled for nuzzling instead.

"Feels good to have that heavy thing off your neck, doesn't it?" She rubbed behind the dog's ears as he wagged his tail in apparent agreement. "Let's get this cleaned up, and then I'll give you a tour of the place."

Despite his size, Rhyswr wasn't clumsy in the least. Morgan had expected a bull-in-a-china-shop scenario, with visions of him bumping into her furniture as his great black tail swept things off tables and shelves. After all, that would be par for the course with most large dogs. However, nothing of the sort happened, even though Rhyswr was clearly pleased to be with Morgan. She could almost swear he was being deliberately careful, a quality unknown among most canines—their enthusiasm got the better of them most of the time.

She put together a salad at the kitchen counter for dinner, with the big mastiff sitting quietly next to her. He could easily see over the counter—and reach everything on it if he'd been so inclined. Instead, he was perfectly well behaved, happy to simply listen as she talked. That was a surprise to her too: how pleasant it was to have someone to talk to at the end of the day. She could definitely get used to it. "I always thought that being a vet meant I wouldn't have time for a dog of my own, that I couldn't offer it a good life. I keep pretty long hours—guess I should have warned you about that."

The black dog simply thumped his tail on the floor.

"I'm glad it's okay with you," she continued, as she pulled up a barstool to the counter and ate her salad. "I'm thinking you should come to work with me as much as possible. Unless I'm out on a farm call or something. I just don't want you to be alone all day, Rhyswr. I want you to be happy."

The dog laid his enormous head on her thigh, and she rubbed his soft ears. Half an hour later, his head was in the same position as they sat on the couch and watched the news on TV together. Morgan had always loved animals, but Rhyswr had brought something new to her home, as if it was suddenly filled with life. *A house is not a home without a dog.* Or a cat or a bird or a goldfish. She didn't understand how it worked, although she'd heard pet owners speak of the phenomenon many times. But now she was feeling it. Strange—she loved her house and had never noticed it lacking anything before. Now, because of the dog, there was somehow *more*.

Usually she did paperwork, caught up on reading veterinary medical journals, and did other tasks before falling into bed. Tonight, Morgan made popcorn—including a very small bowl that she left plain to share with Rhyswr—and put in a DVD. His behavior was impeccable. He didn't jump up or get excited about the popcorn (and she'd seen plenty of dogs do backflips for it). Instead, he gently took pieces from her fingers as she offered them. The only time she had to tell the big mastiff to sit down was when he tried to lick the tears from her face during the sad parts of the movie. "You make a pretty perfect companion," she said to him after the credits rolled. "You didn't even complain that it was a chick flick."

At ten, she almost changed her mind about having him sleep in the laundry room. *Almost.* If it hadn't been for her certain knowledge of the volume of his snoring, she would have given in and let him sleep in her room.

The thick, comfy bed she'd made for him made the spacious laundry room look small. She hoped he'd be comfortable.

Rhyswr obediently sat in the middle of the bedding, but his eyes looked alarmed as she went to leave the room. Morgan put her arms around his big neck and hugged him. "It's just for tonight. If you really hate it, we'll think of something else tomorrow, okay?"

Rhyswr thumped his tail and lay down, and Morgan headed off to her room. She knew she needed her sleep, needed every minute of it that she could get, but still it took all her willpower to leave the dog in the laundry room.

As she curled up under her blankets, she wondered why she hadn't allowed herself to get a dog sooner. Her last thought before falling asleep was that she'd obviously been waiting for the right one to come along.

～

He'd known that the shattering of the faery-forged collar would summon the attention of the Tylwyth Teg, but Rhys hadn't expected messengers so soon. Ancient beyond counting, beautiful beyond imagining, two beings stood in the room with him and banished the darkness with their living light. He squinted up at the Fair Ones, recognizing Tyne and Daeria of the queen's own court, and waited.

Tyne studied the fragments of the collar that Morgan had placed in a box on the laundry table, then placed a single shard in the waiting palm of his consort. Daeria simply closed her delicate, long-fingered hand around it without taking her iridescent eyes off the large dog before her.

"What a surprise you've given us." Her voice struck Rhys's sensitive ears like hundreds of tiny bells chiming at once. Alluring, yet there was an underlying menace, darkness lurking beneath the light. The sound danced up and down his spine, and it was all he could do not to shiver. As a dog, he could make no reply, but none was wanted. "The queen was most impressed by the news. No grim has ever escaped his collar, and certainly no barghest has ever traveled so far. It's provided fascinating conversation throughout the court."

That could be good or bad. The Tylwyth Teg were immortal beings, but the burden of living for endless millennia was tedium. It was one reason that the Fair Ones tended to play terrible pranks upon mortals. Like bored children, they sprang upon the unwary, seeking diversion. So it had been when a weary Celtic warrior turned reluctant gladiator had fought his way to freedom at last. Wounded and near death, pursued by his former captors, he'd blundered straight into the territory of the Tylwyth Teg in the steep hills northwest of Isca Silurum...

"We came to see how this was done," Tyne chimed in. "And now it is apparent that a mortal has had a hand in this. A most unusual mortal, in that she has beckoned you and actually sought you out instead of avoiding you. Offered you food and dressed your wounds. Each unselfish deed has weakened the links of our spell, and now the spell is unmade. This has never happened, not in all the ages of time." He smiled, and it was like the sun in the high arctic. Bright but without real warmth.

"You've upset the balance of things. While it's true that harmony was restored when you purchased this woman's mortal life with your immortal one," continued Daeria, "*we* remain unsatisfied. And therein you have provided the court with a very great puzzle. We wish your continued servitude, yet this mortal has managed to purchase your life with her unusual devotion. You are hers. Of course, *her* enslavement would provide redress for her interference."

Rhys knew the game. He'd seen it countless times. They were baiting him, hoping for a reaction. He dared not give them one, forced himself to appear disinterested, as if Morgan's fate didn't matter to him. The couple waited, but he simply stared at them steadily.

Tyne shrugged finally. "The queen—"

"The *queen* revealed that she knew this mortal's ancestor of twenty generations past." Daeria delivered this tidbit with relish, like someone revealing juicy gossip. "Some say they were friends and the queen permitted the woman to visit the faery court freely."

"And leave as she chose," said Tyne.

Rhys knew better than most how unusual that was. No human entered or left the royal court save by the will of the Fair Ones. He'd seen many hapless mortals there over the centuries, some invited, most captured. Like him, they were forced to provide service or amusement for the Tylwyth Teg. Few ever left. If there had once been a mortal woman who was an actual friend to the queen, he hadn't noticed. But then, he only ever saw the powerful monarch when she was in the throne room. Most of the time she did not deign to grace the chattering court with her presence.

"I suppose it was because of her blood," explained Daeria, ignoring the glare of her consort, who clearly wanted to tell some of the tale. "There was a silver thread of fae blood in her mortal veins and in all her female descendants since. Royal fae blood. Including the woman who has showed you such uncommon kindness."

Tyne nodded. "That is true. Though she is mortal, she is of us."

There was nothing he could do—even with a canine face, Rhys couldn't hide his astonishment at such news. He saw pleasure spring behind their otherworldly eyes, pleasure in knowing that they had managed to surprise him. He could picture them returning to their hidden land beneath the Welsh hills, delighting all with the gossip they brought. *That foolish warrior didn't even know that the woman was fae…*

No, but he *did* know that Morgan was nothing like the cold-hearted creatures before him.

Tyne put his hand on Daeria's arm, and she waved an irritated hand as if giving him permission to speak. He made a slight bow, not to her but to Rhys. "In deference to that bloodline and to an old friendship, the queen has made her appearance in the throne room for the first time since the king expired."

The king had not expired, thought Rhys. Having witnessed death in every form possible, he knew that only the sick and the weak could be said to *expire*, releasing their last breath and having not the strength to take another. The king of the Fair Ones had not only resisted his death by iron blades in the hands of power-seeking traitors but had fought to purchase time for his wife to cast an enchantment that bound the murderers. He saved her life but died mere seconds before she could save his.

"Her Supreme Highness, Ruler of the Nine Realms, called upon the entire court to witness not one but two declarations. One, that Morgan Edwards is henceforth *eithriedig*—"

She had immunity? Rhys's control nearly slipped again. She had been afforded an extremely rare protection—at least from those who dared not disobey their remaining monarch. His Morgan was essentially safeguarded from all faery malice, from simple pranks to spells and violence. With otherworldly threats thus removed, Rhys was confident that he could protect her from all else.

"The court was appalled. Such a valuable gift to be bestowed upon an insignificant mortal." Daeria spoke the last word with a hiss of disgust.

Her companion frowned at her but continued. "The second declaration is that the Tylwyth Teg will relinquish our claim upon you, dark grim, until such time that this mortal woman relinquishes hers by the power of three. You are ours no more—"

"—until *then*," finished Daeria, and there was no mistaking the threat.

The Fair Ones vanished, and Rhys was alone in the dark, relieved yet disturbed. *Until then.* Until a time when he no longer belonged to Morgan. The idea was surprisingly painful. He'd have to make sure that didn't happen. He'd be a model dog, a devoted servant, a perfect animal companion and protector. She'd have no reason to ever make him leave.

FIVE

⌒⌒⌒

M organ had gone to bed hoping for another visit from her fantasy lover and wasn't disappointed. A dream whisked her away soon after her head touched the pillow, and she found herself walking the edge of a calm, silvery ocean. A bright moon shone high and full as a warm breeze licked along her naked skin. She dipped a toe into the water, then waded slowly into the shallows, the soft waves caressing her.

She saw him then—her familiar stranger, her lover—swimming toward her. Saw his powerfully muscled body emerge from the waves as he set foot in the shallows, saw the silvery droplets of seawater fly from his skin as he approached. Heat radiated from him as he enveloped her in his strong arms, and his mouth burned against her lips. An answering heat blossomed between her legs, and she wanted him to touch her there, please, please, *please*...

Instead, he feasted on her breasts. His powerful hands cupped and squeezed them while his clever mouth worked the eager nipples relentlessly. Her clit began to pulse in rhythm with the magic he was making, and she tangled her hands in his thick dark hair to hold him to her. Something deep within her began winding tighter and tighter, and she knew she'd shatter when it let loose—

Without any warning, the dream shifted and changed.

Morgan's lover vanished abruptly, along with her pending orgasm. *Damn it!* She gritted her teeth with frustration as she found herself wandering long, darkened hallways through a house that resembled hers yet didn't—when had it been so far to the kitchen? She wasn't quite sure it *was* her own house until she entered the laundry room, wasn't entirely certain she was still asleep even—until she saw her new dog communicating with glowing alien beings!

Good grief. It was almost a relief to have to slap the damn alarm clock off.

Morgan opened her eyes, contemplating her dreams for a few moments. She briefly considered getting out her favorite vibrator, but that mood was long gone, ruined by the bizarre visions of extraterrestrials among her baskets of dirty towels and jeans.

That'll teach me to eat popcorn late at night.

She had the day off but wasn't interested in sleeping in—after all, she had a new dog. And that dog was probably dying to go outside for a pee. Later she wanted to place an overseas call again in hopes of contacting Gwen—Morgan had been looking forward to telling her about the dog for two whole weeks now. She slipped into her bathrobe and barefooted her way to the laundry room to let Rhyswr out. She hadn't been sure about the choice of accommodations, and he hadn't seemed thrilled either. Small wonder. Although the room was large, it was on the opposite end of the house. But she couldn't imagine getting much sleep with the great snoring creature in her room. Where could she put him so he could be close by? Maybe she could rearrange things in the kitchen area. Would the entryway be better? Deep in thought,

Morgan was several steps inside the laundry room before pure shock brought her up short.

There was a man, a naked man curled on the dog bedding. A very big, very powerful, completely naked—

Morgan spun and ran. All the terror of the attack in the parking lot gave her speed as she raced through the house and straight out the front door. She headed for the only vehicle in the driveway, the clinic van, and tried its doors frantically. All locked, even the cargo doors. *Damn it!* Heart pounding, Morgan kept the van between her and the house as she peered back toward the front door. She'd left it wide open—a clear signal to the intruder as to where she had gone. "Crap! What am I going to do?" she muttered. "Think, *think!*"

The keys were in her purse in the house. Her cell phone was in her purse too. And her purse was—where the hell was her purse? Dining room table? Entryway shelf? Kitchen counter? Bedroom dresser? She'd found the stupid thing in all those places before. Where had she put it last night? And did she dare go back inside to look for it?

"There's got to be something else." Hers was the last farm on the rural road. She'd liked the privacy when she first bought it, appreciated the fact that only the occasional tractor or combine passed by. It had been such a welcome relief from the busy city. Now it felt isolated and dangerous. The nearest neighbors, Jorge and Katrina Klassen, were three miles away. Normally, she could walk the distance easily. Barefoot, however, would make it very tough going.

Morgan turned away from the useless van and left the driveway. It was the first place the intruder would look for her, although there was no sign of him yet. She jogged to a thick stand of trees and huddled down behind the bushes. Her stupid white bathrobe was sure to give her away if she wasn't careful, but there was no point taking it off. Not with brilliant pink pajamas underneath. She watched the house while stealing glances at the old barn and the machine shed. Could she hide in one of them? She was just contemplating the grain bin in the stable when she remembered the dog. Where was Rhyswr? Why hadn't he barked or chewed the intruder's leg off?

The black dog certainly hadn't been in the laundry room. Obviously, the stranger had let the dog out, but where would Rhyswr go? Her property bordered a forested area around a creek. Maybe the big mastiff had found a rabbit or a deer to chase? Morgan sighed heavily. She'd have to search for her dog later. Right now, she had much bigger problems.

Although there was no activity that she could see in the house, she couldn't stay hidden long. She had to either sneak back in and try to find her keys, hide on the property somewhere, or start off walking to the neighbor's house. She had just decided to follow the creek through the woods, which would take her from her own land and into Klassen's pastures, when a loud whoop from the house had her flattening herself behind the bushes.

∼

He was human. Human! Rhys leapt up from the floor and nearly fell over. He grabbed for a chair to steady himself. By all the gods, human! He was a man again, although he felt like a newborn foal with strange legs that didn't want to support him. Slowly, he drew himself up, teetering just a little. It was almost dizzying. He'd been among the largest of dogs, but he hadn't seen the world from a man's height for millennia. And he'd completely forgotten all the colors. As a dog, the world had looked very different. There was color of a sort, but nothing like this. Everywhere he looked, he was assaulted with hues that had not even existed when he last walked on two legs. Suddenly Rhys wanted, no, *needed* to get outside. One thing would be the same, no matter how much time had passed.

He had to see the sky…

His body felt awkward, but it was still as physically powerful as if he'd awakened from an ordinary night's sleep and not a centuries-old spell. Years of battle against the Roman intruders had strengthened it. Years of fighting in the ring for his Roman captors had honed it. His walking improved with every step, and gradually he stood straighter and didn't need to brush his hands along the walls for support.

The door stood wide open. Beyond it, Rhys could see a sprawling expanse of brilliant green. Had mere grass always been that incredible color? He had to rub sudden moisture away from his eyes with the heel of his hand. Walking over the threshold and into the light was akin to being born, and although his heart leapt, he didn't look up. Not yet. Instead, he stepped carefully off the porch and onto the grass, strode barefoot through the bright, tickling blades until he was well away from the building. Then he extended his arms, palms up, tilted his head back, and stared up into the clear, bright blue of the sky.

The intense color dazzled him until he let himself fall backward onto the grass. Rhys lay there for several minutes in a state of near rapture, unable to take in the splendor, unable to look away from it. Blue was a sacred color, and he ran his fingers over the tattoo of a blue hound on his collarbone. Although the image had caused merriment for the Fair Ones and had inspired his sentence at their hands, the blue hound was his clan emblem—its color a part of his identity, part of his very soul. Looking up into the sky, the color filled him, soothed him.

Each unselfish deed has weakened the links of our spell, and now the spell is unmade.

Morgan had done it. He was free because of the woman who had befriended him, cared for him, even saved his life. Rhys closed his eyes for a moment in reverent thanks but opened them quickly when a sharp metal point pressed against his throat. He was shocked to discover his benefactor on the other end of a long-handled hoe.

~

"Who are you?" she demanded, forcing her voice to be steady, although she didn't feel steady in the least. A close look at the stranger's face had revealed eyes the color of ale and old gold. His features were as familiar to her as her own. He was the man from her dreams—but how was that possible? More, the blue symbol tattooed high on his collarbone was a perfect match to the enameled animal on Rhyswr's collar. Shaken, she pressed the hoe harder and saw the man's golden eyes widen.

"Rhys. My name is Rhys." His voice was deep. A little raspy but melodic with an accent that sounded all too familiar.

"Okay, *Reese*, what the hell are you doing here? You've got no car and no clothes. How'd you get here?"

"My name is *Rhys*," he corrected, pronouncing it with a single roll of the r, just as Nainie had said her r's all her life. As did every Welsh person Morgan had met on her trip, from the hotel clerks to the shopkeepers to the tour directors. "You brought me here."

"I'm pretty sure I'd remember that. What the hell are you doing here?"

"I was a warrior of my clan until I was captured by the Roman invaders. They forced me to fight in the arena at Isca Silurum and named me the Bringer of Death for my skills. I thought I knew *hell* then, but I had not truly found it until I escaped from them."

Good grief, was he high on something? The Bringer of Death…Somebody had been playing way too many video games. "Good for you. Ten points for originality. Let me guess, you were drinking last night, and your friends decided to play a prank on you. They stole your clothes and dumped you at the wrong place. Am I close?"

"A prank." He seemed to consider that. "Yes, you could say that a bit of a prank was played on me. I found a cave, but it turned out to be an entrance to the world below. The Tylwyth Teg found me there, and there aren't greater pranksters to be had."

She nearly dropped the hoe. "How do you know about the Tylwyth Teg?" Except for her grandmother, she'd never heard anyone on this side of the ocean speak of them, never mind pronounce their name correctly. The tourist shops in Wales did a booming business in faery merchandise, yet she hadn't heard the ancient name of the fantasy creatures used very much even in *that* country. She narrowed her eyes at the man, daring him to answer.

He shrugged a little. Although she wasn't pressing on his neck anymore, he remained prone. "The Fair Ones are cousin to men but very much older. Ancient as the mountains. It was the custom of our clan to leave offerings for them outside the village. The Fair Ones are often bored, and they think nothing of toying with mortals for sport."

Nainie Jones had often spoken of her childhood, told of her mother leaving milk and bread on the back step for the Tylwyth Teg. It was an offering, a gift of hospitality, she said, so they wouldn't play tricks on the family. Morgan gripped the hoe harder to keep her hands from trembling, yet she couldn't help but be fascinated.

"You cannot enter their territory without permission or payment," he continued. "I had nothing to offer when they discovered me. Not even my life, as I was dying. I thought they would finish me, but instead they healed me. And that was their prank. Because then they changed me, so they could take their payment in servitude."

Rhys—if that was even his real name—either believed what he was saying or was a prime candidate for an Oscar. Because try as Morgan might, she couldn't see any evidence that he was lying. He had to be crazy then, but everything about the whole situation was insane. After all, she was standing in her front yard in her pajamas, holding a naked man at the point of a garden hoe. She'd taken assertive action when she'd seen him lying in the grass, assuming he was drunk or something. Well, she'd gotten the upper hand all right. Now what was she supposed to do with the guy? She couldn't keep him there indefinitely. "If I let you up, will you behave? Because I swear I'll beat you with this if you so much as look at me wrong."

"I will not hurt you. I swear it on my life."

It would have to do. "Okay. You can get up." She stepped back, clutching the hoe's handle, ready to swing and swing *hard* if need be. The man rolled away from her and got to his feet, his movements deliberately slow.

Omigod, he's tall. Morgan felt something deep inside her turn over in pure female appreciation. When he'd been on the ground, she'd been focused on his face. Now, her eyes quickly scanned the strong arms and muscled chest, then followed the dark line of hair that traveled down his taut belly and fanned around a very promising cock. She snapped her gaze back up to his face, feeling her cheekbones heat and her body thrum. It was embarrassing, not so much that he was naked but that she was reacting so strongly to him. It was the stupid dreams; it had to be those stupid, sexy, wonderful dreams that were sending her hormones wild. Morgan cleared her throat with difficulty, fought to focus.

Suddenly she noticed something she hadn't before. The man's arms and shoulders showed at least a dozen scars. There were more on his torso, some on his legs. The scars were white, wounds that had healed long ago. They were also curiously wide, as if they'd never been sutured. What the hell had happened to him? An accident? She prayed that he wasn't one of those troubled souls who felt compelled to cut themselves. Worse—had he hurt the great black mastiff?

"I want to know what you've done with my dog."

He looked surprised. "It's me, surely. You called me Rhyswr, but my name is Rhys."

"No, I called my *dog* Rhyswr. And there's no way you could know his name unless you've been watching me." Had the stranger been hiding in the woods last night, spying on her as she walked around the yard with the dog? Or had he seen her with the dog at the clinic and followed her home? Her grip tightened on the garden hoe. Maybe letting the guy get up had been a really bad idea. "Look, I want to know where my dog is right now before I call the police."

He ran a hand through his dark hair then pinched the bridge of his nose as if thinking. "I know not how to explain. You'll think me mad."

"Too late, buddy. Goes with sleeping in a stranger's house and standing around naked."

He flushed slightly, and those golden eyes darkened, but he made no effort to cover himself. "A warrior goes into battle naked, as does a gladiator. But we are not at war, and this is not your custom. Does it offend you that I have no clothes?"

"I'm not offended so much as pissed off that you broke into my house, scared the hell out of me, and lost my dog."

"Your dog is not missing."

"Good. Where is he?"

"I am the black dog you befriended. When they found me, the Tylwyth Teg were amused by this—" he pointed at his tattooed collarbone "—and thought I would make them an excellent hound. I've been a grim ever since, a barghest, bound in service to the Fair Ones for all time. Forced to wear a collar that was forged in faery fire, crafted by faery hand. There was no hope of escape for me until you unmade the spell with your kindness."

Holy crap. The guy was a loony after all. "Stay there. Right there. Understand? Don't make a move." Morgan brandished the hoe as she sidled over to the front door, then dove through it, slamming and locking it after her. Ran to the phone in the kitchen, snatched up the cordless receiver, then dashed through the house to the back door. It was locked. A quick check of the windows showed that they were securely latched as well. How on earth had the man gotten inside?

The sensible side of her said to call 911. *Now, right now!* Yet strangely, she found herself reluctant to do that. Instead, some inkling was fluttering at her brain like a bright luna moth before a window. She strained to discern what it was but came away with only the same vague sense that she knew this man. Intimately. Cared about him.

"That's ridiculous," she said aloud. Obviously she was thinking with her hormones, reacting to a fantasy, to a *dream* for heaven's sake. The guy might be a serial killer. Homicidal maniacs could be attractive, couldn't they? So could compulsive liars. But what purpose would a grown man have in claiming to be a dog? Did he really think she'd fall for something so outlandish? Maybe he had a fetish for veterinarians...

Good grief, why did she have to think of the word *fetish* with the most attractive man she'd ever met standing naked in her yard? Of course, that attraction was beginning to wane in the wake of the fantastical story he'd told her. She found herself feeling a little sorry for him. Maybe he had missed his medication or had a reaction to something he ate or drank. Maybe he'd suffered a head injury that had left him out of touch with reality—after all, *something* had happened to him to give him all those scars. Yet, he didn't seem to be dangerous. If he was, he'd already had plenty of opportunity to do whatever he wanted to her. Yet, he hadn't laid a hand on her as she lay asleep in her bed. Hadn't threatened her in the least.

What to do? The truth was, she didn't want to have Rhys arrested, didn't want to press charges or cause trouble for him. But Morgan was equally certain there was nothing she could do to help him except to report him as the lost soul he obviously was. *I could just mention that he was wandering my property and skip the part about finding him in my house.* Maybe there was a missing persons report on him. Maybe someone would recognize him and take him home.

As she peeked through the curtains with the phone in her hand, waiting for the police dispatcher to pick up, she realized there was *one* thing she did know about the naked stranger in her yard.

He had, without doubt, the finest butt on the planet.

SIX

He was in a cell again. There was no window from which to see the sky but at least there was light. It was clean, unlike the dank and stinking hole Rhys had been forced to live in at Isca Silurum, and it had a plumbing system that the very elite of Rome would envy. Fresh water was available to him at all times. Food—*good* food, not leavings—had been brought to him. Strange that such luxury was given to prisoners. He'd been given clothes too. Although he didn't care for the garish orange color, they were clean and smelled of strong soap.

But a cell was still a cell. He was a man again yet once more a prisoner. Surely the Fair Ones had planned it thus, tantalizing him with freedom, then yanking it away just as he allowed himself to rejoice. He could almost hear their cold, crystalline laughter, devoid of true mirth. Yet the long night brought no otherworldly visitors to mock him.

Strangely, his captors didn't mock him either. They'd spoken briefly but politely when they brought him clothes and each time they brought him food, and he had thanked them for their great kindness. They looked at him oddly then, and he didn't know what he had said wrong. He knew the language fluently—had come to know many languages over the centuries—but of course he hadn't interacted with anyone as a dog. And this country was new to him. Perhaps he had missed something, some custom or nuance of behavior.

Rhys snorted. Obviously he'd missed more than that or he wouldn't be in a cage again. He had committed no crime that he knew of, yet Morgan had clearly expected him to go with the man she had summoned. The blond man had the bearing of a soldier, but Rhys was far larger and more powerful. He could have stood his ground and simply refused to go. Yet to please Morgan, he had automatically done what she wanted as if he truly was her obedient pet.

The longer he was in human form, the less that subservient role appealed to him…Rhys was certain of his vow to protect her, however. He just couldn't figure out how to fulfill it. He'd sworn to stay with Morgan—yet she didn't want him with her. A day and a half had passed, but he didn't bother questioning how long his sentence was.

After all, in his experience, once a prisoner, always a prisoner.

But other prisoners came *and went*. He listened carefully to what few words were spoken between the men and their captors but gained no clues. Where were they going? Only the elderly man in the closest cell remained. The officer had called him Mr. Waterson and treated him like an old friend rather than a prisoner. He'd been drunk when he was led into the cell, but the officer simply helped him to lie down and covered him gently with a blanket. He'd snored all night, but Rhys had heard far worse sounds.

There was a morning meal, everything wrapped in white paper again. Even the cup was paper. Tastes. Textures. Colors. Rhys reveled in every detail until the last crumb was finished. He was startled by a deep, gravelly voice.

"I got an extra hash brown here. You want it, son?

Reverting to old habits, Rhys hadn't yet spoken to his neighbor. He had never talked to other prisoners, not because it was forbidden but because it was better not to know them. It was all too likely he'd meet them in the arena. "You offer your food?" he asked, wondering if it was a joke.

"Food and I aren't real good friends in the morning. You get old like me, your stomach gets testy. I've had more than enough."

Rhys took the proffered potato patty through the bars. "My thanks."

"Name's Leo. Haven't seen you around here before. First arrest?"

"Rhys. I have not been in this prison before."

Leo laughed. "This here's just the local jail, son. Prison's the Big House, and it's for nastier fish than us. Although I see you're in peels, so maybe you're a bit badder than I think."

"Peels?"

"You *are* wet behind the ears. *Peels. Oranges.* You're wearing prison gear. Where's your clothes?"

"I have none."

Leo's shaggy, white eyebrows went up. "Well, that explains what *you're* in for. Me, I drink a little too much now and then. Can't get my old gray ass home sometimes. *Drunk in public.* But not *disorderly*, not since I was a marine at least. Used to be a bit of a hothead in my younger years. Funny how age cools you down, makes you think things through." He laughed again. "Can't remember stuff worth a shit though."

Rhys considered that. His newly restored body was still strong, but was he any wiser than he had been the last time he walked upright? He remembered all the centuries in between, however, and for a moment he envied Leo and his forgetfulness.

Rhys could recall every single face that had recoiled from the sight of the black dog, every hapless mortal over the endless years whose misfortune it had been to witness the grim's appearance.

Finally Officer Richards, the man who had taken him from Morgan's house (in a *car*, a fine conveyance although Rhys didn't care for the enclosed feeling), came and stood in front of his cell. The blond man was nearly as tall as Rhys, but his frame was narrow and wiry. His eyes conveyed a great deal of intelligence, however, and Rhys had no doubt that they took in every detail.

"Mr. Reese, I can't keep you here any longer. You have no record, and you're not being charged with any crime at this time, although I would advise you to keep your clothes on in the future. I'm concerned that you may have a health problem, however, and I'd like a doctor to have a look at you. It would have to be voluntary, however. I can't compel you to see him when I release you."

Rhys blinked. "You are…letting me go?"

"Have you committed a crime I don't know about?"

He shook his head slowly.

"Good. Will you allow me to take you to a doctor?"

"I have no injuries, no need of a physician," he said carefully. Rhys didn't want to offend the man, but he could see no reason to go to a healer.

"I had a feeling you'd say something like that. All right, then. You'll need to change your clothes." Officer Richards opened the door and handed Rhys a green sack. "We can't have you running around looking like an escaped prisoner. Dr. Edwards called, had some things put aside for you at Ellison's Hardware on her own dime, so I picked them up. You'll have some extra socks and briefs to take with you because they don't sell those separately, of course. There's a comb and a toothbrush too.

"You're very lucky that Doc Edwards has been concerned enough about you not to press charges, never mind make sure you're dressed. She's a kind woman, perhaps too kind. My wife probably would have shot you if you'd showed up buck naked in *our* backyard. I figure when you get on your feet, you can pay the woman back for the clothes—but I'm going to suggest that you bring the money to me to pass on. I can't enforce it, but I think it would be wise if you didn't bother Dr. Edwards again."

Kindness again. "My thanks," Rhys managed. "I will repay her for these."

"I'll be back to get you in about twenty minutes. You too, Mr. Waterson. I've got some paperwork to fill out and then you'll both be out of here."

Richards left and Rhys considered the green bag. It was strange material, almost thin enough to see through and slick to the touch even though it was dry. *Plastic.* He pulled the clothing from the bag and set it out on the bed. It was so very different from what he had once known. Sure, he was aware of what each item was and how it was worn, but seeing and doing were sometimes different things. The orange shirt and pants were closer in design to the pullover tunic and simple *braecci* he was accustomed to wearing in his previous life.

Luckily the plastic packet of three small white things had a drawing on it. The idea was vaguely similar to a Roman loincloth but was all made of one piece. He chose one and knew enough to put it on first, but it took a couple of tries—and Leo clearing his throat meaningfully—to decide which way it should face. The braecci—*pants*, he corrected himself—were a fine dark blue that reminded him of woad, a dye his mother and sisters had made of fermented leaves, but the garments weren't woven out of wool. In fact, none of the items were made from wool. The fabrics were strangely soft, except for the pants, which felt more like stiff linen.

"Are there no sheep here?" he asked Leo as he rubbed the material between his fingers. "This cloth is strange to me."

"Cotton. Comes from a plant, you know? They make everything out of it."

Like linen then, Rhys decided. But finer. Softer.

Finally he was dressed. Leo had informed him that the little white square in the collar of the black *T-shirt* was meant to be hidden inside at the back of his neck. The pants, which the old man said were more properly called *jeans*, had a *zipper*, which clamped together like wolfen teeth when Rhys pulled on a small metal charm. He'd pulled it up and down a few times, amazed at the clever mechanism—and promptly learned that the tiny metal teeth could snag cloth! Thankfully he was able to pull the hem of his T-shirt free.

"You'll want to take care there, son," said Leo drily. "You get your dangling bits caught in that and you'll be singing soprano."

Rhys didn't understand all the words, but the inference was plain. He'd definitely be careful.

The final fastener on the jeans was also metal—Leo called it a *button*. There had been no buttons in his previous life. And although he'd seen them in use since about the thirteenth century, he'd never had cause to touch one. After a moment, Rhys realized that it operated somewhat like the bone toggle on a leather pouch he'd once had. He pressed it through the fabric loop and was pleased when it stayed. The buttons on the overshirt, however, were an entirely different matter. They were tiny and flimsy, mocking his big fingers.

"You're doing it up wrong," said Leo. "Get over here and let me show you."

Rhys stood near the bars and frowned as the old man undid the two fasteners he'd just managed to put together.

"Start here, son. You have to line up the bottom-most hole with the bottom-most button. Otherwise everyone will notice that your shirt's crooked." Leo did up the first button and waved at Rhys to continue.

"My thanks," he said and struggled to do the rest himself. Despite the annoyance of the fasteners, he liked the shirt and its fine bold check. His people had favored woven checks and stripes, and a couple of the women in the village—his mother included—could create even more complicated patterns on their looms but none as bright as this. It was blue, the sacred color, and purest black. The material was thick and soft. Still not wool, but heavy enough to remind him of it.

"Stop there," Leo said as Rhys fastened a button at chest level. "You can't button it all the way up to your chin or you'll look like an idiot. Or an old man and even *I'm* not that old yet. You gotta let the T-shirt show through."

The shoes were odd, not leather at all. They had long strings hanging from them, which he ended up simply tucking inside. There was a packet of strange white mittens in the bag, but the weather was warm and he left them on the bench at first—until he recalled that they were not mittens at all, but something called *socks*. People of his clan had stuffed shoes with dried grass for warmth. No one had ever thought to weave coverings for their feet at the time. He put them on, but they felt strange.

"Heel's on backward," commented Leo. When Rhys looked puzzled, the old man called for him to toss a sock his way. "It fits this way," he said and laid the sock along his own foot, puffing a little with the exertion of bending so far.

Rhys turned his socks around and found that they now conformed to his feet. "Better," he said. "I feel like a child, to be needing so much help to put on my own garments. Truly, you have been kind."

Leo shrugged. "No big deal. My brother, Ed, was in an accident. It left him so he couldn't recall how to do anything for himself—he was perfectly capable, mind you, just couldn't remember from day to day. Short-term memory loss is what they call it now. We all had to help him with little things like that, just remind him how stuff was done. From the looks of your hide, I figure you've had your own troubles."

It was a moment before realization dawned. The man was referring to Rhys's scars. He'd all but forgotten he had them. "They do not come to mind often. It was a very long time ago."

"Good plan. Always best to go forward if you can. I used to say that to one of my buddies when we served together, but some of the shit we saw during the war just ate away at him. Shot himself a few years after."

"The burden of battle is greater for some."

"It surely is. But there wasn't much help for someone like him in those days. Me, I had nightmares for years, still get a few, but I don't dare let myself dwell on it. Drink more than I should sometimes if I get to remembering too much. Got out of the war with most of my hide intact and my brains unscrambled, so I just keep moving forward. Settled here and built a pretty good life.

"Say, mind if I ask where you're from? You got an accent that's kind of familiar."

Rhys remembered Morgan's incredulous reaction when he'd tried to tell her the truth about his origins. Officer Richards's eyebrows had nearly met his hairline when Rhys repeated his story—and one of Richards's fellows had overheard and made circular motions with his finger to his head. The gesture might be modern, but Rhys had no trouble translating it. And he'd come to the realization that his current imprisonment had as much to do with his claims as it did with his state of undress. In order to exist in this time and culture, especially in order to protect Morgan as he had sworn to do, he would have to adopt a new tactic: *truth, but not all of it.*

"Wales. I was born in Wales," answered Rhys. And never mind that his country hadn't been called that at the time or that his nativity had occurred two millennia ago.

Leo nodded. "I thought it was something like that. During the war, our unit was temporarily stationed with some British troops. Good guys, every one of them, in spite of that damn tea they drank, but two of them spoke the most complicated language I ever heard. When they spoke English, they had an accent kind of like yours, and the captain said they were—er—*from Wales.*" He put up his hands in a gesture of peace. "Damn it, I nearly used the nickname there. Sorry. Nowadays you have to be careful of what you say, especially what you go around calling people. What used to be okay when I was a kid is politically incorrect now—and it should be, no doubt about that. But I forget sometimes, especially if I've had a couple beers."

This country had a lot of rules, thought Rhys. In fact, modern-day Wales probably had a lot of new laws as well, but as a grim, he'd had no need to pay any attention to them. He'd better pay attention now, though, if he expected to stay out of prison.

"So, where are you going when you get out of here?" asked Leo.

"I don't know." He hadn't anticipated his freedom, never mind how he was going to use it. More than anything he wanted to return to Morgan, but perhaps she needed more time. She wasn't accustomed to having a man around for one thing, and for another, he'd given her a fright. Not that she remained frightened for long. His mouth quirked as he recalled her determined expression while she threatened him with the garden hoe. No, Morgan was a very brave woman—who else would have attempted to pull a great savage dog from a man's throat? And as for himself, what other voice would have broken through his killing rage?

Truth be told, he didn't know what to do now. He had never feared battle, yet now he was at a loss as to how to approach this woman. He didn't want her to send him away again. Somehow he had to prove himself useful. She had a farm that had gone fallow, its once-fine buildings and fences in disrepair. Perhaps he could work for her, set the place to rights?

But not yet. He had to repay her for the clothing when he saw her again—and at present, he had no coin with which to do so. "I have no destination," he said to Leo. "Your advice would be most welcome."

"Well, I don't have much in the way of advice, but I *do* have an empty house. You can stay with me till you figure out where you're going. You look like you know how to work, and I got chores that need doing. You could earn your keep, right enough."

Rhys nodded. "That I'd be pleased to do."

SEVEN

⌒ʎ↾↽⌒

Leo Waterson had a very large home. He insisted that it wasn't
all that big, but the place was enormous compared with the
thatch-roofed roundhouse Rhys had grown up in. Rhys didn't
mention that, however. Instead, he ran a hand over the wide
wood frame around a window—so smooth and even, everything
straight and squared. "The workmanship is fine," he said, and
meant it.

"Quarter-sawn oak, classic Craftsman house. Built in 1914
and we bought it in 1966. I wanted something newer, of course,
but Tina loved it, and it fit our budget at the time. It's always been
a bugger to heat, though," said Leo. "In the winter now, I just
close off the upstairs altogether. Since Tina passed on, I've taken
over the bedroom behind the kitchen. I think you'll do well in
the north bedroom, on the right at the top of the front stairs.
That was my son's room. Could be a mite dusty now because my
knees don't enjoy the trip to the second floor, but that room usually stays cool in the summer heat. Though I expect we won't get
much more of that now that it's September."

"Grateful I am for your hospitality. Have you some work that
I can do?"

Leo waved a hand at him. "No shortage of it. I'm behind on just about everything you can name. I'll show you the yard if you're curious, but for God's sake, don't feel like you have to jump right into it. You'll make me feel guilty."

Just then, a small spotted terrier entered the room. Age had whitened his entire face and his eyes had a blind bluish cast to them. "That's ol' Spike. He's gone completely deaf now, so it takes him a while to realize I've come home," explained Leo. "Usually I have him locked up if someone's coming over."

"Why?"

"He'll bark at you for sure, but lately the little bugger bites. Just stand still, okay?"

Spike's gait was unsteady but determined as he sniffed his way to his master's side. Despite his small stature, when the dog laid his head against Leo's leg and closed his eyes in bliss, he reminded Rhys of his father's loyal old wolfhound. Suddenly Spike's body stiffened as he belatedly realized there was a stranger in the room. Piercing staccato barks exploded from the small dog, underscored with snarls and growls.

"Damn it, Spike." Leo made a grab for the terrier but was far too slow. Spike had already launched himself in Rhys's direction.

Instead of trying to avoid the attack, Rhys simply waited. The snarling snapping teeth came within an inch of his leg—and then the dog abruptly quieted. The fur along his spine still standing up, Spike's nostrils flared. Rhys lowered himself until he was kneeling on the floor, and the dog didn't react except to sniff at his hands. Apparently satisfied, Spike climbed into Rhys's lap, curled up, and began snoring almost immediately.

"I'll be double damned," said Leo, his eyes wide. "He must like you—I've never seen him do anything like *that* before. In fact, I've never seen him take a liking to anyone much, not even when family visits. What did you do, put a spell on him?"

"No magic." Rhys stroked the spotted fur as the dog slept on. "My father taught me about animals. I like them and maybe I have a bit of a knack."

"A knack he says." Leo shook his head. "They say that animals are good judges of character. If that's true, you just got a helluva reference from Spike."

～

Rhyswr was nowhere to be found. Morgan spent hours searching the woods and the fields around her home, but there was no sign of the great black mastiff. She called her neighbors, put an ad in the paper, phoned the pound, but no one had seen the animal. Although she hadn't known the dog for long, losing him hurt more than she'd expected.

Even less expected was her concern for the man who had claimed to *be* the dog. She didn't believe for a minute that his name was really Rhys. That was just too much of a coincidence. But she found herself thinking about him a great deal, wondering if he was all right. Bill—Officer Richards—had assured her that Rhys's fingerprints weren't on file. She had breathed an enormous sigh of relief over that point. The man might be crazy but at least he wasn't a criminal. Probably.

And he hadn't been charged with indecent exposure, thank God, since he'd been on private property, and she didn't wish to complain. *Ha.* Rhys was hot enough to bake cookies on. Tough to complain about eye candy like that! Yet according to Bill, no one had filed a missing persons report on anyone with his description. No one had showed up to identify or claim him. Not only did he have no idea where he belonged, he remembered no other name but his first one. And that was questionable.

In the end, since he couldn't provide ID or even an address, Rhys had simply been written up for vagrancy and placed in a cell overnight. That surprised her. She thought the authorities would have sent Rhys to a psychiatrist or even a social worker, but the man hadn't committed any real crime. His mental condition would therefore be his own business. And as Bill had pointed out, plenty of people were wandering the streets these days with far worse problems than Rhys.

Where he was now, though, was anyone's guess. All she knew was that the man had simply left upon release. According to Bill, there had been no incidents of Rhys turning up naked in the streets.

If only Morgan could say the same about her dreams.

∼

"Hold it this way. That's it, you got it now," said Leo. "We'll make a handyman out of you yet."

Rhys drilled a hole through the plywood and admired the perfection of the circle when he finished. He'd seen electrical tools before, of course, but had never touched them to see how they worked. His people had been adept with ironwork, and he himself was skilled with many hand tools—but even the most basic of tools looked and worked differently in this time and place. *So many new things to learn…*It was exhilarating to have so much to think about, and by all the gods, it felt good to use his hands again.

Best of all, Leo was unfailingly patient as a teacher. Rhys was truly thankful that the old man had been placed in his path, because he definitely needed a guide in this strange new world.

"I think I'll take a break now," said Leo. "Never used to need one, but now I find I gotta shut my eyes for a little while in the afternoon. Recharges the batteries." He sniffed and chuckled. "Although they don't seem to hold a charge for long these days."

As the old man headed for the house, Rhys made his way to the garden. He'd built a wide and sturdy bench for Leo and placed it in a sunny spot near some enormous purple and white flowers called *dahlias*. It was a good spot for Rhys's latest project too. He pulled out a large block of dark wood from under the bench and a handful of slender cutting tools from his pocket. Studying the piece, he began shaving away thin curls of wood and enjoyed the sun-warmed smell of them. Initially he'd begun carving the piece with a simple knife, but Leo had borrowed some very fine implements from a neighbor who made lifelike wooden ducks.

What Rhys held in his hands was not a bird. It would be a gift for Morgan one day, perhaps even a peace offering, if she would accept it. Just as he'd swapped one tool for the next, however, a flicker of movement in his peripheral vision caught his attention. Rhys stilled, casting his gaze about for the source. There was movement in the middle of the garden, and yet he could see nothing but the rich brown earth he had spaded over earlier in the week. Some bits of straw, the dried yellowed stems of a few leftover garden plants poked up here and there—

Suddenly a strange brown bird stood up from the midst of the dirt and shook out its feathers. Rhys thought it was a grouse— until it turned bright-blue eyes on him. In a heartbeat, the bird became a tiny man with a wizened, coppery face. Brown leaves stuck out in all directions from braided brown hair and covered his strange little body. He frowned at Rhys, planting long twig-like hands on scrawny hips.

Then disappeared in a puff of dust.

An ellyll, thought Rhys. *A stranger to this side of the waters and probably spying for the Tylwyth Teg.* But then, had he truly expected the Fair Ones to leave him alone? Reason said they'd be watching, one way or another.

Waiting.

EIGHT

⌒⫯⌒

It was her turn to be on call, and Morgan felt she'd missed enough shifts. Jay and Grady had argued with her for most of the week in favor of continuing to cover for her. They'd both been overprotective after the attack, and doubly so after what was now referred to as the Naked Man Incident. Their concern was sweet and supportive, but it was time to get on with her regular responsibilities. Normal—she wanted lots and lots of just plain *normal*. Morgan left her car in the parking lot and took one of the clinic pickups home for the night. The cargo box was equipped with everything she was likely to need for most emergencies.

Pager on her hip, Morgan picked up a few badly needed groceries and then made a quick house call on her way out of town. She wanted to check on Berkley, a sweet-natured basset hound and unrepentant escape artist. On his most recent yard break, he'd stumbled into a hole where a construction crew was working on a sewer project. Berkley now sported a cast on his left front leg—and an enormous plastic cone around his head to keep him from chewing on the cast. All dogs looked ridiculous wearing a cone, but Berkley's ears were so long that they draped over the edges and dragged on the floor like twin mud flaps. Morgan struggled not to laugh as she made a careful inspection of the leg and assured the anxious owner that there were no swelling or circulation problems. Once back in the truck, however, she let loose the laughter she'd been holding until tears ran down her cheeks.

Despite the long day, the silly basset had done her a world of good. Morgan felt herself relax, looking forward to the peace and sanctuary of her country home and feeling more in control of her life. *Normal is good.* But as she pulled into the treed driveway of her property, she spotted a blue sedan parked in the yard and an old man sitting on her front step.

"Leo! Is Spike all right?" she called from the window as she parked the pickup next to the car.

The old man heaved himself to his feet as she pulled her grocery bags from the truck.

"Ol' Spike's at home holding the couch down," he said with a broad grin, automatically taking a bag from her. "I was thinking of helping him with the job, but I volunteered to give my friend a ride out here instead. He's just taken a walk around the farm—" he glanced around for his companion but apparently didn't see him "—so I thought I'd enjoy the shade for a while. I remember back when Earl Hornsby used to run this farm. 'Course that was long before your time."

"Well, come on in and tell me all about it. Gosh, if I'd known you were coming, I'd have hurried home. I've got some iced tea in the fridge." And that was about all there was in the fridge, except for condiments. Thank heavens she'd given in to temptation and bought a package of cookies at the store.

Before Leo could answer, a familiar figure in unfamiliar clothes came striding around the corner of the garage. His purposeful gait was fluid despite his height. And that blue plaid flannel shirt didn't hide his broad shoulders or muscled arms in the least.

"Good it is to see you again, Morgan Edwards."

The timbre of his voice combined with his accent—an accent that still spoke plainly of Wales—made her hormones do a double backflip. She wrestled them into an unquiet submission and wondered if it was going to be necessary every darn time she saw him.

And exactly *why* was she seeing him now?

"What a surprise," she managed, smiling weakly. *Nainie told me not to talk to strangers. What would she have said about* deluded *strangers?* But every part of Morgan responded with recognition—and even a crazy kind of joy—as if the man was anything *but* a stranger. Either her instincts were right and she was in no danger from this man, or her many dreams about him had created a false sense of relationship. *I'm betting on option two.*

Thank heavens old Leo Waterson was with him, though she couldn't imagine why. And since Leo was both a client and a friend, for his sake she would be nice and give Rhys-or-whatever-his-name-really-was the benefit of the doubt. *For now.* Looking into the tall man's eyes, she was intrigued anew by their amber-gold color. Even better, she saw no particular sign of insanity—although she wasn't really sure what that would look like. Just the same, she put her hand in her jeans pocket and withdrew her cell phone, keeping it palmed but ready.

"I'm guessing you already know my friend, Rhys," said Leo. He didn't laugh, but she could see the humor in his eyes. Obviously he knew at least some of the story.

"We've met, yes."

As if to change the subject, Rhys swept a hand toward the fields and outbuildings. "This farm is yours?" he asked.

"All two hundred acres."

"A great deal of land. Yet you have no horses in your stable, nor cattle in your barns. Your sheds have no grain in them. Where are your hired men?"

"They have the decade off." She heard Leo snort at that. "Besides, it's not like the land's going to waste. One of my neighbors leased a hundred acres from me this past summer to plant extra hay, and the local college planted twenty-five acres in test plots."

"You have nothing for yourself?"

Rhys seemed genuinely interested, but his questions made her a little defensive just the same. He wouldn't be the first critic of her decision to purchase the farm. She resisted her sudden need to explain how much the place meant to her. Instead, she took the offensive. "So, good to see you're wearing clothes today."

It didn't seem to throw him off in the slightest. "Officer Richards said you gifted me with these. I've come to thank you for your kindness and I've brought coin—*money*—to repay you for them."

Now she was *really* surprised. The money didn't matter to her, of course. After all, Morgan had fully expected the man to disappear into the sunset once he was free. But his desire to pay her back spoke of character, and that did matter to her—and more than she thought. "I appreciate that."

Rhys pulled a few folded bills out of his shirt pocket and extended them to her. "Leo thought this would be the right amount."

"Thank you," she said, sliding the bills into her pocket without counting them. "I'm sure the amount is just fine. Shall we go inside now? I don't know about you fellows, but my feet are killing me."

She poured iced tea for the three of them at her kitchen table, thankful that she'd been too rushed to eat breakfast that morning because the dishes would likely still be there. She put the cookies on a plate in the center and sat down. The rest of the groceries sat on the counter, and they could stay there for the time being. She hoped the milk and margarine and such could manage the wait.

"You look tired, Doc," said Leo. "I'll bet you put in a long day—and here we are taking up your time."

She smiled at him. "I don't get many visitors, so it's a treat. And all my days are long, it seems. I've got Jay and Grady hunting for another vet for the clinic."

"Now that's smart thinking," nodded Leo. "You've got a lot of regular customers now. Why, the last time I brought Spike in, there wasn't a single chair left in the waiting room. That receptionist of yours, Anne-Marie, she brought one in straightaway though. Kindhearted girl, that one."

"Like Morgan." Rhys smiled.

As her hormones swooned yet again, Morgan focused her eyes firmly on her drink. *There's no such thing as a coincidence this big.* That a good-looking Welshman would appear in her life right now was about as plausible as the moon being made of cheese. And what about the similarity between his name and that of her missing dog? *Jay would have a field day with this, I just know it.* "So has Leo's dog bitten you yet?"

"Ah, Spike. We get along well."

Leo simply nodded in agreement—although Morgan could swear he was trying not to laugh. She leaned toward Rhys. "Are you kidding me?" she said in a stage whisper. "Grady had to have stitches in his thumb the last time Spike came in."

The old man burst out laughing, and Rhys chuckled too. "The dog is formidable for his small size, but most of it comes from fear. Now that he cannot hear or see, he is easily frightened and feels he must attack first in order to be safe."

"That makes a lot of sense," she admitted. Did Rhys really understand animals, or was he just repeating what Leo had told him? Come to think of it, Morgan wasn't sure that even Leo understood Spike quite that well.

"So, Rhys, you must have a job?" It was out of her mouth before she could stop it. So much for being subtle, but she was keen to hear his answer.

"I've found much to turn a hand to, thanks to my friend here."

"Rhys has been boarding with me, Doc," said Leo. "He's already made over my entire yard—and you oughta see my garden now. It's never looked so good. Rhys caught me up on a lot of chores around the house too. Split a whole season's worth of kindling for my stove, so I can look forward to a smaller fuel bill this winter. 'Course now all my neighbors are competing for his time, and they're able to offer a wage. He's a man in demand."

A man in demand…I'll bet he is. Morgan shook her head to rid it of the sudden enticing image of a shirtless Rhys swinging an ax as his bared muscles gleamed with sweat. For a moment, she considered swallowing the ice cubes in her drink. Whole. Anything to cool herself down.

Rhys chose that moment to place his hand over hers, and every nerve in her body seemed to jolt with sudden electricity. "I have yet to apologize for the last time we met," he said. "You showed a great deal of courage when you found me, though you must have felt fear."

"I'm not admitting to it," she said, sliding her hand out from under his and putting it in her lap out of reach. She held his gaze boldly despite the fact that her insides were fluttering. "But Nainie used to say that without fear, there could be no brave deeds."

"Your grandmother was very wise."

"Yes, she was." She had to admit, it was refreshing to find someone so easy with Welsh terms. Most people thought *nainie* was some sort of childish endearment. But then, this man also knew about the Tylwyth Teg. His accent, his name...He was either a superb actor or the genuine article. Maybe with Leo present, she'd finally get some answers. "So, Rhys, tell me about—"

She jumped as her pager went off. Pressing the noisy device on her belt into silence, she flipped open her cell phone and speed-dialed the clinic dispatcher all in one smooth, practiced movement. A horse had gotten itself tangled in a wire fence at the Kendrick farm, and the hysterical owner couldn't free the animal. The situation was beyond bad—what Jay would describe as a red-hot mess.

"What have I got for help?" Morgan asked the dispatcher. Any accident involving a horse required as many skilled hands as possible. The big animals usually panicked, making things worse for themselves and endangering the humans around them.

Knowing this, the dispatcher had automatically paged Jay and Grady, plus all three of the clinic technicians as well. Jay and Russell were already up to their armpits in a bovine C-section— apparently someone had forgotten to notify the dispatcher that Morgan was taking her own shift tonight. No one else was answering their pages, and she remembered why: Grady had taken the other two techs, Cindy and Melinda, to a distant farm fair, not for fun but for further training. *Murphy's Law*, she sighed inwardly. She thanked the dispatcher and flipped her cell closed.

Normally a veterinarian would draft the owner at the scene, but she knew that this particular farmer would be of little use. She needed to find somebody else and fast—

"What troubles you?" asked Rhys.

—and the universe had plunked a *very* able body right in front of her. Morgan shoved the phone into her jeans as she stood up. "I'm sorry, guys, but I've got one hell of an emergency. Leo, I need to borrow your *man in demand.*"

"Seems to happen a lot these days," the old man chuckled. "I'll put your groceries in the fridge for you before I go, but I warn you, I may have to eat some more of these cookies first."

She gave him a quick hug. Then turned her attention to his companion, who had stood up when she did. He towered over her, all rugged power and muscle, but she was assessing his usefulness this time, not his appeal. Morgan had a patient waiting, and she was all business now.

"Rhys, I need your help."

"My sword arm and my shield are yours to command," he said solemnly.

Uh-huh. "Actually it's your hands I'm going to need."

~

The only thing in their favor was that the Kendrick farm was just a few roads over from her own. Morgan was grateful for that and for the double suspension in the clinic truck as she drove as fast as she dared over potholes and gravel.

She spotted the horse as she turned into the Kendricks' driveway. The big dapple-gray Percheron was on her side in a drainage ditch by the machine shed, thrashing wildly as an older woman, Julie, stood by in helpless tears. Instantly Morgan was out of the truck and had the rear hatch open, grabbing pliers, bolt cutters, and two sets of rope hobbles. Finally, she snatched the big blue gym bag of medical supplies for large animals.

She ran for the scene, only to find that Rhys had gotten there first. To her amazement, he was seated on the ground with the horse's head in his lap. He gripped one of the horse's ears in his hand while his other hand stroked the sweat-lathered neck. The big mare was quivering as he spoke soothingly to her in a language that sounded somewhat like Welsh, yet Morgan didn't recognize the words. Whatever he was saying, the animal must have been listening because, miraculously, she had stopped thrashing.

Rhys looked up and nodded at Morgan. "Her name is Lucy. She'll not move now," he said.

Morgan approached cautiously, instinctively kneeling in a spot where she was less likely to be kicked, and surveyed the damage. It was bad, very bad. She glanced over her shoulder at the owner's reddened eyes. It would do her no good to watch this. "Julie, why don't you go to the house and put on some coffee? We've got a handle on things here, but it's going to take some work, and we'll need a break afterward."

The woman fled gratefully.

"You did that woman a kindness," said Rhys.

"It'll be kinder if I don't have to put her horse down." Morgan took a deep breath and took up the hobbles. "I've got to restrain the legs so I can work on them."

"The mare will be still, I promise you that."

"What, are you magic or something?"

"I need no magic for this. I took my first steps under a horse's belly, and I was riding before I could walk. Believe me when I say that this fine *ceffyl* will lie quiet for you."

From anyone else it might have sounded like boasting, yet Morgan sensed that Rhys was merely stating facts. And only someone truly experienced with horses could have calmed the panicked animal. *I hope you're right.* Morgan applied the hobbles around the fetlocks just the same, but she breathed easier while she did it. Then felt carefully along the terrible wounds and began snipping the rusted wire.

Hours later, they shoved and heaved with all their strength, encouraging the big mare to roll to her knees. The horse hesitated for a long moment then fought her way to her feet. She was unsteady but remained standing, sides heaving. "There, my *cariad*," Rhys crooned, allowing her to rest her head on his shoulder. She shivered but was quiet.

"The mare will heal. And she'll be sound," he declared to Morgan, who was checking the animal for any wounds that might have been missed.

She shook her head. "We don't know that for sure. So many of the lacerations are deep. And that left rear leg is a helluva mess." Morgan shoved her hair from her face, leaving a broad smear of blood across her cheek.

She looked exactly like a warrior after battle, Rhys thought admiringly. And a true fight it had been to stop the bleeding and put things right. He'd counted 253 stitches in all, and every one of them was finely done. No warrior of his clan had ever received such skilled treatment of his wounds, nor had even the best of gladiators. "Skin and muscle are very badly torn, but the sinews are not cut. More than that, the mare has a strong will to live."

"She's going to need it. It's going to take a ton of antibiotics to stave off infection. And she'll have to have round-the-clock care. I couldn't suture some of the deeper wounds—they have to drain, and they have to heal from the inside out. Everything will have to be checked over and fresh dressings applied twice a day, maybe more at first." Morgan sighed. "I know poor Julie can't manage it. She's just too squeamish."

Rhys's eyebrows went up and she explained. "Don't get me wrong, she loves her animals and treats them well. But most farmers learn to give shots, dose livestock, treat injuries. Not Julie. She once brought a dog into the clinic twice a day for two weeks, just so we could give it a pill. The dog was perfectly calm, but Julie just couldn't deal with the whole idea. Besides, this horse is going to need to be watched by a trained eye for symptoms of septicemia, edema, any number of things. I'd rather not move her, but there's no help for it. Lucy will have to be taken to the clinic."

"A very busy place, and noisy as well. And who will be watching the mare throughout the night?"

Morgan sat on a stump with a deep sigh. "The clinic *is* busy. We have three vets and three technicians, and all of us run full tilt full time. But I've got to give this animal a chance. I have a couch in my office; I can sleep there for a while. I've done it before."

Most recently, she'd done it for him, Rhys thought. "Let me do it."

"Do what?"

"Bring the mare to your farm and let me have the care of her."

Morgan studied him for a long moment. "You'd have to stay with her," she said at last.

"Of course." Rhys studied her as well. She was a clever woman and knew full well that there was much more than the horse involved. If she agreed, she would be granting him a high level of acceptance. She would be welcoming him onto her turf, the same turf she'd sent him away from only a short time before. He'd gone because she'd wished it and because he was still half-stunned with the shock of being a man once more. But he wouldn't leave again. He had a vow to fulfill.

"Well, there are hired man's quarters off the back of the stable. Nothing fancy, but it's got plumbing and electricity. The place hasn't been used for a couple years, though. Not since Jay and his wife stayed there for a week while their house was being painted." She ran her hands through her hair, considering. "Right now it's dusty and God knows how many mice have moved in. Jay fixed the shower, but I couldn't speak for how well the woodstove works—they didn't use it. There's a bed and a table and chairs, but that's all. It wouldn't be much better than camping, especially now that fall is almost here."

He shook his head. "I'll sleep in the stable where I can hear the mare if she stirs. You've no cause for concern over my comfort. I've spent the night in fields many a time, waiting for foals to be born." That the open fields had been far better accommodations than his Roman captors had allowed him didn't bear mentioning.

Morgan was thoughtful for a few moments, then nodded. Decision was written in her face. "I'm going to owe Leo big-time for stealing his handyman, but you have yourself a job."

NINE

⌒ᴧᴨ⌒

The barn was old and empty, but it was clean. There was a corner box stall for the big mare. One of Julie Kendrick's neighbors had dropped off a few dozen straw bales and some hay and feed, promising to bring more. By the time night fell, Lucy was as comfortable as Rhys and Morgan could make her.

Human sleeping quarters were easily set up in an adjacent stall. Rhys turned down Morgan's offer of a folding cot from her guest room. Instead, he broke open some straw bales into a great heaping pile and topped it with the blankets and quilts she'd brought him. She had to admit it looked a lot more comfortable than the narrow cot would have been for his large frame. He welcomed a few other amenities, though, which she set up alongside the grain bin on the opposite wall. A lamp, a small table, a pair of chairs. Rhys didn't want to leave the injured mare alone in her new surroundings, not yet, so the last thing Morgan brought was a tray of sandwiches and a thermos of coffee.

They ate side by side, watching the big dapple-gray horse. The mare looked worn and tired, her big head drooping and her white mane falling forward over her half-closed eyes. The only thing that gave Morgan hope was that Lucy was surprisingly steady on her feet. The mare favored the worst leg, but the others weren't weak.

"What is the mare used for?" asked Rhys. "I could find no trace of harness marks on her."

"She's more of a big pet than anything. Julie's father used to have a team of heavy horses that he used for special occasions. He drove a wagon in local parades and gave hayrides and sleigh rides and such. Lucy has a good temperament for it, but it's Julie that doesn't handle the crowds well. I think she finally realized it just wasn't for her and she sold the wagon, but couldn't bring herself to sell Lucy. Julie used to ride her sometimes, but a saddle big enough for a draft horse weighs a ton and she can't lift it alone. So now, Lucy simply spends a lot of time in the pasture."

"It's a shame. She's a fine ceffyl, strong and steady. My father would have given his eye teeth to breed her to our stallion, Draig."

"Draig?" She knew she'd heard that word in Nainie's stories. "Doesn't that mean dragon?"

"Aye. He had a fiery red coat, and he was dragon tempered for sure. The only horse that ever bit me, and he did it for sheer spite."

"I had a poodle do that to me in my first year of practice. I swear he smiled after he did it too."

"I think Spike enjoys it at times too. I think he must have been a terror when he was young."

"So far he's bitten everyone at the clinic except me and Anne-Marie, our receptionist. He hasn't gotten you yet?"

"So far, no." Rhys rapped his knuckles on the wooden grain bin and grinned.

Mentally, Morgan grabbed the reins of her hormones as they threatened to stampede before that winning smile. *Just don't look at his face.* She changed the subject for good measure, trying to focus on something, *anything*, else. "So I just came back from Wales and I saw so many wonderful little places. Gwen seemed to like the bigger cities, like Swansea and Cardiff, best, but I think I fell in love with the villages. Which one are you from?"

"Who is Gwen?"

"She's an older woman I met on my tour. We roomed together and had a lot of fun, and I was hoping we were friends."

"I'm certain that she'd want to be friends with such as yourself."

Morgan laughed a little. *Such as yourself.* Nainie would have phrased the words the same way. "I've tried and tried to contact Gwen since, but I've had no luck. The phone rings, but no one ever answers it. Jay says she's probably off traveling somewhere. I'm probably just extra disappointed because she reminded me of my grandmother so much."

They talked about her trip to Wales for well over an hour, but it felt like only a few minutes. Rhys was familiar with the places she'd visited on her trip and was able to add a great deal to what she'd already learned about them. Of course, if he'd been reading her the phonebook, she probably would have been just as fascinated. She loved the cadence and lilt of his words, his manner of phrasing. Morgan enjoyed a deep, rich voice in a man, but mixed with a Welsh accent, the effect was devastatingly sexy. As if he needed the help! The physical packaging of the voice was drool-worthy enough. The fact that he was intelligent and insightful as well made him practically irresistible. If she didn't leave soon, she wasn't sure she'd want to.

And it was that, more than anything, that decided her.

"I'll say good night now, Rhys. I have to get up in the morning." It wasn't quite true. She didn't work until noon on Saturdays, but she had to get up sometime, right? "Thanks for all your help today and especially for watching over Lucy." She tried to stand up, but he stopped her with a big hand on her arm.

"You have a very kind heart in you. 'Tis a rare thing and beautiful to see. My thanks to you."

Her heart pounded in her ears as she studied his powerful hand, the strong fingers resting gently on her arm. Warmth radiated from his skin to hers, and she wondered what that hand might feel like on other parts of her body...

She murmured, "You're welcome," and left as fast as she could, hoping it didn't look as if she were running away. Even though she most definitely was.

It was only later, as she set her alarm clock, that she realized Rhys never answered her question about where he'd been born. And he'd managed to reveal exactly *nothing* about his life, his background, or anything else.

Damn it.

∼

Rhys leaned against the doorframe and watched the house for a while. Light shone from the windows, warm and golden against the blues and blacks of the nightscape. The mare whickered in her stall.

"I'm here still, cariad." He closed the door against the cool air, not because he minded it himself but because it wouldn't be good for Lucy to take a chill in her condition. He checked the big horse over one more time, wanting her to be as comfortable as he could make her before he turned out the light. Then he stripped and settled into his own makeshift bed in the adjacent stall. The smells of clean straw and horse were soothing and familiar, but sleep didn't come immediately. Instead, his thoughts were all for Morgan Edwards.

Her pulse had jumped beneath his hand and not from fear. Attraction had kindled the moment Rhys had touched his fingers to her skin. There was no mistaking the flush of color at her throat, the change in her eyes. He could see that Morgan felt the pull and the want, just as he did. He could also see that she wasn't prepared to act on it. His mouth quirked, remembering the speed with which she'd left the barn.

And by all the gods, he'd missed her immediately—the sound of her voice, the quickness of her mind, the look of her in the lamplight, and even the scent of her. They hadn't done a thing but talk, and he hadn't wanted it to end.

Deliberately, he turned his thoughts to the farm. There was a lot of land here still not under plow and buildings that were badly neglected. He wondered what he might do to take the farm in hand, to restore it to usefulness—yet he didn't know if that would please Morgan or annoy her. She was an independent woman. Perhaps she didn't *want* a man in her life? Perhaps she didn't want anyone. Why else would she choose to live out here by herself on this broken-down farm?

One of the women in his village had been like that. Rhiannon was fair to look upon, but she'd chosen to live alone. Under Celtic law, she'd divorced a man who had dared beat her and kept all her land and belongings. She'd also kept her freedom forever after, scorning the company of any man, though many tried to win her affections.

Morgan was far different, he thought. She lived by herself but not necessarily by intent. A skilled healer, she was deeply devoted to her work, and it filled her life. Her unwavering passion for animals had given him his own life back. Yet Rhys thought he sensed a great loneliness in her.

Or perhaps it was his own he was feeling. Strange. He hadn't thought much about being *lonely*. He missed his family, his friends, his clan, his village, all of them. But not in this way. Since meeting Morgan Edwards—especially since meeting her as a man—he was aware of a space within him that he hadn't noticed before. An emptiness, even though there was much to keep his mind and hands busy.

He chuckled, thinking of how Morgan had apologized for his current accommodations. She had no way of knowing that not even a clan chief in his time had had a home as fine as what passed as hired man's quarters here. Water flowed at the touch of a hand. The shower was Rhys's favorite—not only had his people bathed as often as the Romans, they had been the ones to introduce soap to the so-called civilized world, the same world that called them barbarians. There were soft cloths here—*towels*—and blankets. A fine bed waited for him for when Lucy could be left to herself at night. Morgan couldn't begin to know what luxuries these were to him, not until she accepted who he really was and what he had been.

That was going to take time, perhaps a very great deal of it. He sensed a war within her, the sensible and scholarly side of her arguing with the child she'd been, the part of her that had sensed the truth in her nainie's stories. Rhys had faith that Morgan would one day come to understand, but in the meantime, he had to have patience.

He snorted at that. *What I need do most is take care. I cannot lapse for a moment.*

It was easy to allow that he was born in Wales, yet it had not been called that at the time of his birth. Rhys could speak many languages, including the present Welsh, fluently. It was true that Welsh was derived from the Celtic language of his clan, but it wasn't the same—and it was the older tongue that still sprung first to his lips. He knew the modern country of Wales intimately, although it was as an observer rather than a participant. He'd thanked all the gods that he'd been able to answer most of Morgan's many questions about the people, the history, and the customs.

It would be much harder to answer any questions about himself. Thankfully she hadn't yet asked, but he wasn't foolish enough to think she wasn't going to. And when she did, he would not lie to her.

But he wouldn't reveal the entire truth just yet either.

As for Lucy, the gods themselves must have sent the creature. Striving to save and heal the injured mare had built a bridge, a bond of common purpose, between him and Morgan. He had gained a great measure of the woman's acceptance and even trust. What would she say if she knew that she had gained his heart?

He felt that powerful twinge in his chest, both sharp and pleasant, each time he saw her run a hand through her thick red-brown hair, each time her smile lit her pale-blue eyes. There was a powerful ache in his groin too, each time he saw her bend to reach something. Images arose in his mind as his cock rose up against the quilt, images of seizing those fine hips and revealing that lush bottom, thrusting himself deep into it until he was lost. It had been nearly two millennia since he'd bedded a woman, but by all the gods, he wanted Morgan Edwards and only her.

Would she want him?

~

No news on her missing dog. Not a word, not a sign, not a whisper. *It's like Rhyswr never existed.* Morgan sighed as she contemplated the black mastiff's picture on the bulletin board in the clinic waiting room. Sadly, she was beginning to believe that Rhyswr had somehow returned to whoever owned him.

Her partner Jay locked the front door and turned the plastic sign to Closed. "Have you noticed that this is exactly the reverse of what we were doing before?" he asked. "We did all that work to try to find the owner in the first place. Now you're the owner, and we're trying to find the dog. And both times, there's no clue, nothing. I'm wondering if maybe there's nothing to find."

"That's a strange thing to say."

"It's a strange situation, don't you think? He's too damn big to lose. He could have stepped through a portal for all we know. Or maybe he was a ghost all along."

"Jesus, Jay!"

"No, really. Maybe it's crazy, but I'm thinking something unnatural's going on here. It's spooky, like *The Hound of the Baskervilles* or some damn thing."

"Well, he sure bled a lot for a ghost dog. And he ate half a bag of dog food in one sitting."

"So he assumed corporeal form when he entered this dimension. You know that collar that fell off?"

Morgan resisted rolling her eyes. Maybe Jay was just joking around, perhaps trying to cheer her up in some bizarre male fashion. "It's in a box in my office—I was thinking of getting it repaired and I just haven't had time. What about it?"

"I borrowed this chunk of it, the part with the animal on it, and took it to a friend of mine at the university, Zak Talman." He pulled the gleaming segment from his pocket. The links hanging from it tinkled lightly as he put it into her hand. "Zak's a major expert in metallurgy, and he says it's old."

"What, like an antique or something?"

"Not just antique but *ancient*. Around two thousand years ancient. This little blue animal is a hunting hound. It looks Celtic, although no one's ever seen this particular design. The inlaid stone is azurite. But it's the metal that's really amazing. It has no business being in this condition—it should be black with tarnish, pitted, corroded, something. And get this, Zak's never seen anything like the silver it's made from. He even ran tests to verify it."

"Silver's not rare, it's not even very expensive. Most of my jewelry is silver."

"Yeah, but it's not this pure. Most jewelry is 0.925—it means it's 92.5 percent silver, alloyed with other substances to give it strength. Bullion silver for trading is 99.9 percent, but it's so soft, you can't make anything durable out of it. It bends, dents, warps."

"This collar is 100 percent silver, Morgan. One hundred percent. It's not supposed to be physically possible to produce it, but the real kicker is that it's also strong. Really strong. Something in the way it's been created, worked, forged, I don't know. Zak says there's no process today that can duplicate it."

"If it's all that strong, then why did it break? I'm telling you, Jay, it just fell on the floor and shattered like glass."

"We can't duplicate that either." Jay pointed to the coils that surrounded the piece. "We experimented on this little partial link on the end right here. Nothing Zak had in the lab would touch it. Not a damn thing. Not a chemical, not even a hammer and chisel."

She couldn't think of a thing to say to that, could only stare at the wonder in her hands. What was it Rhys had said? *Forged in faery fire, crafted by faery hand.*

"Look, this is where I have to apologize to you. I didn't know the collar was valuable, or I'd have never taken a piece of it out of your office," Jay continued. "I'm really sorry for that. The good part is that I didn't tell Zak who you were, or where you found it, or even that there's more of it than just the piece I showed him."

"Why? Are you worried about something?"

"Let's just say I'm concerned enough to suggest you lock up the collar somewhere for safekeeping until you figure out what you want to do with it. Thank all the stars, Zak is an honest guy and gave the piece back to me, although I'm sure he cried himself to sleep last night. He'd like nothing better than to do more tests and bring in experts, because if this thing is real, it would be the find of a lifetime. A lot of museums and collectors would pay a fortune to have a single link of this collar, Morgan. I think you have enough in this box to ransom Bill Gates."

Her legs felt wobbly, and she plunked into a chair. "Omigod," she managed and looked up at her partner. "How? How did something so rare and valuable end up around a dog's neck?"

"No idea. That's why I think there's something weird going on. As in otherworldly. Paranormal. Supernatural. Hell, maybe even extraterrestrial."

"Jay!"

"Come on, Morgan. That guy, what's his name, *Reese*, just happens to show up exactly when the dog disappears? With a tattoo matching the dog's collar? That's not a coincidence."

"No, but I'm sure there's an explanation."

"Yeah, like maybe he was telling you the truth."

"No way. Not possible." Morgan was on her feet then, waving a hand in front of her emphatically. "Look, I've been thinking about what the guy said, and I think he's involved in a role-playing game. It's probably a club or something that's adopted the blue hound logo. Somebody in the group owned the dog, and that's why the dog was wearing the collar, why it had the same symbol as the guy. And whoever dumped the guy on my property took the dog. Everything can be explained, Jay."

He folded his arms and shook his head. "You'd like it to be, but it can't. For one thing, my wife and I play those kinds of games. We belong to one of those clubs, and if there was a group like this, we'd hear about it. And nothing, *nothing* explains the collar. I told you, silver that's 100 percent pure and stronger than titanium is not possible according to any physics that we know of."

"Then your friend Zak must have made a mistake."

"Why, because what he discovered doesn't fit into a category you can believe in?"

"Come on, Jay, think about what you're asking me to believe. Both of us have studied biology, chemistry, natural sciences. We practice them every day. We have to deal with reality, not fantasy."

"I'll bet they said the same thing to Newton and Einstein. Look, what is fantasy but science we haven't discovered yet? Right this minute, they're figuring out how to prove that there are more than three or four dimensions, that maybe there are a dozen. That used to be science fiction, Morgan. How could they have even imagined that without being open to possibilities?"

It gave her pause. Nainie Jones had talked of not just being openhearted but being open-minded more than once. "But isn't there such a thing as being too open?" she asked. "Can a person be too willing to discard the rational in favor of the fantastic?"

"I don't think you have to choose between them. I mean, why is it always either/or? Can't both exist at the same time? The known and the unknown?"

"And you think this is a case of the unknown?"

Jay held her gaze and nodded solemnly. "You can laugh at me if you want to, Morgan, but I'm thinking that the collar does not fit in the natural world as we know it. And that means your dog and your naked guy don't either."

"Good to know. Especially now that *my* naked guy—" she made quotation marks in the air with her fingers "—is living at my farm as we speak. Should I worry about being dragged into the Twilight Zone?"

"Too late for that," said Jay. "I think we're already there."

TEN

~⟨⟩~

E nough for now, cariad. Rhys finished leading Lucy in a long, slow circle around the grassy field north of what Morgan had called the *machine shed*. The fallow ground was little more than an overgrown pasture, but it was a good place to exercise the injured mare. The soft earth was much less jarring to her wounds than the hard-packed corral over by the barn. "Time to go back and rest."

It felt good to be around a horse again. To be in this place, close to the land again. He hadn't always been a warrior. Men must eat, and it would be foolish to know only the skills of war. When peace returned, what then? It was said in his clan that a man must have a bow in one hand and a plow in the other. He had ridden a horse since he was able to stand, practiced daily with sword and bow, but he had helped his father and older brothers in the fields too. He'd learned to plant all manner of crops, aid the birth of foals, trade cattle.

True, this was a different time and a different country. He had seen farming practices change and develop over the centuries, but Rhys remained confident. What he didn't know, he could learn. *Would* learn. For Morgan, certainly, but also for himself. Why, a man could—

Without warning, Lucy balked, planting her feet and refusing to move forward.

"Come along now." Rhys made soothing sounds at the big gray mare. "True it is that it's a fine day, but you're not healed enough yet to be walking o'er much." Instead of obeying, however, she flared her nostrils and threw her head, yanking back on the lead rope and even showing the whites of her eyes.

He didn't urge her forward again. Many a warrior had been saved by heeding his mount's warning. Horses could hear sounds too soft and too high for human ears, and Lucy was too steady a beast to start at nothing. Rhys stood where he was and carefully studied their surroundings for something, anything, out of place.

The September afternoon was warm and still, a pleasant remnant of late summer. Yet there was no birdsong and even the insects had gone silent. There were no bees laboring in the nearby clover. No sound at all except for the quivering breath of the horse beside him. Then Rhys frowned at a large patch of tall grass just ahead.

How was it managing to wave without a breeze?

The stems appeared to be disturbed from underneath the soil. A burrowing creature, a mole perhaps, might move a few blades of grass as it moved through the earth. But the area affected was much wider than Rhys was tall. Suddenly a great mound of sod began to rise slowly like yeasted bread until it tore away from its surroundings. Clods of dirt rolled off the quivering earthen sides as *something* heaved itself upward. An icy calm settled over Rhys, as it always had when it was his turn in the arena.

Thanking the gods that Morgan was yet at the clinic, he took firm hold of Lucy's halter. He had no time to see her safely to her stall. Instead he turned her away and led her as quickly as he dared into the shade of the machine shed where she couldn't see whatever happened. Tying her lead rope to a post, he prayed for the sake of her wounds that she wouldn't break loose and run.

He needed a weapon. Rhys eyed the tools that hung in the shed and quickly settled on a long-handled spade. He hefted the thick hardwood shaft in his hands—oak, he hoped—and approved of the pointed steel blade at one end. It was old, but heavy and solid. He would have preferred a sword or even a Roman trident, a *fascina*, but in the ring as in battle, one learned to use whatever came to hand. Armed, Rhys headed out to face whatever was invading the farm.

The mound, now chest high, had split along its base on the side facing him, like a long, gaping mouth with snaggled roots for teeth. The darkness within seemed blacker than shadow ought to be on a bright afternoon—and a pair of eyes flashed in the depths, many handspans apart. Rhys allowed himself a quick glance at the house, reassuring himself that no one was home, and braced to meet the unseen enemy.

A handlike appendage reached from the darkness, the flesh pale like something long buried as it grasped at the dirt with four long, thick fingers. It hesitated as if testing the strength of the sun—and suddenly the moist white skin flushed a deep and mottled brown. Nostrils flared on the sides of the blunt nose that followed. The flat, arrow-shaped head was as wide as a wheelbarrow and swiftly became the color of the earth as well, as it emerged from the gaping crevice. Silvery eyes the size of apples flashed in the daylight but didn't flinch or blink.

Blind but far from harmless, thought Rhys, as the creature's mouth opened to reveal double rows of conical teeth, some longer than a spearhead. He'd seen these monstrous salamanders before. It was a *bwgan*, a creature from the darker side of the faery realm. Like the faeries themselves, *bwganod* lived almost forever.

Unlike the fae, they relished the taste of human flesh—and the creature turned its great head in Rhys's direction, tracking his location by smell.

Rhys took the offensive immediately, not waiting for the rest of the beast to emerge from the darkness. He ran forward and leapt over the bwgan's head, stabbing downward as he passed with the spade as if using a spear. He'd hoped for a killing blow between the eyes, but the big creature was fast and the skull was solid. Still, the spade slid along the bone and sheared off a portion of the bloated face, taking one of the eyes with it. The roaring hiss that followed was like water on a blacksmith's forge as the salamander writhed, its dagger teeth spitting droplets of amber venom in all directions as dark, bluish blood poured from the wound. Rhys jumped just in time to avoid being hit by the long, swollen tail, the color of a drowned corpse. The tail didn't turn brown in the light as other parts had previously. Perhaps the creature was weakened? Rhys searched for an opening and—

The bwgan charged out of the cleft in the earth like an angry dragon, broad-toothed jaws snapping together like bronze shields clashing. It probably anticipated that its intended prey would dodge left or right, but Rhys had long ago learned to *always do the unexpected*. He ran to meet it head-on and used both his momentum and the creature's to shove the spade as far down its throat as he could. The teeth splintered the protruding wooden shaft, but it was too late—the head of the spade was steel, and iron was poisonous to most of the fae. Rhys dove and scrambled to get out of reach of the venom and gore. The bwgan's body paled to its original ghastly shade and flopped back and forth like a cut snake on a hot rock.

He watched the monster's death throes with mounting anger.

Bwganod do not live on this side of the ocean. Not only had the vicious thing been deliberately sent by some faction of the faery court, it had been magically transported. Rhys knew it would have taken a great deal of power to move the earthbound beast over so much water. And for what purpose?

After Morgan had broken the spell that bound him, the ruling fae were restrained by their own laws. They could not place a finger on him directly—but Rhys knew all too well that they had no shortage of other faery creatures to send in their stead. He'd seen the ellyll, after all, and knew the Tylwyth Teg were watching him. And he should have known that simple spying would never satisfy them. Obviously they wanted him dead.

By all the gods, they wouldn't find him easy to kill.

At last the bwgan ceased its thrashing, and its remaining eye darkened. Rhys was thankful the ugly creature had landed right side up because there was one last task to perform. Drawing a utility knife from a sheath on his belt—a gift from Leo—he peeled the cold, clammy skin from the broad forehead. As the skull was revealed, so was something deeply embedded in the bone. Rhys held his breath as he applied the tip of the knife to gently pry out the object. It resisted his efforts at first, then popped from its cavity with a sound like a joint dislocating. Wiping away the dark, bluish blood with the edge of his T-shirt, he examined his prize in the sunlight. It was somber in color and oddly shaped, like a rounded triangle—flat on one side and as big as a duck's egg. But no egg shimmered so. The light played over and around it as if it were a darkly iridescent pearl.

Rhys knew that what he held in his hand was incredibly valuable, but the value didn't lay in its beauty. Bwgan stones were rarer than the most priceless of jewels. Few of these deadly creatures produced them, and there was no way to tell if a bwgan had one or not until it died—a rare occurrence in itself. Druids prized the stones, magi sought them, and the Fair Ones themselves esteemed them highly.

He had no idea what he would do with it or even what he *could* do with it—he was certainly no druid—but the gods had delivered it into his hands, so he thanked them for it. Perhaps a use for it would become apparent later. In the meantime, he had other things to do. He jogged to the corral and was immensely relieved to see Lucy still standing where he'd left her. She whickered when she caught sight of him, but he dared not go to her right away, not stinking like that predatory monster. Rhys headed instead for an old metal barrel that caught water from a rain gutter and immersed his hands and wrists, rubbing away the gore that coated them. Finally, he peeled off his shoes and clothes and dropped them into the water, leaving them to soak—but not before knotting the stone into a sock. It would be safe enough in the barrel for the time being.

Naked, he untied the gray horse. "There's a brave *llafnes*." *Big girl.* He spoke soothingly to her, crooning a mix of Welsh and Celtic words. They had to pass the dead salamander in order to get to the barn, but he walked Lucy in a wide arc around it. Her nose quivered and her ears were in constant motion, alert for danger, but she didn't balk. "You'd make a very fine warhorse," he said. Her solid build and her responsive, steady temperament were ideal. She was slow right now and favored her left rear leg, but he had confidence she would grow strong again. "A shame it is that no one has need for such steeds in this age."

They left the grassy field and headed toward the barn that held both her stall and his quarters. He was grateful now that Leo had insisted he buy a few more clothes. Rhys had thought one set more than sufficient for his needs, but he hadn't counted on getting them bloodied in battle. *Another good reason to fight naked.* At least the bwgan's death was likely to discourage any other creatures from showing up. For a while.

It didn't do a thing to discourage human visitors, however.

He was a hundred feet from the barn when a strange truck pulled into the farm's driveway. Rhys swore aloud but there was nothing he could do—he wouldn't rush the injured horse nor walk her across the hard-packed corral, even though it would have been the faster route. He was just forty feet from getting his nude self out of sight when the truck—followed by a second one drawing a trailer—pulled up beside him.

Rhys had only a fleeting moment to wonder if the gods hated him after all before a man jumped down and walked toward him. His hair was long and bound in a tail, while charms and fetishes bounced around his neck. His orange T-shirt proclaimed "Zombie Apocalypse Survival Team," which made no sense to Rhys at all. But he recognized the man from the clinic, a healer of animals like Morgan.

"Hi, I'm Jay. You have *got* to be Reese." He handed Rhys a thick, checkered shirt, like Rhys's own, only this one was red. "I see we caught you at a bad time. Thought you might be able to use this."

"Rhys," he corrected and took the shirt, tying it around his waist like an apron or a kilt. He took Jay's hand then, noting that the man's grip was solid enough, despite his wiry build. "And I thank you for the loan of the shirt. I was not expecting guests to arrive."

"I figured that." Jay laughed as he made a quick inspection of the horse's bandages. "These dressings look really good. Neat, clean, no seepage. Morgan said you were taking great care of Lucy. So...you go au naturel often?"

"In truth, I'm feeling more than a little foolish now. My work for the day was done, my clothes were filthy, and I stripped them off. I was just taking Lucy back to the barn and enjoying a bit of sun before making use of the shower."

"And along come a bunch of strangers. Sorry for the rude surprise. Morgan lets us borrow the corral in order to practice, so we bring our horses out here every couple weeks." Jay waved toward the others—five men and three women who had clustered near one of the vehicles.

Most of them were trying to avoid looking in Rhys's direction. There was embarrassed giggling from two of the women, however, and more than a few stolen glances. Strange behavior—women of his own village would have been bold enough to walk up to a warrior and invite him to their bed had they favored what they saw. Nudity and sex were normal parts of life among the clans, and there were no customs or laws decrying them. Women as well as men chose their partners as they pleased, and no one thought ill of it nor attempted to deter it. In this time, however, there were rules aplenty, written and unwritten, and so many social mores that Rhys wondered if he would ever remember them all.

"Next time I'll be certain to dress for the occasion," Rhys said and made his escape. For a moment he considered placing his body on the far side of the horse, but customs be damned, it wasn't in his nature to hide—and besides, he'd rather keep the group's attention on *him* than the rest of the farm.

Particularly with a dead bwgan still lying in the field.

If the group kept to the corral, they wouldn't be able to see the monster salamander—if they could see it at all. Now that Rhys was mortal, he wasn't certain why *he* could see the thing, but perhaps it was because he'd once been a fae creature himself. As a boy, he'd known people who had *the gift*, as it was said, meaning they could perceive the Fair Ones readily, but over the centuries fewer and fewer had the ability. It was unlikely that any of Jay's group had a latent talent for seeing faeries.

Morgan, however, might be different. If she really did possess some fae blood as the messengers had claimed, would she see what others could not? Rhys had no idea how he would explain the bwgan's existence, never mind its presence.

First things first, however. Rhys made the horse comfortable, checked the bandages again, paying particular attention to those on the left hind leg. He filled her bucket with fresh water, and she buried her nose in it, drinking long and deep.

He sought water too, standing under the shower in his quarters as he pondered his biggest problem. How did one dispose of a bwgan? He didn't know how long Jay and his friends were going to linger—he didn't even know what it was they were here to *practice*. Morgan was sure to be home soon as well. That meant the bwgan could not be dealt with until after dark, but he hated to leave it so long. He was still thinking it through as he toweled off and dressed, deciding to go barefoot until his shoes dried. Maybe he could—

A sudden sound set every nerve alert. Unmistakable and impossible at the same time, it resonated again. And again. A ring of steel on steel that Rhys had heard countless thousands of times over the centuries but never in recent history.

Swords.

ELEVEN

⌒⫛⌒

Despite Jay's urgent warning to take the pieces of the silver collar home, she'd managed to drag her feet for a couple more days. Now Morgan plunked the box in the backseat of her car. It wasn't the only task she'd been putting off. She'd been intending to get the collar repaired, just as she'd told Jay, and hadn't done it—but it wasn't because she hadn't had time. She could have made the time, *would* have made the time. Except the real reason she'd thought to have the collar fixed was not so she could put it back on the dog. It was so she would have something to remember the dog by.

Which would mean she'd given up on ever seeing Rhyswr again. And so she'd stuck the box in her office where it was guaranteed to be buried by papers and books and samples of veterinary pharmaceuticals. Out of sight, out of mind.

The silver links were very much on her mind now, however. And so were Jay's words. And what Rhys had once said too. Good grief, was she starting to believe that *faery-forged* crap? But what other explanation was there? She'd thought she had it all figured out, but the news about the silver blew all her theories away. Now her brain hurt from trying to make sense of the impossible.

Needing a friend to talk to, she'd tried phoning Gwen several times but hadn't succeeded in reaching her. She wished with all her heart that she could talk to her grandmother. For some reason, it seemed that Nainie might have been the one person who could decipher the strange situation. What if Jay was right? Morgan sighed then and shook her head as she climbed into the car. *No.* She wasn't ready to start accepting faery tales as truth. There was a perfectly logical explanation, a scientific explanation for all this. There *had* to be. She just hadn't figured it out yet.

She turned her car into her driveway and was surprised to find Jay's green pickup parked by the barn, as well as a big gray truck attached to a horse trailer. Was it *that* day already? Jay and his role-playing buddies came to the farm to practice archery, swordplay, and occasionally even jousting activities that didn't readily fit in suburban backyards.

Morgan parked beside the other vehicles and had barely gotten out of the car before she was captured in a hug by Jay's wife, Starr.

"I'm so glad to see you! Did you just get off work? You must be starving—we've laid out a picnic since it's so nice outside, and there's lots and lots of food. Let me find you a plate. Oh, and you have to try the fruit bars I made," Starr chattered as she led Morgan around the corner of the barn.

"Thanks. If they'll give me your energy, I could really use some," said Morgan with a laugh. *If it would give me some of your style, I'd like that too.* Starr had straight black hair that hung to her waist, intricately braided with beads and tiny bells. She always dressed in bright gauzy layers of hand-dyed cloth, long skirts and shawls and scarves. Starr's unique bohemian fashions enhanced her appearance rather than detracted from it, and next to her, Morgan always felt plain as a jenny wren (to borrow a phrase from Nainie). And yet she was certain she'd trip on her own skirt or be choked by a scarf if she ever tried to dress like that. She certainly couldn't work in such clothes...*And what do I ever do but work?*

The air was suddenly rent with loud cheers and decidedly male hoots that belonged more to a football game than to archery. Still chuckling, she turned to look—then stopped in her tracks and stared.

The group was cheering for Rhys. Riding without saddle or reins, he was guiding a big black Friesian in an easy circle as he drew a medieval longbow. His aim was astonishing—he nocked arrow after arrow and all flew into the center of a straw target.

"Can you believe it?" asked Starr, a little dreamily. "He's directing Brandan's horse with nothing but pure body language. I guess that's how dressage is done, but Boo's never been trained for it."

Body language. Rhys's body was certainly communicating something to hers, Morgan thought, unable to take her eyes off him. The black T-shirt he wore only seemed to emphasize the heavy muscle beneath. He was an imposing figure on horseback, yet as always, his movements were graceful, fluid. Both bow and horse seemed to be part of him, moving as a seamless whole. She'd never openly admired a man in her life, but there was no help for it—every sensuous dream she'd had replayed in her mind as she watched him.

Jay's voice sounded in her ear, making her jump. "You think that's good, you should see Rhys with a sword. He's been helping all of us with our techniques." He rubbed his left arm and shoulder. "What a workout! Mike's had the most training of any of us, years of it, but he says he learned more in an hour with Rhys than all of it put together. Footwork, balance, the way you keep your upper body facing forward at all times—I'm sure I've heard it all before, but when he says it, it sounds different. It makes sense. Especially when he knocks you on your ass."

"He hit you?"

"We were practicing. I learned pretty quick that if I don't keep my feet wide enough apart, my opponent can dump me. The only thing that made me feel less foolish is that Rhys took Mike down too."

"Mike? But he's so tall—you're always complaining that gives him an advantage."

"That's what I thought. But Rhys used it against him so fast he didn't see it coming. You know what this means, don't you?"

"You have a new playmate to invite to your Renaissance fairs?"

"He'd sure make a helluva impression." Jay lowered his voice then. "And that's just the point. Morgan, this guy of yours is hyperskilled with weaponry."

"That's pretty obvious. But so what? Brandan and Mike are too. So are the rest of you. Starr's a whiz with her bow, while I can barely hold one steady."

"Maybe you're not experienced enough to see the difference. Look, even Mike and Brandan agree with me that Rhys is different. *Really* different. He seems to be a good guy and all, don't get me wrong. I like him, even though I think Starr's infatuated after seeing him naked, but—"

"She saw him *naked*?"

Jay shrugged. "He was naked when we got here. We surprised him, that's all."

"I've got a naked guy wandering around my farm and you're defending him?"

"Hey, I know people who like to be naked. Very natural and healthy. Think of the vitamin D his body is able to make on such a sunny day—"

Morgan put her hands over her ears. "I don't want to think about that, thank you!"

"The point is, no one was around, so I figure, hey, it's his business. And I know you can still hear me."

She sighed and put her hands down. "I really wanted to believe that the nudity was a one-time thing. Now I have to be concerned about it—jeez, Jay, he's living here. With me. On my property. What if he's a pervert?"

"Has Rhys ever walked around naked when you're here since that first time?"

"No."

"Ever made a move on you?"

"No."

"Ever said anything, insinuated anything, given you any reason to *suspect* he's a pervert? Even just given you a creepy feeling?"

"No, no, and no." She threw up her hands. "So he's not raising any alarms. But maybe I'm just easily fooled. For all you know, I have faulty predator-detection instincts."

"Bullshit. Veterinary medicine is as much an art as a science because our patients can't talk to us. You have to have not just good instincts, but *great* instincts to be good at it. And you're good at it, Morgan. Maybe better than Grady and me put together."

She was surprised and touched by the compliment and would have said so, but Jay wasn't finished.

"So I figure Rhys is safe enough or you'd know," he said. "But you gotta consider this weaponry thing. Morgan, I'm telling you, his level of skill with a sword or a bow or even a horse doesn't come from taking classes or attending Ren fairs."

"How do you know?"

"Because he's on the offensive constantly. And all of his moves are instinctive; he's not thinking about them. But he *is* thinking about how to pull his punches, so to speak. Everything he does is designed to take advantage of his opponent's weaknesses, and *fast*. He got under Mike's guard and took him down, like I said, but if Rhys hadn't drawn back at the last moment, Mike would have lost one or both legs."

"Jesus, Jay! First you tell me he's naked, then you tell me he's some kind of psycho!"

"That's not what I mean at all. It's just that his style of swordplay isn't *play*. It's kill or be killed. It's the real thing, Morgan. And you can only get that kind of skill one way."

She didn't want to know but asked anyway. "And what is that?"

"From living it, Morgan."

Oh, good grief. "You really think his warrior story is true, don't you?"

"I'm remaining open to all possibilities."

In other words, he did. If Jay had asked her to accept the existence of unicorns, she doubted that it would have felt much different. "Look, it's one thing to be receptive to new ideas, but this is really *out there*."

"That's not a valid reason to discount Rhys's story. What about Sherlock Holmes?"

"What does he have to do with anything?"

"Sherlock Holmes said, 'When you have eliminated the impossible—'"

Jay stepped back suddenly, and Morgan turned to see what he was looking at. She had a split second's view of the great black horse bearing down on her. There was no time to react before she was whisked skyward and clamped tight to a broad chest.

"What the hell!" she sputtered. She was seated sideways on the horse in front of Rhys like a storybook princess. It wasn't a secure feeling, despite his obvious strength. "Put me down!"

Her captor only laughed at her. As the horse circled the archery range at an easy canter, Morgan gradually lost her initial fear. She couldn't fall if she tried, held fast by Rhys's iron arms. And as far as she could tell, Rhys himself was part of the horse. She gave up and relaxed. They circled the field twice more, and Morgan found herself actually disappointed when they came to a gentle stop in front of the cheering group. Rhys gave her a final squeeze then set her on the ground as easily as if she'd been a child.

He dismounted and walked the horse over to his owner. Morgan couldn't figure out how he guided Boo so easily without a lead rope. Rhys's hand rested on the muscled neck of the big draft animal, but Boo weighed close to a ton. If the horse decided to go in another direction, there'd be nothing to stop him. Yet he followed as if he were simply a large, companionable dog.

Morgan's heart squeezed. The horse was behaving just as her big black mastiff had, taking his every cue from his human. As Rhyswr had looked to *her*—and damn it all, she missed him. Seeking some privacy, she stepped around the side of a truck and scrubbed the moisture from her eyes with the heel of her hand. Sniffed and chided herself for getting so emotional—

"It's strange to see sadness on such a bright day. Are you well?" There was concern in Rhys's strong face, a softness in his gaze that contrasted with the hard muscle of his body.

"I'm just missing my dog, that's all. It's probably silly—I didn't have him all that long."

"Aye, but it's not the number of days that decides the strength of the bond." He rested a massive hand lightly on her shoulder for a moment, then strode back to the corral where Mike had finished saddling Boo.

Surprised by the simple wisdom, Morgan was left to wonder if he was speaking about her dog or something more. For the next couple of hours, she watched Rhys instructing each of the group, even Jay, who could barely ride, in the art of horsemanship. No matter who the student was, however, she only had eyes for Rhys. The way he moved was deeply familiar to her, as if she'd been watching him for years, not mere days.

She ate from a plate Starr had brought her, barely tasting the food. Barely hearing the excited conversations around her. Instead she considered the long conversations she'd had with Rhys each evening over supper. They were so easy together, so familiar. Sometimes she even knew what he was going to say before he said it. How had this man, this *stranger*, slipped so seamlessly into her life in so short a time? How had he stepped from a dream and into her every waking thought?

It's not the number of days that decides the strength of the bond...

She still didn't have the answers she wanted—and she sure as hell wasn't ready to consider Jay's suggestion—but in the past few days, she'd managed to come to one conclusion at least.

Nainie Jones had said that someday a leap of knowing would come to her. Morgan hadn't understood then, but now it seemed that she had indeed inherited a little of her grandmother's ability to sense the future. Modern science allowed that intuition, extrasensory perception, and presentiment existed. Plus, hunches and feelings counted for a lot in Morgan's own work. There were numberless times that she had sensed more than tested her way to a diagnosis. So she could accept that she had a portion—a very *small* portion—of Nainie's gift. After all, that would explain all the dreams she'd had about Rhys. It explained how she felt that she knew Rhys before she met him and why she trusted him when all logic said she shouldn't.

It didn't explain the rush of desire Morgan felt every time she was within a hundred yards of the man. But one day soon she just might try to answer that question on her own.

∾

The sun was down before the group finished loading up their horses and their equipment and left. Rhys had enjoyed their company immensely. They seemed to appreciate his instruction, and it felt good to heft weapons again, even if they weren't exactly what he was used to. Both the bows and the swords were light for their size, more like toys than tools, and while the longbow was powerful, it wasn't suited for use on horseback. But the principles were the same and they worked well enough, as evidenced from the blood when Mike had taken a hit from Brandan. Mike had held up well. He'd accepted what they called *first aid*—was there second or third aid as well, and what might they consist of?—and then carried on with his swordplay as if nothing had happened. Mike's instincts were good, and Rhys thought he'd have made an excellent warrior in his own clan's time.

Thanks to Jay's wife, Starr, much of the leftover feast had ended up filling the shelves of Rhys's refrigerator. It appeared that Morgan would be free from having to concern herself with feeding him for days—and for her sake, he was glad not to trouble her. He hoped she would still come to the barn to visit. Tonight, however, the guests stayed long. By the time everyone left, Morgan had pleaded weariness and retreated to her house. He missed their time together, just the two of them, at the end of the day, but this time he was grateful she was gone.

He had a bwgan to bury.

There wasn't another spade in the machine shed, but Rhys found a long steel pry bar. And amid the clutter, he unearthed a heavy yellow-and-black-striped sack—its label promising an even better tool than the bar: rock salt. He heaved the bag over his shoulder and carried both it and the pry bar to the field.

The dead bwgan looked ghastly in the moonlight. The bloated white body lay close to the crevice in the earth from which it had emerged. The mound that it had raised seemed smaller, however, and the gaping tear in its base narrower—was the earth trying to heal itself?

Salt, or *halen* as it was called in Wales, was a pure and sacred substance, and had been used since ancient times to repel evil and unnatural forces. As if he were sowing seed, Rhys scattered heavy crystals of salt over everything—the ground, the blood, the carcass. The salt pitted the pale hide of the monster, and a stinking smoke arose as the body unexpectedly began to collapse on itself. Encouraged, Rhys threw fistfuls of salt on the bwgan until its bulk was considerably diminished. Finally he used the pry bar to lever what was left of the creature into the hole.

As he stuffed the last of the tail as far into the pit as he could with the steel bar, a whoosh of dank air caused Rhys to spring backward. He landed on his arse but quickly tucked his knees to his chin, barely avoiding having his feet crushed as the rend in the earth slammed shut like a huge dusty mouth. Inwardly, he cursed the Tylwyth Teg in every language he knew as he swiped the dust from his eyes with his sleeve and stood up. Cursed aloud as he realized the highly useful pry bar had gone with the monster salamander.

He still had salt left, though, and plenty of it. The white crystals glittered like quartz in the moonlight as he spread them thickly all the way around and on top of the slight depression that marked where the mound had once risen. He hated to damage the soil in such a manner—nothing would grow in this spot again—but Rhys knew that the underground was the natural realm of the Fair Ones. In the British Isles, there were *ways* that were many miles long, yet the faery mounds, thus connected, seemed like adjacent rooms. And once a way for traveling through the earth had been created, there was nothing to prevent other creatures of that realm from using the same route. Because of the salt, however, unwanted travelers would find the door sealed shut on this end.

By all the gods, the earth will not open here again.

Not here, that was certain, but what about the rest of the farm? Rhys straightened from his task and looked around. He'd drawn them here, faeries and monsters—and the gods only knew what next—to Morgan's land. And all she'd done to deserve it was to show kindness to a dog. True, the faery queen had declared Morgan to be eithriedig, and as such she should be fully protected. But would the bwgan have hesitated to prey on her? They were known for their ferocity, not their brains.

Perhaps that was why the Tylwyth Teg had sent the creature in their stead. The royal edict officially tied their hands from directly harassing Morgan, but the darker side of the fae realm was filled with things that often bit first and asked questions later. If at all.

For a moment, Rhys wished he could warn her…then realized that even if she believed him, it wouldn't be nearly enough to keep her safe. No, it was up to him. He'd vowed to protect her, and he would find a way.

TWELVE

⌒⟨⟨⟩⟩⌒

Morgan had been called out just before dawn to attend a goat. The owner had expected twins for certain, perhaps triplets because of the doe's sizable abdomen. However, when labor set in, the doe strained without result. When Morgan arrived, she found a kid presented crosswise and had to coax it into proper position. Once she did, it practically popped out like toast. And so did three more behind it! The owner was ecstatic and so was Morgan. Quads weren't unheard of, but they weren't common. And such healthy and strong quads were rare. It was one of those gratifying cases that made her glad to be a veterinarian. As she left, the mother was munching grain, and all four of the kids were behaving more like spring-loaded toys than newborns.

She wondered if goats would do well on her farm and made a mental note to ask Rhys about it. The man seemed to know all sorts of things and was proving himself just as capable around the farm as he was with horses. She'd discovered the empty garden plot neatly turned over and prepared for planting next spring. The old apple orchard north of the barn and all the berry bushes were pruned, as were the rose bushes around the house. Roofing was repaired on the outbuildings, and fences were mended.

Thanks to Rhys, the farm was gradually losing its overgrown and neglected appearance.

Morgan found herself less inclined to stay late at the clinic doing paperwork. She was still devoted to her patients and continued to put in long days when they needed her, but she looked forward to Rhys's company in the evenings.

The Celtic warrior and faery grim stories had not been repeated. She couldn't begin to guess his reasons for telling her such crazy tales in the first place but decided to give him the benefit of the doubt. Maybe he'd just been embarrassed by being found naked in a stranger's home; maybe he was trying to avoid revealing his identity. At the time, she hadn't gotten close enough to smell his breath—maybe he'd been under the influence of alcohol, perhaps even a so-called party drug. It certainly wasn't unusual for people to get naked when they'd overindulged. *Or get strange.* She'd had an instructor in college who, when he'd gone over his limit, often claimed to be the offspring of an extraterrestrial pairing with a human! Jay would no doubt have been fascinated...

As far as origins went, she still didn't know a lot of personal information about Rhys. He recalled plenty about Wales but didn't seem to remember how he managed to show up in Spokane Valley, Washington. Jay could believe that faery curse song and dance if he wanted to, but Morgan preferred to read up on topics such as clinical amnesia. Leo had suggested short-term memory loss, and she studied that too. There just *had* to be a rational explanation for Rhys's mental condition, something scientific and solid, something she could accept.

Because if she didn't find satisfaction for her mind, would it ever allow her to follow her heart?

∾

Rhys pounded the last nail in place and stepped back to look at his work. A large horseshoe was fastened over one of the doors to the barn, its open end on the right-hand side.

"Won't that let all the luck spill out?" asked a familiar voice.

"Leo! Good it is to see you again." Rhys went to the old man at once and clapped him firmly by the shoulders. "I didn't hear your car."

"Probably because you've been pounding nails for the last twenty minutes. Plus, I parked by the road so I'd remember to pick some of those crab apples by the front gate—they make a good jelly, you know—and I walked up. Been sitting over there on Doc Edward's porch swing, watching you."

"You should have hailed me."

Leo shrugged. "You looked pretty intense about what you were doing, so I thought I'd just wait. Besides, the swing's in the shade, so it was no hardship to watch somebody else work. I thought you'd just be putting up one or two horseshoes, though. Instead, you got every shape and size of them over every doorway in the place."

"I found a few stacked on a rafter in the machine shed," said Rhys, stalling for time to think of how to explain his strange task. He decided right away to keep quiet about the barrel of rusty iron nails he'd already used up. Nor was he going to reveal that unnatural creatures had watched him as he did it. Or that they'd crept and slithered, flown and trudged around the perimeter of the farm, leering and hissing at him from the other side of the fence as he hammered nails into the top of every wooden post on the property. More than likely, the small fae beasts had been the unwilling forerunners of the bwgan. Rhys imagined that even the Tylwyth Teg had needed to practice a little before they could successfully send the monstrous salamander over such a distance. He wondered how many failures there had been, how many lesser fae had perished in the attempts. Of course, the Fair Ones would neither notice nor care.

No, Rhys wasn't going to talk about any of that to Leo. Nor mention that he'd buried nails deep in the hard-packed soil between gateposts so that there was a perfect ring of protection around the farm. Nails even studded the corners of the roof of Morgan's house, and Rhys had pounded two or three nails into the trunk of every tree on the property. The trees would be unaffected, but they were now poisoned against lesser fae. The Tylwyth Teg would be unable to send any more minions to the farm. If they wanted to cause trouble, they'd have to do it themselves.

"You call that a *few*? I counted about twenty or so horseshoes. And how come they're all on their sides? Looks like the letter *C* or something."

Rhys looked at the horseshoe and back at his friend. "They're just as they should be."

"My dad always said horseshoes were for luck, kind of like four-leaf clovers. And if you didn't hang them with the opening at the top, all the luck would pour out. But maybe it's different in Wales."

Rhys considered what to say. He wouldn't talk of the Fair Ones to Morgan at present—she would equate that with madness for sure, and who knows what she would do? Perhaps even call Officer Richards again. Leo, however, was different. "The Welsh hang their horseshoes like this so they look like the crescent moon. The sign of the moon plus the iron will repel faeries. The very presence of iron weakens them, and its touch will burn or poison them."

"Never heard that one before. Seems like a mean thing to do to a cute helpless faery."

"In Wales, faeries are neither cute nor helpless, and often humans must protect themselves against them. There are many different kinds of fae—the greater ones, the Tylwyth Teg who rule over all, cannot be repelled by the presence of iron, though they can be injured by its touch. All of the lesser fae and the darker ones, now, they're the faeries that cannot abide iron at all. They'll not come near it."

"All this faery stuff reminds me of my first-grade teacher, Mrs. Farnsworth. She was English, and if we behaved and got all our work done, she'd tell us faery tales. Stories about sprites and brownies and pixies and such, and all the squabbling they did with each other. Used to be that I couldn't wait to get to school in hopes we'd hear a story that day." Leo sighed and picked up a horseshoe from a stack. "So if I put this up over my front door, I'll have no more trouble with the little people?"

"Take two. You need to cover both doors, front and back," said Rhys, then did a double take. "No *more* trouble?"

"A couple days after you left, I started finding things out of place. Books, knickknacks, that kind of thing. They'd be on the shelves when I left the house and then there'd be a dozen on the floor when I came back. And no way was Spike responsible—he can barely get around. But nothing was ever broken.

"And then it started happening with the plates in the kitchen. Again, nothing broken, just taken out of the cupboards and stacked on the floor every morning. Never any doors or windows unlocked, no sign of anyone having gotten in, so I couldn't blame it on a prankster. Almost had it figured for some kind of damn poltergeist, like in the movies. But today I finally saw the little guy. All brown, about two or three feet high, dressed in leaves and with leaves in his hair. He was throwing my tools around my workshop like he was having some kind of tantrum."

Rhys frowned. It could only be the ellyll. "I'm thinking I should be paying a visit to your house then," he said. "I'm done with my tasks here for now. I'll just be checking on Lucy and changing her dressings and then we can go."

Leo looked relieved. "I'd like that. I'd appreciate a second opinion."

Rhys thought Leo might come with him to the barn, but he said he wanted to spend a little more time on Morgan's large and comfortable porch swing. That was fine with Rhys—he needed to think. He'd spotted the ellyll briefly while in Leo's garden, but he'd expected that any creatures working for the Tylwyth Teg would follow their target to the farm. After all, the bwgan had come directly here—*and thank the gods for that*. Why had the ellyll lingered? Perhaps it had expected Rhys to return and was simply making a nuisance of itself in the meantime.

He unwrapped the old gauze and applied new, his fingers deft and sure yet gentle. The mare twitched and lashed her tail, letting him know that she didn't like having the dressings touched where the wounds were the worst, but still she permitted him to work on them. "*Fy un hardd*," he murmured. *My beautiful one.* A fresh outer layer of cloth bandaging protected the dressings. As he finished the last, he heard Morgan's car drive up and hoped she had brought more from the clinic—

Morgan. Leo. Together. Rhys cursed and left the barn at a jog, hoping he could interrupt their inevitable conversation before Leo could call her attention to the horseshoes—or, worse, mention what creatures they were meant to keep at bay. He found Morgan sitting in the chair beside his friend. "Lucy's looked after now," he announced, more brightly than he felt. "Afternoon to you, Morgan."

"Same to you." She smiled at him, and was it his imagination or was there just a little more warmth in her gaze than had been there yesterday?

Leo cleared his throat. "I was just telling the doc that *I found some more work for you to do*, so I need to steal you back for a little while."

Rhys relaxed. "I'll be pleased to help, as always. I won't be gone long," he said to Morgan.

"No worries. I've got plenty to keep me busy." She waved at a thick folder of papers in her lap. "Have a good time, you two."

A good time? A strange thing to say to a man who was about to turn his hand to a task. His puzzlement must have showed because Leo leaned forward and cupped a hand to his mouth in a stage whisper. "I may have let slip there was a baseball game on TV tonight."

"Your secret male plans are known to me," said Morgan with a laugh. "Make sure you order pizza from Gibby's. They've got a special one with nachos. Don't worry about coming home early to check on Lucy—I'll do that before I go to bed. Happy bonding!"

As she went into the house, he followed Leo to his car, grateful that the subject of faeries hadn't come up. "What does she mean by *bonding*?"

"She's just referring to a fancy new catchphrase: *male bonding*. Don't know why somebody had to go and give it a name. It's just guys getting together and having a good time doing guy-type things without women around. You know, like watching sports and drinking beer and eating a lot."

"Men have been doing that for many centuries."

"Exactly. But now it's got a damn title," said Leo as he turned the car onto the highway. He was quiet for a long moment, then sighed. "So it seems I got a few questions to ask. I never saw anything like this faery creature in my whole life. For a moment, I thought I was seeing things, that maybe my mind was finally starting to go. Then that little guy looked right at me and asked me where *you'd* gone to and when you were coming back. Asked for you by *name*, that is." The old man looked meaningfully in Rhys's direction. "So I'm thinking, is there anything you'd like to tell me about where you're from and what you're doing here?"

There was no help for it. Rhys took a deep breath and told Leo his story. The old man didn't say much as he drove, just listened, asking only a couple of brief, clarifying questions. On Rhys's advice, they stopped to pick up supplies for the ellyll. Leo said little even then, simply paid for the purchases and got back into the car.

After his experiences with Morgan and with the police, Rhys was all too well aware of how insane his story sounded to the people of this time and place. He hated the idea of losing Leo's friendship, and there wasn't a thing he could do about it. The truth was the truth. But by the time the car turned into the old man's driveway, he fully expected to be ordered off the property.

Instead, Leo turned to him, his face a curious mix of expressions—but none of them hostile. "Rhys, I used to think that people got smarter as they got older. Turns out, it doesn't quite work that way. The longer I live, the more I realize I don't know.

"Now you've dumped a whole shitload of stuff I don't know into my world. And I gotta say, if I didn't see that little guy with my own eyes and hear him with my own ears, I don't know if I could have swallowed a story like that."

"You believe me then?" asked Rhys.

Leo nodded. "Don't get your hopes up too high, though. Maybe I'm just crazy too. So let's go visit this—what the hell did you call it?"

"An ellyll."

Leo gamely tried to wrap his tongue around the *LL*, the most difficult of all Welsh language sounds. Then snorted. "Forget it. It's an elf."

"But it's an—"

"Elf."

"An elf, then," agreed Rhys. "But not in his hearing." He didn't know if *ellyllon* liked elves—they were similar creatures but different enough that perhaps being mistaken for one could be insulting. What he did know was that many ellyllon had quick tempers and that the ones he'd met could curse more fluently than any warrior. As elementals, they wielded a very ancient magic and were known to make up charms and spells on the fly—particularly to use against an enemy. "Perhaps it would be best if I spoke for us."

"No argument there." Leo led the way to the workshop on the other side of the garden.

Rhys peered inside. Nothing moved. He pushed the door open farther. No sound, no movement. "It's not here—"

Thwack. A pair of garden gloves struck him in the chest.

"There ya are, ya great *helynt*." The little brown man walked out from under the workbench and pointed a long twiggy finger at him as the brown leaves that covered him rustled and fluttered.

"Me, a troublemaker? Why?" asked Rhys, surprised.

"*Why? Why? Why?*" mocked the ellyll. "If it weren't for *you*, ya *twpsyn*, the Tylwyth Teg wouldn't have marooned me in this strange country. I'm to be their eyes on ya or lose my own." He seized a screwdriver from the scattering of tools on the floor and let it fly.

The tool struck the doorpost next to Rhys's head and stuck there like a thrown knife. He struggled against his fighter's instincts and managed a polite response instead of lunging for the creature. "Far from home you are indeed, good spirit. Might I make you an offering of milk and bread?"

The ellyll's blue eyes glittered, and he dropped the pliers he'd just picked up. "Fair starved I am, 'tis true. My current employers tend to stint on their wages."

"It's strange to me that such a powerful elemental need be employed at all. Surely the earth yields you her abundance."

The tiny man snorted. "Abundance I once had, but not here. Family I once had too, but no one is left of my clan. The Tylwyth Teg fight among themselves, and the harm they would wreak upon one another spills about like a pot overboiled. I am called Ranyon, and 'tis my fate to be alone." He seemed to droop at the last word and sighed deeply. A number of small items tumbled from beneath the leaves that covered him—bits of copper wire, steel washers, and some tiny gears from an old clock made a half circle around the saddened creature.

"I am sorry to hear of it," said Rhys, trying to think of what to say. Like Ranyon, he'd experienced devastating loss, but he knew of no words that could help. All he could do was kneel and gently pick up the ellyll's treasures for him and deposit them in the tiny palm of his twiggy hand. For a moment, he wished Morgan was there—with her kind heart, he was certain she'd think of something to say.

But it was Leo who stepped up. "Well, nobody needs to be alone here, or hungry neither," he declared and held out a hand to the dejected creature. "Ranyon, you come on in to my kitchen and we'll get you fed. We picked up some fresh bread on the way here. Rhys said faeries like butter and cream, so I got some of that too. Oh, and you gotta try the raspberry jam that I made this summer. It's my granny's recipe. She was always taking home blue ribbons from…"

Surprised, Ranyon took the hand that was offered and found himself led to the house like a child, as Leo talked about food and baseball. Rhys followed behind, wondering if his friend knew what he was getting himself into and not daring to tell him.

An ellyll was extremely loyal.

As it turned out, the ellyll was an instant baseball fan too. Leo and Rhys sat on the long sagging couch with Ranyon between them, and within a few minutes, the little brown creature was standing on the cushion and loudly cheering on the Blue Jays. Rhys leaned toward the Cardinals himself, and Leo, as a Mariners fan, declared himself neutral but couldn't help but get caught up in the close game. The three of them polished off a pair of large pizzas. Despite his size—and despite having already consumed the bread with butter and jam—Ranyon ate most of one pizza by himself. He did share a few crusts with Spike, who was more than happy to accept them from him.

"Did you notice that Spike didn't even bark at Ranyon?" Leo whispered to Rhys during a kitchen break. "I know the dog's deaf and blind, but there's nothing wrong with his nose. He *always* gets upset at strangers."

"An ellyll is an elemental. He's of the earth itself, so Spike wouldn't scent anything odd or out of place."

"You mean Ranyon smells kind of neutral—like a rock or a tree or something?"

Rhys nodded. "He's much like a tree in many ways."

"You don't mean to tell me that all those goddamn leaves on him—"

"Grow there. Aye, they do."

Leo shook his head as if to clear it. "Hope the damn dog doesn't pee on him," the old man muttered as he carried a second tray of nachos to the living room.

When the Jays surged ahead at the bottom of the ninth inning with three runs and finished seven to five, the ellyll could no longer contain himself. He bounced off the couch, vaulted the coffee table, careened off the bookcase, and somersaulted several times in front of the TV while howling and hooting with delight at the top of his lungs. His many small and shiny treasures peppered the floor.

Leo slapped his knees and laughed until tears ran down the leathery creases of his face. Rhys laughed too but with a watchful eye on his friend in case he was unable to catch his breath. He needn't have worried.

"Goddamn," wheezed Leo at last, wiping his face on a pizza-stained paper napkin. "Goddamn, I almost pissed myself. Ranyon, you are a cutup. I haven't had a belly laugh like that in heaven knows how long."

"And I haven't had such a fine meal nor such solid companions in an age and a half," chuckled Ranyon, lying on his back in the center of the room with a hand on his distended belly. "Truly, it's been a *brammer* of an evening."

"I take it that's a good thing," said Leo.

Rhys nodded. "Aye, it is indeed." He moved to gather dishes, planning to take them to the kitchen.

"Leave 'em be," said the ellyll, with a wave of his twiggy hand. "I'll be taking care of those myself tonight. It's the least I can do fer such fine hospitality."

Leo protested immediately. "You're my guest, and guests don't wash dishes."

"Ellyll likely don't wash dishes either," whispered Rhys over his shoulder, as he put the plates back on the coffee table.

"Aye," said Ranyon, as if Rhys had spoken aloud. "I've a charm fer that. It'll all be put right by morning."

Leo glanced over at Rhys, but he had no idea how to begin to explain and just shrugged. The old man opened his mouth, then closed it again as if he'd thought better of asking any questions. He was likely still mulling over what Rhys had told him about Ranyon's leaves…

In the end, Rhys agreed to stay overnight, partly because he didn't want to trouble Leo to make the long drive out to Morgan's farm in the dark, and partly because he wanted to see what his friend was going to do with the ellyll. Things played out much as he expected—Leo simply assigned Ranyon a room of his own upstairs, down the hall from the one Rhys used.

The little brown man was delighted and bounced upon the bed. "Lookit this fine bit o' comfort here!" Burrowing under the covers, Ranyon sighed happily, and it wasn't long before loud snores all out of proportion to his size were echoing along the hallway and down the stairs.

Back in the kitchen, Rhys peered at what the ellyll had left on Leo's table. A blue coffee mug had a fork and a potato peeler attached at strange angles to its handle with a carefully wound length of copper wire. The mug was half-filled with water, and in it were three smooth white stones, a sprig of something that Ranyon had called *soapwort*, and an ancient green toothbrush. The brush had a tiny copper bell wired to it.

"I don't know if it's modern art or a setup for TV reception," grinned Leo. "I guess I'll display it on top of the fridge, like the artwork my great-grandkids send me. I didn't understand what the little guy was saying when he put it together, but he was sure proud of it when he was done."

"The ellyllon do not create art. 'Tis a charm, and a strong one."

"*That?* Shit, what's it do? Is it dangerous? Goddamn, I didn't know he was *serious* about that stuff."

"Nay, it's not dangerous, although I don't know its purpose. A charm is designed to be helpful in some way. And an ellyll takes everything seriously, especially friendship. He's not likely to leave your home now."

Leo shrugged. "Yeah, I kinda figured that. But after having you around, I found I liked having someone in the house again. The kids don't live close so they don't visit much. And it's pretty obvious you won't be here much anymore."

"The agreement is that I should stay at the farm to tend the horse. Once Lucy is fair mended, there's little reason for Morgan to keep me about."

The old man chuckled. "Buddy, if you believe that, I have a bridge to sell you."

"Why would I be wanting a bridge?"

"Okay, forget the bridge. You like this woman, right?"

"More than like, 'tis true."

"And you've told her that, right?"

"Not in so many words," said Rhys, then relented. "No, not a word at all. My story is a strange one, and she thinks me touched in the head. Would you have believed me if not for Ranyon?"

"It certainly would have been harder," Leo agreed. "But we're friends, and that means I would have *tried* to believe. I would have at least entertained the possibility, even if it was only for a few minutes. Building a relationship will help Morgan be able to believe too, because she'll know you and trust you."

"I'm thinking I need to be patient with Morgan. She needs more time."

"But she knows how you feel, right? You've let her know that much, haven't you?"

Rhys frowned at him. "I labor on her farm. I take care of the horse, but there's much to be done on Morgan's land to make it yield again. Surely she knows my intentions from my work."

"Wanna bet? Any hired hand could do the same. A *stranger* could do the same. Your work shows her you're not lazy, and that's good, but it doesn't do a thing to make her feel romantic toward you. Maybe it was different for the women in your time, but it's been my experience that modern women want more from their men."

"More what? I cannot bed her until she accepts me."

"You don't seem to understand that there's plenty to be done between showing off your work ethic and having sex with her. You know, when I was younger I thought like you do, that my gal simply ought to 'know' how I feel." He made quotation marks in the air with his gnarled fingers. "Later, I caught on that women didn't work that way. I needed to show her she was *special* to me, and after we were married, I learned I had to keep on showing it."

"Special," repeated Rhys.

"Exactly. I brought my Tina flowers and little surprises, did nice things for her. Hugged and kissed her and told her I loved her as often as I could. It's always those little things, the little attentions that count the most. And thank heavens, I did better at it as I got older."

Rhys considered his parents, his sister and her husband, his friends—all the relationships he knew. In his former life, Rhys's motives and intentions would have been perfectly clear. Or would they? According to Leo, a man courted a woman much the same in any age. Perhaps he had been a warrior, in the company of warriors, much too long.

"Think of it this way—women are just like gardens. You do a lot of little things every day for a garden to make it grow, right? Well, a woman's needs have to be met in order for your relationship to flourish." Leo grinned then. "Even *marriages* have to be nurtured, and ours was happy for fifty-three years. Guess we were damn fine gardeners, Tina and I."

Leo looked over the strange coffee cup charm one more time and shook his head, then headed off to bed with Spike in tow.

Rhys went upstairs to his own bed, where Leo's words kept him from sleep for a long time. He tried to see things from Morgan's point of view and realized that his friend might be right. Why would she consider him as anything more than a hired man? What had he really done to persuade her otherwise?

Meanwhile, it was both disquieting and comforting that he'd finally told Leo *everything*. Had it been foolish to do so? Was it dangerous in some way that Leo now knew his secret? At least Rhys hadn't had to struggle to convince his friend—the physical presence of the ellyll verified his story. *Perhaps I should invite Ranyon to the farm to meet Morgan.* He snorted at the notion. Not that it wouldn't work, but he didn't want Morgan to believe because he'd brought her living evidence. He wanted her to believe him because—

Well, because she *trusted* him. A man needed his woman to have faith in him. And there was no doubt that he wanted Morgan to be his. Truth be told, he wanted to be hers too. It put him in mind of the last family gathering, when his sister, Arwyn, wed one of his cousins, a blacksmith from a neighboring village. Arwyn was barely a year younger than Rhys, and she had learned to heft a sword when he did. She made up for her smaller stature by being bold and brave and *fast*, and had bloodied his nose more than once when they were growing up. Most of the time he'd seen it coming—but not always. On this day, however, Arwyn didn't look anything like a sparring partner, or someone who was dangerous with both bow and dagger. She wore a fine red dress that showed off her dark hair plaited with flowers, and he remembered her smile as she held hands with Urien in the circle of their families. There'd been much happiness that day...

He sighed. Foolish to think of his family now after nearly twenty centuries had passed. Foolishness and folly. He thought he had come to terms with the loss of them over the long millennia. Instead, the hurt surprised him—both that the ache and the emptiness in his chest were still there and that the pain was still strong. No doubt it was Ranyon's tale of his aloneness, somewhat similar to Rhys's own, that had stirred up the memories like silt at the bottom of a deep pond.

Leo had said, "Always best to go forward if you can." But for a long moment, Rhys allowed himself to imagine facing Morgan in that circle of everyone he loved, holding her hands in his own...

When he started imagining other parts of her he'd like to hold, he had a whole new set of thoughts to keep him awake.

THIRTEEN

⌒⫯⌒

Some days it sucks to be a veterinarian.

It was a sign that one of Morgan's professors had kept posted prominently in his classroom. She hadn't understood at first—she'd had a huge supply of idealism that carried her for a long time. But by the time she'd graduated, reality had taken some of the shine off her idealism. She had no doubts about the career she'd chosen—she had a true passion for it—but she'd also come to realize that the best veterinary training in the world didn't make that world a perfect place. There were aspects of her job that weren't so lovable, plus a few things she just had to try to get through. Just like every other vocation in life.

Knowing that didn't make it one bit easier when you were having one of those days.

Her morning had begun with a dental procedure on an eight-year-old border collie—a basic teeth cleaning. Rory's owner brought him in annually for the procedure. Not all dogs needed it that often, but despite Rory's general good health, he had dreadful teeth. Cindy, the senior tech, started the IV drip. When the dog relaxed, Morgan intubated him and administered the gas. With Cindy carefully monitoring the dog's vital signs, Morgan began scaling and polishing the teeth. It should have gone like clockwork.

Instead, Rory stopped breathing. Quickly Morgan switched off the gas, removed the tube, and held the black-and-white muzzle closed, breathing into the nose while Cindy compressed the chest. One breath, three compressions. One breath, three compressions. Over and over. Nothing. She injected a respiratory stimulant. Nothing. Morgan tried everything she knew until sweat mingled with tears on her face. But the dog was simply, inexplicably *gone*.

It hurt like hell to lose a patient. It hurt even more when she had no reason, no explanation, nothing to point to. The pre-op blood work had been normal. The anesthetic had been the same one used in Rory's previous dental cleanings. Her favorite instructor had often said that sometimes things went wrong even if you did everything right—but it didn't make it one bit easier to accept. Helplessness, anger, and grief flooded her gut.

After having to tell Rory's owner that his canine friend had died while under her care, Morgan wanted to go home and punch something, pound nails, dig a hole to China, cry, yell, something, anything to vent her emotions. But she had patients to see, and the waiting room was full. Jay and Grady were booked up too, so there was no way she was going to ask them to take over—even though she knew full well that they would do so gladly. Instead, she mentally *pulled up her socks* as Nainie had called it, and carried on.

Thankfully there were no more surgeries on her slate. Instead, Morgan made her way through a sea of vaccinations and check-ups, pregnancy checks and digestive upsets, skin conditions, infections, ticks, and ear mites. Normal, everyday things. Slowly, gradually, she eased into the rhythm of the work. As if sensing her distress, her patients seemed unusually cooperative. By the end of the day, her eyes felt gritty, her back ached, and she could swear her feet were threatening to sue her, but she'd regained a somewhat fragile equilibrium—especially after a comical pair of pugs stood on the exam table and insisted on licking her face while she tried to listen to their hearts.

The phone rang three minutes before closing. The receptionist was already gone so she could make a deposit before the bank closed, so Morgan reached for the receiver herself. Late calls were never good news, and this one was no different. The O'Neils' cat had been hit by a car and was on his way to the clinic—and Jay and Grady were both out on farm calls.

Her techs were looking at her for direction. Cindy had taken Rory's death every bit as hard as Morgan—perhaps harder, judging from her red eyes. It would be natural to let her go home, but it might not be a kindness. What if Cindy took it as a lack of confidence in her skills? Morgan sighed inwardly. She wouldn't mind going home and having a damn good cry herself, but right now another animal needed help, and *somebody* had to keep it together, somebody had to be a leader. She elected to offer a choice.

"You heard the phone call," she said to her staff. "We've got an emergency on its way. Cindy, do you want to take another chance on my surgical skills, or do the three of you want to draw straws and see who gets stuck with me?"

"I'm staying," said Cindy.

Russell and Melinda looked at each other. "Us too," said Melly.

Just then Jack O'Neil came bursting in the front door with the blanket-wrapped feline in his arms, and everyone sprang into action. The bloodied blanket was removed as Norman the cat was quickly and carefully prepped for surgery, and Morgan felt her heart stutter. The damage was extensive...*Crap. Not again, please not again.* The good part was that the poor cat wasn't conscious, so he wasn't suffering at the moment. The bad part was that Morgan knew that the chances of saving him were slim to none.

She also knew that she had to try, that she would give it her best and then some, anyway.

~

Rhys found Leo sitting in a chair in the kitchen staring at the strangely ornamented coffee cup on the table. Around him, countertops gleamed, the sink shone, and the windows were spotless. Every dish was clean and put away, the floor swept and washed. And the living room held even more surprises than the kitchen. Leo had always kept the place tidy, but this was more than mere cleanliness. The colors and textures of the furniture, the walls, even the drapes—all looked fresh and bright instead of faded and worn.

"New as the day Tina and I bought them," Leo had whispered, as if Ranyon might somehow hear him. The ellyll's snores could still be heard from the second floor. "And all the worn spots on the arms of my recliner and the tear in the couch cushion? Gone, like they'd never happened."

"The ellyllon are masters at making charms. They use an older magic than even the Tylwyth Teg command."

"I don't know what to say to him," said Leo, glancing over at the stairs.

"Surely you don't fear him now? Your thanks will be sufficient, and your company. He's just a creature alone as you and I are, and if he's done this, then he's determined to be your friend."

"I would have been his friend without all this." Leo waved a hand around.

"Aye, you would have. And that's why he likes you. You show great kindness to all and expect no favors. You're a good man, Leo."

The old man recovered himself then. "Well, all I know is that this kitchen is too damn clean," he declared, getting up from the chair and straightening his suspenders. "Gives me the heebie-jeebies, and I'm going to do something about it."

Rhys nodded. "I'll go put the workshop to rights then. The tools are still scattered about."

An hour and a half later, Rhys returned to find that Ranyon had been lured from sleep by the aroma of freshly baked apple pies cooling on the kitchen table. "Fair day to ya! Smells like this side of paradise," grinned the ellyll as he scrambled to get up on a kitchen chair.

"A good morning for sure, and we're gonna start it off right," said Leo. He plopped several scoops of vanilla ice cream on top of a still-warm pie, stuck a large spoon in it, and pushed it in front of the ellyll. "Oh, and one more thing." He pinned a dish towel around Ranyon's neck as a bib of sorts. "You don't want to go getting your leaves all sticky."

Sighing happily, the little creature dug into the treat with a will. When Leo left to drive Rhys to the farm, Ranyon couldn't speak for all the food in his mouth. He could only wave with one of his long-fingered hands, his eyes half-closed in pie-induced ecstasy.

Rhys had hoped to catch sight of Morgan in the morning, but she'd left for the clinic long before Leo dropped him off. He put his pie in the fridge—Leo wasn't about to let him leave without one—and turned his attention to Lucy and to the work he'd planned out for the day. By evening, Rhys was anticipating

Morgan's visit to the stable, but a pale crescent moon had cleared the horizon before her car pulled into the driveway.

From the barn he saw her enter the house. Two hours later, he guessed she wasn't coming out to visit. No doubt she needed sleep more than company at the end of such a long day, but it was a disappointment just the same. He chided himself and checked Lucy one last time, then climbed into his own bed in the next stall. The mare was doing well enough that she likely didn't need such watching. He could sleep in his own quarters now and have no fear for her. Truth be told, however, he preferred to bed down where the scent of hay and straw and horse was familiar and comforting.

As always, he woke the moment Lucy stirred in her stall. Rhys listened carefully in the darkness, ready to get up and see to the mare, but she shifted and settled again of her own accord. Rhys rolled over, but found himself unable to go back to sleep. He was also unable to steer his thoughts away from Morgan. Was something wrong?

He rose and dressed in the dark, then slipped through the barn door like a shadow, hoping not to disturb the horse. The night was cloudless, the height of the moon and the position of the stars announcing it was well past midnight. There was no sense of danger, no instinct that prompted him to seek a weapon, yet Rhys was disquieted. He walked around the buildings, seeing nothing out of the ordinary, until he passed the old garage and could see the house. A blanket-wrapped figure was sitting on the porch swing.

Morgan was staring off at the constellations climbing above the eastern horizon, when suddenly she felt *his* presence, just as she did in so many of her dreams of late. Had she fallen asleep at long last? She turned her head to find Rhys standing at the bottom of the porch steps. *How does he manage to look so tall even there?*

"What ails you this night?" he asked.

"*Ails*—I don't think I've heard anyone use that word since Nainie."

"What *troubles* you then," he amended, obviously humoring her. "It's a cool night indeed to be sleeping out of doors."

"Yeah, well, there's not much sleeping going on tonight. So I decided to watch the stars instead."

He nodded. "My mother taught me about the stories in the sky. I like to watch them too sometimes, when my head needs clearing and my heart needs settling." Before she could think of a response, he was sitting beside her on the porch swing. "You have that look about you," he said. "A soldier who's lost a friend in battle."

Morgan sighed. "I lost two patients today. *Two.*"

"You fought hard for them."

"How would you know?"

"It's your way. The best of healers are warriors at heart. I've seen it—" Here he stopped and seemed to search for the right words. "I saw you fight for Lucy," he said at last. "You gave her everything you had in you. Most would have shaken their heads and given the horse a quick and merciful death. Instead, you fought with skill and with spirit, and now she'll be sound and whole again."

"I sure wish the successes took the sting out of the losses. I didn't win today and it makes me feel like I failed. And I knew these animals, personally—I feel like my patients become my friends. My teachers used to say that I cared too much, that I'd burn out early because of it."

"You have a heart for animals. If the day should come that you cannot care, that's the time to be walking away from it. No one can fight for long without a cause they can feel in here." He put a hand to his chest and slid the other around her shoulders. "And you feel cold to me. How long have you been out here?"

"A while." Most of the night, actually. She allowed him to pull her close and rested her head on him. Relaxed a little, then a little more. Rhys's powerful arm around her was warm and solid and oh so welcome. She was tired right down to the bone, physically and emotionally. Not only was she tired of battling the injuries and disease that threatened her patients, she was pretty damn tired of fighting her attraction to this man.

So when he leaned into her, she met him like she met everything else in her life—square on. Except he wasn't a battle to be won. His lips were firm but soft, and they teased at hers, nibbling at the corners of her mouth, darting the tip of his tongue along her teeth, gently sucking her bottom lip until she shivered—and not from the cold. Arms around her, he grazed his lips along her cheekbones and over her eyelids, glissed them over her brows until the furrows in them relaxed, kissed his way to the peak of her forehead and somehow eased the headache that had been pounding there. Morgan wound her fingers into his hair and drew him back to her lips, lips that were throbbing now, wanting. His mouth settled warmly over hers, gave and filled and soothed and aroused with only kisses…

She came up for air to find that he'd somehow tucked her into his lap. Or perhaps she'd slid into it herself—she didn't know and didn't care. Gloriously half-stunned by the storm of sensation he'd caused, she simply settled back against him in delicious warmth and wonder, her head under his chin.

"What do you see in the sky?" he asked. The rumble of his voice, so close she could feel it as well as hear it, was like a caress.

"I always find the hunter, Orion, first, and then I look for his dog."

Rhys chuckled. "It is no surprise that you should choose that one. What you call Orion, my father called Lludd of the Silver Hand. The god of healing. Lludd has a dog too—right there—a great deerhound that could cure any disease with a lick of his tongue." He then pointed to the crescent moon. "When the moon is like that, we called it Dwynwen's Bow. Like most Celtic women, Dwynwen was a huntress and a warrior, but she also became the patron of all sick animals."

"I sure could have used her help today," said Morgan.

"Perhaps she *is* helping. Dwynwen also looks after all true lovers. She brings them together and comforts them when they are apart, and strengthens the tie between them. Perhaps she was the one who woke me and told me something was amiss with you."

True lovers...Uh-huh. She decided to let that lie for the moment. "Is that why you're awake? You thought something was wrong?"

"I felt it. So I came."

It was so matter-of-fact, it reminded her of her grandmother. Always sensing things, knowing things, as if she could pluck the information out of the air. Morgan couldn't imagine what that would be like—or could she? What about the vivid dreams she'd had of Rhys before she'd met him? Hadn't she decided they were premonitions of a sort? A ripple of pure pleasure shot through her as she recalled how incredibly sexy those dreams had been—and realized they could be true. If she wanted them to be. If she wanted Rhys. *True lovers...*

Her sensible side intervened at once. She hadn't had enough sleep. She was too tired to make relationship decisions. She had to get up early. And she hadn't known Rhys all that long—and still didn't know much about him. If he remembered his last name, he hadn't announced it. And if he'd forgotten something that basic, what if he'd forgotten he was already married with six kids and a mortgage? With anyone else, she'd just ask them outright. But with Rhys, would she trust the answer?

Fiery arousal fizzled abruptly, doused with the cold water of reality. She could practically hear the hiss of steam as she struggled to her feet.

"I'd best go inside," she said.

He rose as well. "Aye, you've been awake overlong. And I'd best see to Lucy."

Neither of them believed it was best, she thought, as he gathered her in his arms and kissed her forehead. "I hope you rest well," he said and headed down the steps and across the yard.

Damn.

Even in jeans, even when the light was dim, even when she was doing her darnedest to quell her attraction, he still had the best butt on the planet.

It was *so* not fair.

FOURTEEN

~⁊⋀⋩~

Morgan didn't come out to the stable the next night. Or the next. On the third night, she came by to ask Rhys if he still had enough food in his fridge—and of course, he did, but he invented a few things he *needed* just to be sure she'd return. She lingered a few minutes, checking over Lucy's dressings, but he sensed there would again be no companionable visit.

He caught her arm as she turned to leave. "Have I given you offense?"

"No, of course not. I'm just really busy this week, that's all. I've got a new vet joining us on Friday." She looked uncomfortable and more so when he stroked her upper arm with gentle fingers.

"Glad I am to hear you're to be having more help—the gods know you're needing it. But the weight of the world seems on you still. Perhaps I could be lifting some of your burden?"

Morgan shook her head. "Thanks but no. It's something I have to work out myself. Alone." She gave him a weak smile and left.

Aye, he thought to himself as frustration sparked. *You're working out if I'm mad and if you dare get any nearer to me.* There was no help for it, however—she'd made it plain that she didn't want his company while she sorted through her feelings. All he had to offer was patience and more patience.

By all the gods, he was weary of being patient. Leo had encouraged him to court Morgan, but it was impossible to do when she was pushing him away. Or perhaps not…"It's always those little things, the little attentions that count the most." According to Leo's words, maybe there was a way to win Morgan's approval without actually being present.

It was worth a try.

Despite sleeping poorly all week, Morgan was up and ready for work early. She told herself that she had paperwork to do and supply orders to place and correspondence to attend to at the clinic before the new vet arrived that day…anything but the real reason she'd left so soon the last few mornings.

She still wasn't ready to face Rhys, not after the night they'd kissed. Her body and her heart definitely wanted a repeat of that evening. Her mind, however, was more troubled than ever.

The front door locked neatly behind her, and she was both relieved and disappointed to see that the porch was bare. Rhys did a huge volume of work around the farm—and really, how had she managed without him? She hadn't even realized how much there *was* to do. Yet, he'd found time lately to leave small delights on her doorstep for her. A few stems of late flowers from the nearby woods, a handful of wild strawberries that should have been out of season, a spray of leaves that had changed color early. Even a pair of bright feathers that a blue jay had left behind. It was like finding treasure every day.

Unused to such attention, she had wondered if he was just sucking up to her—after all, he had room and board here, even if it was humble—but was immediately ashamed of the cynical notion. Jay repeatedly told her to trust her instincts, and all her instincts said that Rhys's offerings were genuine. Of *course* he had a motive. He obviously cared for her and was trying to show it.

Her attraction to him was genuine too. That had simply increased since the evening that Jay and his friends had held practice. She'd studied Rhys's every move that night, done everything but drool over him, for heaven's sake—and she might have done that as well. Small wonder that her system all but hummed with arousal in his presence. Small wonder that she had sought expression the other night in his arms. And her heart had urged her on.

Which led to her current dilemma. Go forward or back? Allow the relationship to progress or run for her life? She felt she didn't know enough about him—and yet he insisted she knew everything that was important.

Stalemate. A lover's limbo if ever there was one.

Grabbing her bag, she hurried out to the driveway. Just as she put the key in the door handle, she saw something on the hood of her car—and froze. *Omigod.* Morgan put a hand to her throat and took an unsteady breath, then another, moving closer until she could touch what was definitely *the* most beautiful carving she'd ever seen, and assure herself it was real.

A mastiff, just like Rhyswr.

At about a foot and a half high, it was large yet exquisitely detailed, right down to the dog's expression. The canine figure was seated but not stiffly so. Instead its position was relaxed, one hind leg tucked sideways—and she couldn't help but smile because Rhyswr had often sat just like that. The grain of the wood was dark. A little mottled too, almost as if the dog was brindle. Reverently, she stroked her hands over the carving and finally picked it up, marveling at the weight of it as she cradled the wooden dog close to her.

Morgan didn't realize a tear was on her cheek until a large thumb gently wiped it away.

"I've been working at this for a long while," said Rhys, nodding at the carving. "I know you've been missing your dog, so I thought to make you one like him. I wasn't after making you sad again."

She laughed a little and swiped her face with her sleeve. "I'm not sad, not at all. It's just that this is so incredible and so perfect and so— *omigod*, I can't believe you made this. It's beyond beautiful. I don't even know how to thank you properly for such an amazing gift."

"I can help you with that," he murmured, and before she could move, he brushed his lips over hers. *Light. Heat.* Unseen sparks flared to life between them, as surely as if a blade had caressed flint, and every cell in her body leapt with sudden arousal. If she hadn't been holding the wooden dog, she might have thrown her arms around Rhys's neck and—

He stepped back and grinned. "A perfect thanks and plenty. I'll be seeing you tonight."

Both breathless and speechless, she simply hugged the dog to her as he walked away—and was it her imagination or was there a slight swagger in his step? All she knew for certain was that if the kiss had lasted any longer, she'd have made the evening news: "Spontaneous human combustion occurs in Spokane Valley! Story after this commercial break."

$\sim$

Rhys mounted the last of the nest boxes on the inside wall of the old granary. The tiny building had been empty for years, from the looks of it, but the roof was sound. It would make a fine chicken coop. It was late in the year to find chicks, but perhaps someone would give up a few hens rather than overwinter them. He wondered what breeds there might be in this country. *And ducks*, he reminded himself. *There should be a few ducks here as well to eat the garden slugs in the spring.* Some waterfowl would look fine on the pond across from the house. Morgan would like it, he was sure.

He stood back to admire his work and nodded approvingly. He'd always been good with his hands, and Leo had been tutoring him on modern building methods. He didn't agree with all of them of course—after all, a Celtic roundhouse was of sturdy construction, perhaps stronger than Morgan's own house. And some of the materials used in this time seemed flimsy. Yet he enjoyed the learning, and Leo kept him supplied with books on building. Rhys read them religiously, determined to learn everything he could, not only to fit into this world but to thrive in it. Accordingly, he'd insulated the walls of the coop against the coming cold weather and installed a small window he'd chosen from a stack in the barn.

Now he was contemplating ducks, of all things, and it felt completely natural.

Rhys considered what a surprise and a relief that was. After years of battle, some men found that they could only be warriors, that they were no longer at home in the world they had fought to protect. He'd thought that might happen to him. As the Bringer of Death, his world had been awash in blood and carnage—first fighting the Romans, then fighting for his life in the arena. After all that, how would he ever be able to return to who he was? Or be anything else but a destroyer?

Yet here he was. Surrounded by fertile land that called to him and work that was satisfying. It was the way of his people to grow crops and tend cattle—and in this short time, he'd come to know that he *could* live that life again. Perhaps all the centuries of watching humanity had eased some of the lust for battle in him. And like water over rock, the countless years seemed to have worn down the worst of his memories, so he wasn't as haunted as some. He had good friends, and best of all, he had a woman who stirred his heart.

By all the gods, he'd relived those recent kisses countless times. He was restless, left wanting so much more than Morgan was prepared to give. She'd pulled back after he'd kissed her under the stars, and he didn't know if she was afraid of him or of herself. Probably both. His strange story troubled her deeply, yet she was undeniably attracted. A quandary to be sure, and one she refused to share. *Ha.* As if he wasn't sharing in the hell of it just the same.

He was startled out of his reverie by the barely audible sound of a footstep outside. Hammer in hand, Rhys sprang from the newly refurbished coop in a heartbeat only to discover Jay Browning trying to take a step back, tripping, and falling on his backside.

"Easy boy," said Jay, his voice a bit shaky and his eyes wide. "It's just me."

"Aye, I remember you just fine." Rhys lowered the hammer, tossing it to one side and offering the younger man a hand up. "I didn't know anyone was here."

"I walked in from the road." Jay dusted himself off, still eyeing Rhys with apprehension. "Starr's picking some of Morgan's crab apples there. I'm damn glad she didn't come up here with me. You'd have scared her with that hammer."

So much for thinking that he was no longer a warrior or that he could blithely be a simple farmer. Habits died hard—even after centuries, his reflexes were battle sharp. Rhys sighed inwardly. "I apologize for that. 'Twas only instinct."

"Yeah, well, that's one of the things I want to talk to you about. Your instincts are out of this world. You've got some incredible skills, and the guys and I have learned a lot from you. I can't wait to use some of this stuff at the Ren fair coming up. What I want to know right now, though, is where did you learn to fight?"

Rhys was silent for a long moment. He hadn't expected anyone to ask him outright. It was one thing to omit the truth and allow people to fill in the blanks on their own. It was another to lie baldly, and he didn't have a taste for that. "Tell me why it is you want to know," he countered.

Jay folded his arms over a black T-shirt with white letters on it—"If the zombies chase us, I'm tripping you." "I know what you told Morgan when she found you. You're not from around here, and you're a helluva lot older than you look. You've been a Celtic warrior, a gladiator, and a dog. Some malicious fairies put a spell on you, and Morgan broke it.

"So I came here this afternoon when I knew Morgan would be busy orienting Tyler, our new veterinarian. She thinks I'm out on a farm call, but I wanted to talk to *you*, buddy. I want to hear from your own mouth if some, or all, of your story's true."

Rhys studied the man. His face was open and honest—and dead serious. "Do you believe I told Morgan the truth?" he asked Jay at last.

"I think I do."

"And if you have my word on it, what will you do then?"

Jay grinned. "Pester you with a million questions about the past, hope for more weaponry lessons, and invite you to our next fair. Other than that, not a damn thing. I'll keep your secret, even from my friends—but not from Starr, you understand—and you have my word on *that*."

They gripped hands, yet Rhys was puzzled. "Why is it you accept the truth and yet Morgan does not?"

"Well, for myself, your story explains a helluva lot—like why you can ride a horse like you're part of it and use weapons like a Jedi Master, yet driving and phoning and changing channels on the TV don't seem to be in your box of skills. Not to mention that walking around naked has been out of style since the sixties."

Aye, thought Rhys. He'd suspected he wouldn't be living that down.

"As for Morgan," Jay continued, "I have to give you fair warning first. She likes you. A lot. In fact, I've never seen her so lit up. I'm guessing you like her too?"

Rhys nodded. "A great deal more than *like*."

"Then one of the things I'm here to tell you today is don't break her heart. As her unofficial big brother, I'd have to get medieval on you, and I doubt that I could take you—but believe me, I'd try. And so would Grady and the guys who were at practice, and probably at least a couple dozen or so of her clients who love her and care about her. Understand?"

"Plainly."

"Good. I can check that off my list. So as far as her belief system goes, you gotta understand that Morgan has worked very hard to earn her veterinary stripes. It takes *years*, Rhys. She's been busy studying while most people are off building relationships and trying things out and figuring out who they are. Then her grandma died while she was at school, and I think Morgan coped with the loss by digging even deeper into her studies. So she's devoted herself to facts, Rhys, to *science*. She's safe there. And it's not because she doesn't feel, but because she *does* feel, and deeply—she uses her knowledge and skills to serve the animals she cares so much about."

"And what about me?"

"Well, you're different. She cares about you plenty, as I said, but your story just doesn't stand up against accepted science."

Rhys had seen the march of progress over the centuries. "Science once said the sun revolved around the earth. That didn't make it true."

"I know. But eventually it was overcome by proof. I don't think we can prove your story to Morgan."

He could, actually, but he didn't want to. "I'd rather she trusted me."

Jay simply shrugged. "For both your sakes, I hope she comes around sooner rather than later. I think her exceptional heart will lead her to the truth—but it could take a helluva long time, so you're going to have to be patient."

More of the same, then. Well, patient he could be. "My thanks to you for your honesty and also for your trust. Morgan is fortunate to have such a friend. So—were you saying something about a fair?"

"There's a Renaissance fair in two weeks," said Jay. "The guys and I were wondering if you'd join our team for the medieval combat events. We'll follow your lead, adopt whatever strategy you decide on. And we'll practice with you from now until then so we don't embarrass you too much. But, um…" He looked uncomfortable. "There's just one catch, Rhys—it's not real, okay? The whole event is for entertainment. You'll have to promise not to kill anybody."

"Well, now," said Rhys. "There goes all the fun of it."

He burst out laughing at Jay's horrified expression and clapped him on the shoulder. "I'll be proud to join your little band. And you have my word, I'll not be slaying anyone."

~

I hope this is a good idea. Morgan slowed the car, straining to keep a watchful eye on the gravel road and read the mailboxes at the same time. Good idea or not, she was determined. She'd taken Rhys's exquisite carving into the house that morning and set it on the floor next to the stone fireplace. The beautiful wooden dog seemed to belong there, and yet she felt there was something missing, something huge.

Maybe she couldn't have Rhyswr, but the great black canine had shown her that she had ample room in her home and her life and her heart for a dog. A big one.

She'd considered going to a reputable breeder, and she'd talked to many wonderful people over the phone and in person when trying to find Rhyswr's owners. But while she might have room in her busy life for a canine companion, a young puppy would need far more attention, training, and routine. Besides, Rhyswr had saved her life. Maybe she couldn't do anything for the big black dog now, but she could pay the gift forward and save the life of another dog. Sure, rescued dogs weren't necessarily perfect—but the dog wouldn't be getting a perfect owner either. And she'd witnessed in her own practice that simple love really could work wonders.

A few minutes later, she wondered why she hadn't done it sooner. Gentle Giant Rescue was located on a farm that was even older than her own. The owner, Ellen Gunderson, had a red bandanna tied over her white hair. Her startling blue eyes looked out from a weathered face, but there was kindness in them and laugh lines around them. She led Morgan along a long row of spacious grassy runs shaded by trees. Each run had a doghouse that looked to be the size of a garden shed.

"This here's my *pony* farm," Ellen laughed. "It's been an extra-warm day so most of the dogs are lying around. Since you're a vet, you probably already know that mastiffs can't tolerate a lot of heat." She clapped her hands together loudly. "C'mon, boys and girls, we have a visitor."

Enormous canines emerged from their sleeping spots. Several had been in their doghouses, others in hollowed-out spaces under the trees. Ellen went from pen to pen, introducing Morgan to each of the dogs, fourteen in all. Most were English mastiffs with fawn coats, the familiar tawny color with black masks. Five more were brindle, having stripes and streaks of gray or brown in a darker or lighter coat. One had a bright golden coat with black stripes.

"That's Tigger," chuckled Ellen. "You can see how she got that name. And this one over here is Roy, and the charcoal-gray one standing by your elbow is Andre. Andre's a Neapolitan mastiff from Italy. We don't see too many of those. Gertie, Duggan, and Diesel are bullmastiffs. That's a pure breed too. And then there's Tank—he's a mix. A little Anatolian shepherd, a little Great Dane, and a sprinkle of Newfoundland, I think."

"Whatever he is, he's certainly big," said Morgan, trying to pet him and getting her hands washed with his massive tongue. "He's even taller than the mastiffs, and I didn't think that was possible."

"Narrower though. Some of our mastiffs weigh well over two hundred, and he's more like one hundred sixty or so."

Still bigger than me. Sheesh! "Thank goodness they're friendly."

"They've all got pretty good temperaments, at least toward people. Minnie and Apollo, now, they don't like other dogs much. The rest are fine with just about anything, even cats."

Morgan couldn't imagine such big dogs interacting with cats—they looked like they could inhale them without even trying.

"The air's cooled down now," said Ellen, "so I'm going to let a few of them out to play. Will you be comfortable with that?"

"No problem."

Moments later, Morgan was surrounded by snorting, drooling canines with huge noses that snuffled curiously at waist height. She petted as many as she could reach, and they pressed in closer, vying for the attention. Some began licking her hands and her clothes. "Omigosh, it's like being in a herd of calves!"

"They're strong, and they're overwhelming if you're not used to it. Let me know if you're uncomfortable, okay?"

"I'm used to farm animals, so I'm okay—it's just that most cows and horses aren't trying to persuade me to pet them. If they get too pushy, I'll push back. They just need to know the boundaries."

"Exactly. Here, let's walk out to the field and maybe they'll spread out a bit."

As they passed the last pen, Morgan caught site of a long, dark tail hanging out of a doghouse. It was hard to see in the shadowed interior, but she could just make out the enormous bulk of a dog. Maybe she sensed something or it was the dog's body language—facing into the house as if it was uninterested in the outside world—but she stopped in front of the gate. "What about that one?"

Ellen sighed. "That's Fred. His owner died on a Tuesday, and the family took Fred to a shelter on Thursday. I don't know if they just couldn't cope with a dog this size—which is understandable, it's a lot to take on—or they just weren't interested in trying. But the shelter called us, and he's been here for over a month and a half now, just like that. Hardly eats, hardly moves."

"Animals grieve," said Morgan. "In fact, dogs may mourn as deeply as humans do. And it's so hard because you can't explain to them what's going on. He's lost his owner and his home in one fell swoop. Is he an older dog?"

"Not at all. He's about four. I thought if I just gave him some time, he'd snap out of it. Thought he would be running and playing by now, or at least show some interest in something. But nothing yet. Got a vet to come out here and check on him—in fact, I think it was Dr. Grady from your clinic—but Fred's healthy enough. He's lost some weight, though. I try to spend time with him, but he's not interested. He's just not responding. He needs to find his forever home, but at this rate, I can't see it happening anytime soon."

"Can I meet him?"

"Sure. He doesn't seem to be territorial—hell, he doesn't seem to be much of anything right now—so he doesn't mind a stranger in his pen. I'll take the rest of the crowd out to the field. I've got a few tennis balls that'll keep 'em occupied while you visit."

Morgan stood by the enclosure until Ellen and the dogs left. It took a while, since a few dogs came back to see if she was coming too. She noticed that, while definitely enthusiastic, none of them bounced like Labradors. Their gait was almost dignified, and for a moment her heart squeezed hard as she remembered watching Rhyswr walk around her farm with that same stately pace. *Okay, Rhyswr, wherever you are. Let's see if this is a dog I can help.*

"Hi, Fred," she called out softly to the unmoving dog in the doghouse. There was no reaction, but she hadn't expected one. She continued in the same soft, steady voice. "I know you're sad right now, and that's okay. I understand that. I was sad for a long time when Nainie died, and some days I still feel sad about it, even though she's been gone for a while. It sucks, I know, but that's the way it is when someone you love is gone." She entered the gate, continuing to talk. "I'm just coming in to sit with you for a while. I hope that's okay with you." She moved slowly toward the doghouse but took a wide arcing path rather than a direct route that might be perceived as threatening. She kept talking, soft and low, as she reached the doghouse and sat down on the ground beside it. The tail hung over the threshold of the door, utterly unmoving.

Morgan talked about Rhyswr and how she missed him. How she was trying to move forward by being open to adopting another dog. She found herself talking about Rhys too. Here in the peaceful shade, without a sound except for the noisy breathing of the big dog and a slight breeze stirring the leaves above, her feelings for Rhys seemed simple, natural, normal. If it wasn't for his crazy story, she could see herself getting a whole lot closer to him.

"What a mess, Fred," she sighed. "If Rhys believes his own fantasy, then he's seriously disturbed. If he's just making it up on purpose, then he's got something to hide. Either way, I can't see having a real relationship with him."

Except that she wanted to. Common sense said no, but the heart said *yes, yes, yes.*

"Nainie always said that I should follow my heart. Well, my heart says that Rhys and I have feelings for each other. My gut says it's okay to trust him. My hormones want to jump him every time I'm near him. But my brain says that the idea of getting involved with Rhys is the stupidest thing it's ever heard." She sighed again. "So far, I've been listening to my brain, but the rest of me would like to stage a revolt.

"How about you, Fred? Want to weigh in with an opinion?"

The dog's tail never moved, not once. And she still hadn't seen anything but his back end. The rest of him was lost in the cool, cave-like shadow of his house. Fred might have two heads for all she knew.

Morgan glanced at her watch—an hour had sped by. It was a wonder she hadn't talked the big dog's ears off. "Well, I guess our time's up for now. Thanks for listening, Fred. And if it's okay with you, I'd like to make an appointment for another session." She got up stiffly and dusted off her jeans, then stretched until a joint popped. "Omigosh, you might have to get a couch if we're going to do this often…Can't complain about the rates, though."

FIFTEEN

~T~

Morgan pulled into the movie rental shop on the way home. Most couples got to know each other slowly by hanging out together. Maybe if she and Rhys shared some normal dating activities, she'd get to know more about him. And maybe then her brain would quit complaining long enough for the rest of her to get to know Rhys too.

She nearly gave up the whole idea as she tried to select a title. What would Rhys enjoy watching? She didn't know a darn thing about his taste. Jay would pick the latest alien invasion or zombie outbreak flick. Grady preferred war movies. None of those seemed quite right, somehow. She wasn't up for a romantic comedy, not everyone was crazy about animated features, and a docudrama might put the man to sleep. Morgan wandered the new release section and then all the other sections, until her eyes started to blur. Finally, she decided to just get an assortment of fun old standbys and let Rhys choose. Who knew, maybe his choice would tell her something about him. It'd be a conversation starter at the very least, and since they would both have seen the movies before, they could talk all the way through the films if they wanted to and never miss a thing. If she was really lucky, one of the films would prompt a memory from him—*the first time I saw this movie, I was in…*

With six movies in a bag, she walked next door to Gibby's and ordered a couple of pizzas. At least that selection wasn't hard. As far as she could tell, Rhys wasn't picky about food, so she ordered two of her own favorites that she could simply cook in the oven at home—Pepperoni Supreme and Juanita's Taco Special. *If the evening's a bust, I'll have enough leftovers to last me a week.*

When she went out to the barn to invite Rhys, he was nowhere to be seen. Lucy was in her stall, and the dribbles of grass in the corners of her mouth told Morgan that the horse had been out recently. All her dressings were clean and fresh, so obviously Rhys had gone off to work on something else.

Morgan checked around the buildings and finally spotted the man by the pond. He was crouched at its edge, feeding a little flock of black-and-white ducks. "Omigosh, where did you find these?"

"Leo had the idea of going to a feedstore," Rhys grinned. "They knew of someone who had a few ducks to sell. These are called Ancona ducks."

"I don't think I've ever seen this breed, but I love the look of them." She took the crumbles of feed he offered her and knelt beside him. The spotted ducks were obviously used to people—they came to her without hesitation. Morgan laughed at the feel of their nibbling bills on her palms.

"They don't grow very big, but a pair of them would make a good dinner," said Rhys.

"You're *not* eating them!" She looked up, horrified, only to find him grinning at her. She reached over and punched him in the leg, and he laughed.

"Then perhaps you'd let me keep them to eat the slugs from the gardens."

"That's better," she said. "Although there are no slugs in the garden right now—wait, did you say gardens, plural?"

"I've uncovered the soil in two more places where the sun is good and made them ready for planting in the spring. Leo says he'll show me how to start seeds in his greenhouse. In the spring he'll help me build one over by your garage, if it pleases you."

"It pleases me plenty," she admitted, but the pleasure came from far more than the greenhouse plans. Rhys planned to be here in the spring. He *wanted* to be here. More than that, *she* wanted him to be here. Her brain still disapproved, but maybe tonight's activities would remedy that.

"I've always wanted to have time for things like gardening."

"Perhaps with the new vet you've hired, you'll find more time for pleasures." He extended a hand and helped her up, then kissed her soundly.

She could think of all kinds of pleasures she'd like to find time for...Instead, she cleared her throat as she tried to clear her head. "I have time tonight for pizza and movies. Want to join me?"

His face lit up, and she could swear her already sensitized hormones fainted dead away. "Very much," he said. "I'll give Lucy her grain and clean myself up." He walked away, and her gaze automatically followed him until he was out of sight. *Best. Butt. Ever.*

Sighing, she didn't even try to wipe the goofy grin off her face as she headed for the house to put the pizzas in the oven.

Rhys came to the door just before the food was ready. He was wearing clean clothes and his hair was wet—and she immediately had to deal with mental images of *hot naked man in the shower.* It didn't help that her imagination didn't have to make up a single thing, thanks to Rhys's state of undress when she first met him.

Needing a few moments to compose herself (and for her brain to lecture her unruly libido), Morgan handed him a couple of iced colas and a roll of paper towels and sent him to the living room while she pulled out the pizzas. She cut them up and arranged slices of both flavors on each plate—seconds could be self-served in the kitchen—and followed. Rhys was studying the DVDs, which were spread out on the coffee table.

"Did you decide what you'd like to watch?" she asked as she handed him a plate. He hadn't sat on one end of the couch or the other—instead, he'd sat dead center. Should she ask him to move over or just sit beside him and enjoy the proximity? *Well, that's a no-brainer.*

"I think I'd like to try this one." He held up *Jaws.*

"*Try.* Good one. You mean you'd like to see it again?"

"I've never watched it."

She stared. "You're pulling my leg."

"No, but I can if you want me to," he shot back with a grin.

She swatted his shoulder and took the DVD out of his hands. Moments later they were eating pizza on the couch while a giant shark ate swimmers on-screen. Morgan watched Rhys with interest. He was leaning forward, giving the film his full attention. He seemed surprised at every development too (although truth be told, the movie still managed to make her jump at times as well). Was it possible he really *hadn't* seen it before? Where on earth could a person hide in order to miss such a huge chunk of pop culture? Wales wasn't cut off from the rest of the world—unless Rhys had been in a monastery, and there weren't many of *those* still operating.

Besides, his behavior in other areas wasn't monkish in the least. By the time the movie was halfway through, they were cuddled up together as naturally as if they did this all the time. She could certainly get used to it…

And she could certainly get used to the post-movie activity. The embers that had been glowing all along flared into blazing life as soon as the credits rolled. Gentle kisses heated quickly and hands slid beneath clothing. Morgan wanted nothing more than to be skin to skin with this man, but some last living brain cell had her coming up for air instead and gently but firmly pushing free of Rhys's muscled arms.

They kept hold of each other's hands, however, as they sat back and tried to slow their heart rates. Rhys's amber gaze was warm on hers. "You're undoing me."

"Then we're even," she said. "I've been undone since I first dreamed of you."

He sat up. "You've seen me in your dreams?"

"Often." She hoped it didn't sound crazy, then nearly laughed. *Why am I worried? This is the guy who once told me he was a dog.* "It started in Wales, before I even met you. I've dreamed about you most nights since."

"Among my people, that's a very serious thing. My mother read dreams, and she always said they bring instruction. What did you see?"

"This. We were together just like this." She took his work-roughened hand with both of hers, kissed it, and held it between her breasts. "In every dream. I'm not sure what kind of instruction that's supposed to give us. Maybe just some hope."

"Do you only *hope* we'll be together? I'd take it as a powerful sign that we're meant to be."

"It's early yet."

"Ah, but it's not the number of days—"

"—that decides the strength of the bond," she finished. "Yeah, I remember you said that. But it doesn't mean it's a good idea to take things any further just yet."

"What do your instincts say?"

"I'm not talking about instinct, I'm talking about *intellect*. I need to be sensible about this."

"Aye, of course. You're a very intelligent woman. But there's such a thing as thinking overmuch." He nodded his head at the TV screen, where the credits had run their course and only an image of the shark remained. "The people of Amity Island thought they were being sensible. Sharks couldn't be here, they said. Sharks don't behave like this, they said. They wanted proof of it for their minds before they would believe, and until they believed, they refused to act. Many good people were devoured because of it."

Morgan tried to suppress her smile. "Omigosh, are you actually using *Jaws* as some kind of relationship analogy?"

He simply shrugged. "It wasn't until Brody followed his instincts instead of his orders that he was able to save the town from the monster. It's the same with many things in life, including the bond between men and women: instinct often reveals the greater truth."

Rhys had succeeded in surprising her again. "That's very wise," she said. "So I'll admit that my instincts know what I want. But my head hasn't decided if it's good for me yet."

"You mean if *I'm* good for you." He leaned over and kissed her, long and deep until she thought she'd drown in the pure bliss of it. Then he rose. "Perhaps you need to try me in order to know," he grinned. "My thanks for the pizza and the movie."

Morgan watched him leave the room, then sighed as she heard the back door close. Why had she let him leave? Sometimes being sensible felt an awful lot like being stupid.

~

"Lucy looks really good. Far better than I expected."

Rhys looked up to see Morgan in the doorway of the stable. The rising moon highlighted her hair with silver and sharpened her fine features. She almost looked like one of the Fair Ones, except there was genuine warmth in her expression, true feeling in her eyes. But exactly what that feeling was had him puzzled. Something was different, changed. "You did fine work on her," he said as she approached.

"That was just the beginning. It's your constant care that's brought her around. I saw you walking her after supper tonight. She doesn't seem quite as stiff."

"The heat is gone from the wounds. She still has pain, but she knows she must move. It's a very fine balance between moving too much and not enough." He sensed that Morgan was the one walking a fine balance. She hadn't come to talk about the horse, that was certain. At her house, she'd admitted she wanted him— but had she made a decision?

She nodded. "I guess we make a pretty good veterinary team then, you and I."

"I think we would be very good together in all ways," he countered boldly, daring her to reveal herself.

"I think you're right." Without any warning, she stepped into him, but she'd barely begun to slide her arms around his neck before he seized her. Cupping her lush bottom in one hand, he tangled his other hand in her hair and brought her lips to his. Torn between the need to feast and the desire to savor, he explored her mouth thoroughly and was delighted when she held him to her as fiercely as he was holding her.

He nuzzled her ear, alternately kissed and nuzzled his way to her throat, as his hands pushed under her blouse to cup her full breasts and thumb their peaked nipples. His cock had reared up hard to the point of pain, and his control trembled. By all the gods, he was hungry, nay starving, to press her skin against his, to touch and grasp, taste and nip. Ravenous to bury himself deep and hard in all that softness until he was insensible. The urge to take was overwhelming, and he fought to bridle it back as if it were a half-mad warhorse.

Morgan welcomed Rhys's rough palms on her skin, his textured caresses providing a rich sensory overload. She shrugged off her blouse and fought to unbutton his shirt, planting desperate rapid kisses on his chest as she exposed it. Her breasts were tight with arousal and she pressed them against the hard planes of male muscle. Something new was building in her, something primal. She gloried when his strong hands shoved her jeans down her thighs and gripped her bare ass, lifting her until her toes no longer touched the ground. Instinctively she rocked her bottom in the cup of his palms and rubbed her nipples over his chest, wanton and triumphant at the same time. The scents that surrounded her took her back to her dreams, ramped up her arousal until all her senses were electrified and begging for more.

Instantly Rhys responded to her unspoken need, tossing her lightly onto the quilt-covered straw that was his bed. He stripped away her jeans, then stood back as if to admire his handiwork. She should have felt self-conscious, normally would have half-covered herself with her arms and hands. Instead, she welcomed his gaze, reveled in it. She wanted his eyes on her. Suddenly she was inspired to open her legs and circle her fingers in the wetness there. He reeled slightly as if physically punched and quickly skimmed off his own clothes. *Omigod.* Morgan inhaled sharply as he revealed his rampant cock, ran his hand along its length as if brandishing it. "Yes," she breathed. "Mmm, yes."

Rhys knelt at once but didn't give her what she asked for. Instead, Morgan was certain she might die of anticipation as his hot, open-mouthed kisses roamed slowly up the insides of her legs. He nuzzled her inner thighs and pushed her legs wide, breathed on her inner folds. Then ran his tongue along them, in them, up and down, flicking his tongue lightly over her pearl before settling in to feast.

Morgan was wild beneath the onslaught of sensation, knotting her hands in Rhys's hair as he devoured her relentlessly. And when the orgasms burst through her, her screams were both helpless and jubilant, snapping the ropes of his control like weak threads.

He was inside her at once. She was hot and slick and pulsed around his cock like a tightening fist. He pounded into her, faster and faster as she urged him on, higher and higher until the sweet annihilation of release overtook them both.

Exultant, he sank to the quilt-covered straw and gathered Morgan to his heart.

～

Morgan awakened to the sound of geese overhead. The morning air was cool, and she snuggled deeper under the quilts, nestling back against Rhys, who tightened his arm around her. She breathed in the sweet scent of straw, the warm tang of horse, and sighed contentedly, her entire body still in a kind of languor.

Their lovemaking had been like nothing she'd ever experienced. Earthy and raw, tender and fierce, it had unlocked a depth of passion in her that she hadn't known was there.

It had unlocked her heart as well. Nothing had ever felt more right than being skin to skin with Rhys. Nothing had felt so much like home as being in his arms. She'd never felt such an intense connection in her life. Never imagined it was even possible.

That connection was even more apparent as they reached for each other twice more in the night. It sang in her very veins as he whispered to her in a language she didn't know, yet understood just the same. He was a strong man, but his touch was tempered with a tenderness that utterly disarmed her. And through it all, in his arms she felt the sense of belonging that she'd been missing for a very long time.

She snuggled closer, breathing in his scent, and slid back into sleep for a time until she startled awake and found herself alone. "Rhys?"

"Morning to you, *anwylyd*." His voice came from Lucy's stall, and Morgan sat up to look. There he was on his knees, gloriously naked, as he changed the dressings on the mare's wounded legs.

"Morning—what did you call me?" Morgan ran her fingers through her hair to remove some wisps of straw from it.

"Anwylyd. It means beloved or darling one."

A few days ago she might have protested, but today it sounded good. There was something solid and right about it. There was something solid and right about the defined muscle that covered Rhys's broad frame too, and she admired it openly. He moved slightly, and the early sun through the stall window illuminated an odd pattern of silvery lines crisscrossing his back. Clutching a blanket around her against the cool air, Morgan struggled out of the makeshift bed and stood by Lucy's stall.

The first time she'd seen Rhys naked—when she'd threatened him with a garden hoe—she'd noticed a number of wide white scars on his arms, legs, even chest, and thought them profuse. She hadn't seen his back at that time, hadn't seen his back in last night's darkness either. But her fingertips had felt dozens upon dozens of long raised ridges. In daylight, the damage was even more appalling than she'd suspected. Unlike the scars on his arms and legs, these stripes were narrow. They crossed Rhys's spine from neck to tailbone, wrapping tapered edges around his ribs and shoulders and hips. There was barely an inch of skin that wasn't brutally marked. Morgan felt shaky, almost ill, at the ghastly evidence of long-ago abuse before her and sat on the grain bin for support. "What the hell happened to your back? Who did this to you?"

Rhys didn't answer at once. Instead, he finished wrapping the mare's leg, before wiping the salve from his hands on a cloth and putting the supplies away. Finally, he came to stand in front of Morgan. His eyes still reminded her of ale and old gold, and his gaze was steady on hers. "To the Roman way of thinking, a man with the sign of a dog should be treated as a dog. They whipped me for sport as much as for punishment." He shrugged. "It was a long time ago, and their bones are naught but dust now. Truly, the Fair Ones were just as cruel, though they didn't lay a hand on me."

Dust. Romans. The Fair Ones. Morgan didn't know what to say. Her expression must have showed her bewilderment, because Rhys tried to brush her face with his fingertips, and heaven help her, she shied from his touch. She didn't mean to, but her mind was racing like a rabbit from a lynx, panicked and desperate. She cared for this man—crap, she *loved* this man—and he had abruptly morphed into a deluded stranger again.

Suddenly furious, she was upset with him for changing, yet most of her anger was directed at herself. Wasn't this her very own fault? Why hadn't she asked more questions? Why had she rationalized away the strange things he'd said when she first found him naked? Had she thought that if she just ignored them, Rhys's mental problems would simply disappear?

"Look," she said, fighting to steady her voice and losing the battle. "I don't know what you're dealing with, but you don't have to do it alone. We can work on it together, find you some help—"

"Help?" He looked both puzzled and annoyed. "There is no help for the truth."

"The truth? All I'm hearing is fantasy here. You're still trying to tell me that you're over two thousand years old, for God's sake!"

"I told you about the Tylwyth Teg—"

"Those are goddamn faery tales! Stories for kids! They're not real!"

"They were real enough when they changed me into a grim."

Morgan stared at him for a long, long moment. His expression didn't change, his golden eyes remained steady. "Please tell me you don't believe what you're saying. You can't. It's not rational. Something's wrong, something's giving you these delusions, these hallucinations, and we need to find you some help, some treatment, medication, *something*."

"It's you who are needing a bit of help," he said gently. "You'll not allow yourself to believe; perhaps you're afraid to believe that there is more to the world than what you see. There are many things all around us that are old and powerful, and they're to be respected not feared."

Morgan forgot to breathe for several seconds. Those were Nainie's words—exactly what Nainie had once said to her. How could he know, what did it mean? She sucked in a lungful of air just in time to realize Rhys had ahold of her hand. Before she could pull it back, he had placed her fingertips on a scar just under his rib cage.

"You're a healer, and a fine one. Do you not recognize your own handiwork?"

What? Morgan saw at once that this wound was different. It was pinkish and raised slightly, fresh knit. She could discern that it had once been sutured with tiny, even stitches. But it was the shape of it that electrified her—a long straight slash with a hook at the end, like the letter *J*. She'd had to make an incision to enlarge the stab wound on the black dog, so she could repair the damage to his heart and lungs. Her finger traced along the scar almost of its own volition. The scar was located in the same place, oriented the same way…

She yanked her hand away as if from a hot stove. "It's just coincidence. It has to be!" Desperation edged her voice. "Just a crazy and bizarre coincidence, that's all!" Sliding from the grain bin, she edged around Rhys and backed toward the stable door.

He didn't move. "I don't like that you fear me."

That halted her in her tracks. She marched up to him until they were only inches apart and planted her index finger in the center of his chest. "I. Am not. Afraid. Of *you*," she said, emphasizing every word. "But I'll tell you what I am afraid of. I'm afraid that your fantasies are contagious. I'm afraid of buying into your make-believe world. I'm afraid of loving you so much that I tell myself it's perfectly okay to know absolutely *nothing* about you. And it's not okay, not at all."

"You already know everything that's important about me. I've worked every day to prove myself to you, but you refuse to give me your trust."

"My *trust*? You're living on my property. That's a helluva lot of trust, mister. And so was last night, goddamn it. Now you're messing with my mind again, and I don't like it. I want the lies and the games to stop. I want them to stop *right now*."

He reached for her as if to hold her, but she knocked his hand away and headed for the door once more. She could feel his eyes on her and paused at the threshold to face him. "I want you to leave. Take your fantasies and go play with somebody else's life." *With somebody else's heart...* "Go back to Leo's or go to hell, but don't come back, do you hear me?"

Rhys's face darkened, but he didn't move from the spot, only folded his heavily muscled arms across his broad chest. "I hear you fine. And now you hear *me*, Morgan Edwards. I'm not daft or touched in the head. I'm not a liar. And I'm not playing any foolish games. Do you think what we shared here was just a lark to me? You have my heart, and if I'm not very mistaken, I have yours as well. I want to make a life with you, but there'll be nothing between us without *trust* and *truth*. I've given you both. Where are yours?"

She opened her mouth and closed it again, unable to form a coherent response to such an outrageous question. Truth indeed. *Romans and fairies and death dogs, oh my.* Morgan turned on her heel and marched to the house with the blanket flapping around her, angrier than she'd ever been in her life and glad for it, because it kept the pain in her heart at bay.

SIXTEEN

After slamming the door and locking the dead bolt, Morgan peeked out the window and saw nothing. Rhys hadn't followed her, and for some reason, that made her even madder. *Good. Fine. Dandy.* She stalked to her room, muttering and fuming. Balled up the blanket and threw it into a corner.

She showered in the hottest water she could stand, scrubbing herself furiously as if she could erase the memory of Rhys's touch. Remained under the water until it was too cold to bear, but it failed to cool her anger. Morgan toweled off and pulled on clothes in a fury. What the hell had she been thinking? It had been foolish, absolutely stupid of her to let this man, this *stranger*, stay on her property in the first place. And downright crazy to have sex with him.

Sex. Her fury suddenly popped like an overfilled balloon, and Morgan sank to the edge of her bed with her head in her hands. It hadn't been just sex, not by a long shot. Not for either of them. Whether she liked it or not, the connection was real and powerful. She felt as if she had known Rhys all her life, in spite of the fact that she'd only just met him. And she loved him—that was certain. She'd always been on the cerebral side, cautious and careful, inclined to consider all the pros and cons and analyze everything to the nth degree...

This one time—*just one damn time*—she'd followed her heart, her instincts, and now look at what had happened.

She took a deep breath, let it out slowly. She was good at analyzing, and if ever a situation called for it, this one did. *Okay, step one: lay out the facts.* That turned out to be harder than she thought, because the *fact* was that Rhys hadn't exactly committed a crime. He hadn't beaten her, stolen from her, cheated on her, or done anything other than work around her neglected farm and care for a wounded horse. In fact, the entire dilemma lay in his outrageous ancient-warrior-becomes-death-dog story.

Well, so what? That made him a goddamn liar, didn't it?

But was it still a lie if he believed it? Everything in his face, his eyes, his body language, said that he was telling the absolute truth. Morgan had never heard of anything like this, had certainly never seen the situation mentioned in the advice column of the newspaper. And as problems went, it seemed insurmountable. She couldn't just ignore it—it would always be the elephant in the room. And who knew what other strange things Rhys believed or what odd behaviors could develop because of it?

It didn't help a bit that her partner, Jay, believed that the intricate silver dog collar proved that Rhys's strange tale was true. Surely Jay was letting his own wishful thinking cloud his judgment—yet his judgment had always proved sound before. She relied on him at the clinic without hesitation. Why should this case be any different?

Was there any chance, any totally wild, billion-to-one chance that Rhys's story *could* be true?

Oh, for pity's sake, now I'm buying into the fantasy. She snorted, but the derisive sound turned into a sniffle and her eyes filled with unwelcome tears. She sniffed again, loudly, and a mounting headache had her heading to the kitchen for the bottle of ibuprofen she knew was on the counter. Afterward, she wandered aimlessly to the living room with a box of Kleenex under one arm and stood staring at her many bookshelves. Sunlight penetrated the venetian blinds on the windows, and bright rays fingered the numberless issues of veterinary journals, enormous resource books on every species of animal, and texts on chemistry, pharmacology, and anatomy.

Nainie had laughingly called her a bookish child, and the evidence plainly showed she still was one. But the titles on the spines had been very different when she was younger. Faery tales, folklore, myths, and legends. Elves, witches, ogres, and dragons. Spells and curses. Good and evil. All just silly fantasy of course, but Morgan still felt a pang of nostalgia. She had loved every single one of them. How many nights had she pleaded with Nainie to keep the light on just a little longer so she could read more of the wonderful stories?

On an impulse, Morgan hurried to the spare bedroom, where about four dozen boxes were stacked against one wall, each neatly labeled in her own handwriting. She'd intended to settle in, of course, to finally free her belongings from storage and to display all her treasures now that she had a house of her own. Yet there were still a lot of boxes whose contents hadn't seen the light of day since she lived in an apartment. There were even *more* boxes that hadn't been opened since Nainie had passed away and left all her things to her granddaughter.

It was a daunting task, and she'd made little progress. Morgan figured she'd be fully unpacked sometime in the next decade or so—if she was lucky. Now the intimidation she usually felt when she entered the room seemed to dissolve. Her anger over Rhys was slowly but surely nudged aside, replaced by a subtle niggling pressure. *Look, look, look.* Giving in to the compulsion, she began opening boxes.

So many letters, photos, and knickknacks. And books, of course—scores of them, many filled with Welsh folklore. Each one was like an old friend, but she wasn't there to read. Instead, she glanced at each title, then reached for the next one. Morgan had no idea what she was looking for, but she couldn't seem to stop. When she'd gone through all the boxes in the guest room, she went to the closet and found more. And still more. By late afternoon, she was sitting in a sea of open boxes and towering stacks of books and papers.

She sighed heavily. *So far, all I've done is make a helluva mess.* But she might as well finish the job.

There were only five boxes left when she discovered something beneath some of Nainie's favorite cookbooks. It was a small jewelry box from Morgan's fifteenth birthday, made from dark wood with a Celtic symbol carved on it. Opening it, she found a tangle of silver necklaces and plastic bracelets, sterling earrings and wild-colored dime-store ones. And right on top, a snapshot of Nainie. Morgan had taken the photo herself with her brand-new camera, surprising her grandmother in the kitchen as she rolled out pie dough—a slice of everyday life perfectly captured. How many times had she seen her grandmother bake?

She could nearly smell the cinnamon in the air.

Morgan sighed and drew a finger over the photo, gently tracing the shapeless flowered dress, the faded apron, the glasses sliding down Nainie's nose, and the crown of blue-gray curly hair that would never behave. Morgan pulled a tendril of her own wayward hair as emotion washed over her.

"Oh, Nainie, I wish you were here. I miss you all the time." She sniffled hard and rubbed her nose on the shoulder of her shirt. At once she noticed some little white things carefully lined up beside the pastry board. They didn't look quite like dough scraps…Finally Morgan gave up squinting at them and held the photo near the window for better light. She had to get a magnifying glass, however, before the tiny objects resolved themselves into clever knots and triangles and flowers of leftover dough.

"Faery pastries," she murmured, remembering. Every baking day, without fail, Nainie would make a small batch of faery pastries, dripping with honey and raisins. Morgan would receive one on a china saucer with a cup of milky tea. As for the rest, a tiny basket of the diminutive baked goods would grace the back porch at sunset.

An offering for the Fair Ones, Nainie had explained. Some of her words came back to Morgan now. *There are many things all around us that are old and powerful…They're not to be feared but to be respected, and it's long been a gift in our family to know them.*

Nainie had believed the faery stories she told her granddaughter. Which made her the only person in the world who could understand what Morgan was going through. Even though her grandmother had passed on, Morgan felt certain that Nainie would be listening and watching over her somehow.

"I'm trying hard not to be stupid here, but you told me that the heart knows things the mind doesn't and to trust my heart even when things didn't make sense." Tears began, only a few at first, and then the floodgates simply burst. "They sure don't make sense right now. There's this man in my life. I think he's a good man, but he's really confused and so am I…"

She poured her heart out to Nainie's photo for a very long time. Talking to the dog yesterday had been good for her, but her heart hadn't been ripped in half at the time. She wasn't much of a crier by nature, but this time she couldn't stop the tears. It wasn't long before the box of Kleenex was empty and she had to switch to toilet paper. Which seemed somewhat undignified, but it was either that or scratchy paper towels.

By the time Morgan was down to hiccups and sniffles, she still had no answers. She loved Rhys, and Rhys, love her though he might, was obviously crazy. It could be the treatable kind of crazy, like schizophrenia or something like that, but he'd have to agree he had a problem. And she didn't see that happening anytime soon.

With Nainie's picture in one hand and the old jewelry box in the other, she got unsteadily to her feet and stumbled to the kitchen to make coffee and pull herself together. The sun pouring in the windows seemed to mock her mood as she propped the photo against the salt and pepper shakers on the table. She stood back and surveyed it, then went back to the guest room and came back with a frame. It was far too large for the precious picture, but it would protect it. She centered the photo on the glass and closed it up, then took the Truman's Farm Equipment calendar down from the wall and hung Nainie's photo in its place. *Maybe I could get Jay to scan it or something.* A larger copy of the photo could hang on that wall permanently. *Nainie in her kitchen and me in mine.*

For a moment, she almost smiled…

Her grandmother used to say that the best medicine for feeling miserable was to go make somebody else happier. Morgan doubted there was a medicine in the world that could make her feel much better—with the possible exception of Jack Daniel's—but she knew there was one soul who she could visit and at least not make him feel any worse.

She would spend some time with Fred.

~

Rhys kicked a bale of straw across the floor between the stalls, startling Lucy. Steady beast that she was, the horse didn't shy or jump, just flattened her ears and switched her tail. He was far too angry to be sorry for kicking the straw right then.

Morgan had been furious when she stormed out of the stable. Although she'd ordered him to leave, Rhys had lingered, knowing that she spoke from the heat of the moment, from the emotions that were tearing at her. Frustration clawed at him as well. He knew how to ride and how to fight, how to farm and how to build. He knew how to care for an injured horse, yet he had no idea whatsoever how to help the woman he loved. She was compassionate and skilled as a healer, clever of mind, but how could she accept a truth that she viewed as impossible? To be fair, few in this time and place would be able to believe such a thing. The Fair Ones were all but forgotten, relegated to myth, diminished to tiny beings that consorted with butterflies in picture books.

Helplessness didn't sit well with him. Rhys much preferred action, but the situation called for him to give Morgan time. *How much time?* He paced the stable until the mare was nervous, then walked the fields. He didn't go far, however. He'd vowed to watch over Morgan Edwards and protect her, and the fact that he'd made that promise while still a dog didn't nullify his commitment. Even if she didn't want him, he would see to her safety no matter what.

But she *did* want him. Of that he was certain.

At noon, Rhys judged himself calm enough to walk the mare and even turned her out for a short time to graze. He studied the horse's movements, saw that she wasn't favoring that left hind leg nearly as much, and judged that by the next day she would be ready to spend the morning in the pasture. Morgan would be pleased—if she ever talked to him again. He led the mare back to the stable, noting that the big horse seemed content and comfortable. He was neither.

The red car was gone.

He leaned in the doorway of the barn for a long time. Wondering what Morgan was doing. Wondering what she was thinking. Remembering the night she'd spent in his arms. By all the gods, she'd revealed a passion that matched his own, and his groin ached at the thought.

His heart ached more, however, and was much harder to ignore.

When Jay and his friends arrived for practice, Rhys was glad. Not for the company so much, but for the chance to *do* something. And right now, a good fight could only improve his present outlook on life.

~

"The Renaissance Fair Rules of Heavy Combat" turned out to be a little more detailed than simply "Don't kill anyone."

"No maiming, dismembering, mutilating, stabbing, or any other kind of wounding," said Jay, ticking off his fingers. "No bloodshed, period."

Rhys rolled his eyes. "Are we dancing with them or fighting? Can I hit them?"

"As much as you like, as long as they can walk away afterward. Many of the events are full contact, just like football." Jay glanced at Rhys and added, "Ask Leo about football."

At least he'd be allowed to use his fists. That was a relief because the weapons, from swords to maces to flails, had been created out of materials that Jay called safe and Rhys called flimsy. The weight of the weaponry was all wrong and poorly balanced, if at all. He hefted the sword Jay had given him. It was not only wooden but padded—*padded*—like something you would give to a very small child, had he or she been able to lift it. And Jay had said that the actual weapons in the combat event were made of something called *rattan*, which was said to be even lighter. It would be more like a brawl than a battle, but if Rhys was honest with himself, even a fistfight held a lot of appeal right now.

He blew out a breath and centered himself. *Control.* He had to stay in control. The fair was still a couple of days away, and he had no desire to unleash his frustrations on his new friends.

Oblivious to Rhys's inner struggles, Jay and Mike and the rest seemed excited by his presence. Their families had come to watch, as had Leo. Ranyon had decided to come along as well—after all, no one would see the ellyll unless he permitted them to—but Rhys was concerned he'd been a little too thorough in protecting the farm with iron nails and horseshoes. As it turned out, Ranyon had created a charm for himself that would allow him to ride in Leo's car. The thing hung from the rearview mirror like a bizarre wind chime—a strange collection of car keys and brake shoes, twigs and crystals, all bound together with the copper wire that the ellyll seemed to favor. The same charm permitted Ranyon to enter Morgan's farm without discomfort.

Brandan had brought along his big black Friesian, Boo, as usual. But there were three extra horses tonight as well to practice something called *jousting*. The strange sport had been developed centuries after Rhys had first sat astride a horse, but he cheered enthusiastically with the rest of the group as rider after rider was knocked to the ground in a great clanking of armor. When it was over, he was of a mind to ask the victorious Brandan for some lessons. Rhys also wondered how much coin it would take to purchase Lucy from her owner—he felt that the gray mare's powerful build and temperament would be well suited to such a sport once she had fully healed. He'd have to talk to Leo about finding more paying work. But he already knew he couldn't keep Lucy at Leo's house. His friend had explained the difference between livestock and pets and why the former couldn't live in the city when Rhys had proposed he keep a goat. *More rules.*

That meant Rhys would have to ask Morgan about keeping the horse at her farm. Of course, right now the horse was perfectly welcome. It was *him* that Morgan didn't want there. He sighed and resolved to speak to Leo about the dilemma later.

Right now he could do with a little hand-to-hand action.

~

The sun was slipping behind the horizon when Morgan finally drove home. She saw a pickup and horse trailer pulling out of her driveway as she approached, which told her the gathering at the corral had broken up. Brandan was driving, and she waved as she passed the truck.

She loved her friends dearly, but although she was in a much better frame of mind than when she'd left, she wasn't in the mood for company. Fred had been an excellent listener once again, and she'd talked for a long time. A couple of times she thought she saw his tail twitch slightly, perhaps in sympathy. After all, she felt almost as crappy as he did. That thought produced a mental image of her renting an empty run from Ellen and crawling into a doghouse just to be alone for a while. To just lie in the shade and the cool and—

She was in the kitchen before she recalled that she'd left her groceries in the car. As she retrieved them, she saw the light go on in the barn. *So Rhys still hasn't left...*Part of her was furious, and part of her was relieved, and all of her was much too tired to deal with it right now. She'd take it up with him tomorrow. Or the next day. Depending on how long she could ignore his existence, and assuming she knew what the hell she wanted to do about it by then…

Morgan crossed the darkening kitchen awkwardly, her arms full of tall paper bags she could barely see over—the store had been out of plastic. She plunked the bags on the table, forgetting that she'd set the small wooden jewelry box there earlier. It tumbled to the floor, scattering its contents at her feet.

Crap. She backed away carefully, hoping not to step on anything, and slapped on the light switch by the door. Knelt and began gathering the tangled trinkets and treasures. Thank heavens she hadn't put the precious photo back in the box…

A glimmer of silver caught her eye. *Nainie's necklace?*

Morgan's fingers trembled as she gently drew the long intricate chain from the debris. It seemed to separate itself from its neighbors as though glad to be rid of them. She studied it with adult eyes, recognizing several of the small colored stones woven into the spiraling chain—amethyst, citrine, garnet, peridot—but the large carved stone of the medallion was as mysterious as ever. Even with all her books, she'd never been able to name the dark, mysterious gem. Tiny flashes of blue, green, and purple seemed to spark from its faceted surface, and it was both opaque and transparent. How could something look like a pearl and a crystal at the same time? Even Nainie hadn't known what it was.

Set in silver and circled with smaller stones, the design was strongly Celtic, yet unique in a way Morgan couldn't quite pinpoint. Even in Wales, with every gift shop offering Celtic jewelry of every description, she'd never seen anything even vaguely like it—except for the ornate silver collar that had fallen from the neck of the great black dog, Rhyswr. A strange thought occurred to her that the designs, though different, were of the same origin. *Oh, good grief.* That was *so* not possible. She had no reason at all to connect them, it was simply the product of an overstressed mind. Which reminded her, she needed to unpack the Kleenex she'd just bought…

Keep the necklace with you until your heart calls for it. Those had been her grandmother's instructions. Morgan didn't really understand them—why would her heart call for it? And how? She *did* feel guilty that the heirloom had been in a box for so long. Technically it had been *with* her. After all, she'd kept it and it was in her house. But she was pretty certain that Nainie had intended for her to wear it. *It'll help you to have faith and it'll show you truth when you need it most.*

"I sure wish it could. I don't know about the *faith* part, but it'd be nice to have a little *truth* around here," she murmured as she placed it reverently around her neck, looping the long chain twice so the heavy stone medallion didn't hang to her waist. The cool links felt reassuring against her skin, and there was a sense of rightness that lightened her aching heart a little. She fingered the pendant for a few moments, then knelt and began scooping up the other fallen bits of jewelry into the box. Suddenly, the hair on the back of her neck stood up as realization hit. All the bracelets and brooches, necklaces and rings were dulled with time, blackened with tarnish or green with oxidation. Everything was in sad need of cleaning and polishing.

Not so the medallion nor its long chain. She lifted the necklace from where it fell between her breasts and stared at it. The gemstones glittered. The silver gleamed as it always had, just as she remembered it. Just as if it were new. But hadn't Nainie told her that the necklace had been in their family for generations?

Forged in faery fire, crafted by faery hand. That's what Rhys had said about the dog's silver collar.

"Omigod," Morgan breathed. She closed her hand around the medallion and, for a brief and panicked moment, thought of tearing it off her neck. Then sense—what was left of it in her strange situation—prevailed. Her grandmother had worn the pendant her entire life, tucked it safe inside her dress, treasured it close to her heart. Nainie had passed the necklace to her granddaughter with great love, and Morgan wasn't going to fear it now. Besides, hadn't Nainie known every household trick in the book and then some? She might have coated it with something, dipped it in a substance that prevented it from tarnishing, polished it with some old-fashioned Welsh remedy. Or maybe the piece wasn't silver at all, maybe it was white gold or something even more valuable that didn't darken as readily.

See? Morgan lectured herself. *It's all perfectly logical. Jay and Rhys have me spooked, and I'm just seeing things that aren't there. I'm upset today and susceptible to this silly stuff. I just need to stick to reason.*

And reason said that the necklace couldn't possibly have any connection to the heavy chain-link collar that had been worn by the great black dog.

SEVENTEEN

〜✧〜

Rhys strolled through the crowded fair with Leo. The little ellyll had come along as well, sporting a Blue Jays cap similar to Leo's favored Mariners hat. No one could see Ranyon or his bright headgear unless he wanted them to, of course—and so far, that privilege was confined to Leo and Rhys. And to Spike, of course, but the old terrier had been left at home in blissful peace and quiet.

A wise decision, thought Rhys. The fair was bustling with horses and wagons, chickens and cows, entertainers and buskers, while sellers jostled to hawk their wares. It was loud and boisterous—the sounds far different than the mechanical ones that emanated from the city where Leo's house and Morgan's clinic stood. Crowds of people laughed and talked, dressed in vivid colors, while flags and pennants waved high above it all. It put Rhys in mind of a great trading market in Moridunum he'd been to as a small boy—with one outstanding difference.

It was clean.

Even with all the people and livestock, the smell in the air was mostly of baked breads and simmering stews and roasting pig. That's because this was a temporary city, a bright mirror image of what life might have been like in a former age. Jay had explained it to Rhys as a way to keep traditions alive. Rhys could understand tradition, but he puzzled at the playfulness of it all, at the sheer enjoyment exuded by the participants. Why pretend *not* to have cars when you had them? Why play at swordsmanship when people carried guns? Perhaps modern people tired of their toys and their inventions. Perhaps the so-called civilized world was a great noisy burden beneath all its wonders, and it was a relief to let go of it for a while. That he could understand. And he had to admit that the fair was a place where he understood the rules—most of them, anyway.

"Oh, now, *here's* something you'll like." Leo pulled him over to a fire where a great side of beef was slowly rotating. A moment later, Rhys had his hands around an enormous hunk of meat, and the juices dribbled down his chin. His friend opted for a slightly smaller slice folded inside a slab of bread the size of a dinner plate, and a similar one hid most of Ranyon's head. The three of them grinned at one another like small boys. "I swear food tastes better when you can throw manners out the window," said Leo, with his mouth full.

"Aye," said Rhys and Ranyon together. They relished every bite as they watched a troupe of jugglers. Afterward, the threesome licked their fingers and wiped their faces on their sleeves, then washed their food down with ale at another booth. It was weak as water compared with the brews Rhys remembered, but it was refreshing nonetheless. Besides, he wanted a clear head for the events. Mightily satisfied, they made their way along the shops in the direction of the viewing stands.

Rhys examined a fine black leather bridle. It would have to be larger for a ceffyl the size of Lucy, of course, but the color would look fine against her dapple-gray coat. He turned to see Leo searching for Ranyon.

"He was right here a second ago," said the old man. "Oh, wait a sec. He's down there."

Rhys had to look twice but finally spotted the ellyll half-hidden beneath a stand of brilliantly colored T-shirts, rapturously fingering them one by one.

"I guess he likes them," whispered Leo. "But he probably doesn't have any money. Will it insult him if I offer to buy him one? Or can he just conjure up the cash on his own?"

"Nay. The fae are powerful, but magic cannot create something from nothing, nor can it change the essential nature of a being."

"Wait a sec, aren't you the guy that got turned into a dog?"

"What is a human but a type of animal? A man has blood and bone and hair and teeth. The Tylwyth Teg had only to change my shape."

Leo's eyebrows nearly met his hairline. "So they could make you into a mammal—but not a bird or a frog?"

"Aye, that's the way of it. They can't make a cow out of a cabbage, nor a fish from the air. So Ranyon can conjure neither coin nor shirt," said Rhys.

"Well, it's probably not an issue for him. I imagine if he really wants something, he can just make it disappear and walk away with it."

Rhys shook his head. "*Never.* The fae are many things, but not thieves. Most of them could kill you without a second thought, but they will never steal your belongings."

"Great. Honor among the homicidal."

"Some have genuine honor, like Ranyon's people. For the rest, it's pure pride. The Tylwyth Teg will never admit they need anything from mere humans. They *borrow* instead, and only from strangers. When they take something, it's a point of pride to return it to its original place by dawn of the next day. The Law of Benthyg requires it, but they would do so without such a law."

"So if they wanted to read a book, they'd just take it for the night and put it back the next day. I might not even know it had been missing?"

Rhys snorted. "You would likely know at once. Time doesn't move the same way in the faery realm. The book will reappear in its rightful place at its rightful *human* time—but months, even years, may have passed while it was in fae hands. Plus, the Fair Ones tend to wring as much use as they can from a thing before they must return it. A book may be missing pages, the cover torn and dirty, as if you or I had read it a thousand times. But the Law allows for such usage."

"I'll just be keeping those horseshoes over my doors."

Leo bought Ranyon a bright-blue souvenir T-shirt, telling the vendor that the child-size item was for his grandson. It was likely the only modern item for sale in the whole of the market, and it pleased the ellyll tremendously.

Ranyon tried to wrestle the shirt on the moment they were away from the booth, but it didn't work well with his Jays cap still on his head. Rhys patiently untangled him as Leo held the hat and chuckled. "Actually, my grandson is in his thirties. I don't think this would even fit any of the *great*-grandkids. Fits you pretty good, though." He handed the hat back to Ranyon. "Goes with those Blue Jays colors too."

"It fair fits me fine," said Ranyon, smoothing it over the leaves that covered him. "'Tis a *gwych* color. My thanks to ya, my friend. You've a generous heart in ya."

Rhys smiled to himself as his friends walked ahead of him hand in hand. He knew that not only was Ranyon invisible to the rest of the crowd but, like the hat, the shirt had vanished from mortal sight as soon as the ellyll put it on—at least to most eyes. Not Morgan's, however. Ranyon had mentioned that, had it not been for one of his famous charms, she would have seen him at the last few practices at the farm. "Most mortals can't see me because I belong to a different realm. But some can, and glad I am that I had this with me. I felt power leave it and I turned around to see your lady."

The ellyll had said nothing more at the time, and Rhys hadn't brought it up. He knew full well why Morgan had the sight, as his people had called it. By the admission of the Fair Ones themselves, there was a trickle of fae blood in her veins. *Thanks be to all the gods that she didn't wander where the dead bwgan lay in her field.* Rhys could not have hidden it from her. And rather than support his case for the existence of faeries, he would likely have been blamed for it somehow. He sighed. Morgan Edwards was proving to be an incredibly stubborn woman. At least she hadn't enforced her demands that he leave her property.

Yet.

They passed a bakery where *gyngerbrede* was just being taken out of the brick ovens. Leo inhaled the spicy air rapturously.

"Damn, that smells just like my granny's kitchen," he said. "I wish I wasn't so stuffed."

"I've a charm fer that," said Ranyon. Plucking a penny off the ground, he said a few strange words over it and passed it to his friend.

Leo looked at the coin in his palm and was about to speak when a long, loud belch erupted from his throat. Mortified, he put his other hand over his mouth, but a second burp refused to be suppressed. It was louder than the first, and a few heads in the crowd turned to look for the source.

Rhys grabbed his friend's arm as a third burp nearly vibrated Leo off his feet. Quickly, he helped the old man to a bench.

"Goddamn," whispered Leo, obviously afraid to open his mouth very far. No further belches were forthcoming, and he sighed in relief. "What the hell did I eat? I haven't burped like that since I was twelve and trying to burp the alphabet to impress Annie Mae Grissom."

"You wanted room in your belly to fit some sweets," laughed Ranyon. "I told you I had a charm fer that." He pointed at Leo's left hand that was still clutching the penny.

"Shit, I should have known it was you." Leo dropped the penny as if it was hot and shook his fist in mock anger. "You have a damn charm for everything, don't you? I'd better not start farting!"

"Nay, I have pity on these poor mortals around us," grinned Ranyon. "So, are we having gyngerbrede or not?"

As they made their way up the bleachers, a children's costume parade was just clearing the forefield. The next event would be an exhibition of falconry.

Rhys looked around and spotted Morgan at one side of the field, checking the wing of an enormous hawk for any injuries or strains. Jay had mentioned she was on duty during the fair, that a veterinarian had to be on hand during any event that involved animals. *Rules again.* Rhys could see it was a good rule, however. He watched as sunlight glinted on her hair, bringing out its rich chestnut color. She hadn't tied it back today, and the sweep of it as she bent to write something echoed the sweep of the hawk's wing. He wished she was sitting next to him—although it was damned unlikely she would want to do so, considering the way things stood between them. As if Morgan could feel his eyes on her, she lifted her head and looked directly at him before returning to examining the bird. She didn't smile, didn't acknowledge him in the least.

"I take it she still thinks you're crazy," said Leo.

"I've a charm fer that—"

"No!" said Rhys and Leo together.

"Well, 'twould be faster than what *yer* doing," Ranyon muttered.

Rhys sent the ellyll a warning look, then turned his attention back to Leo. "Aye, Morgan does not yet believe where I came from."

The old man shifted his Mariners cap on his head. Ranyon copied the gesture with his Blue Jays hat. "You gotta admit, son, your story is one in a million."

"My tale is far from rare. There are others like me."

"What do you mean *like you*?" asked Leo.

It was Ranyon who answered, however. "There're plenty of other humans enthralled by the Tylwyth Teg. They keep 'em like pets or like slaves. Same thing."

The old man was flabbergasted. "In the twenty-first century?"

"The Tylwyth Teg are immortal," said Rhys. "Time means nothing to them and neither do humans."

"Aye, just trifling and temporary creatures with little use," added Ranyon. "Not to be offending the both of ya. But other than providing a little entertainment from time to time, humans just aren't important to most of the fae."

Leo held up his hands as if to fend off what his friends were telling him. "That's downright cold."

"Aye, it is. But how important is a bee to you?" Rhys asked the old man. "Your lifetime is all but forever compared to its brief span. It lives in a world apart from yours. You might enjoy the honey it makes, but what human would consider a bee's well-being, its happiness? Would it weigh on your conscience if you killed one?"

The ellyll spat—a new skill he'd picked up from watching baseball. A giant pink wad of bubblegum bounced through the floor of the bleachers and disappeared. "The Tylwyth Teg rule over all the faery races, but they have no conscience to speak of. No concern for anyone but themselves, and not even for one another. Like spoiled and hateful children they are. And no one to stand against them."

"There's malice aplenty from some," agreed Rhys. "But you can guard yourself against malice. Most of the Tylwyth Teg are *indifferent* and that's worse. That's what makes them so dangerous."

Ranyon put his Jays cap on backward and sighed. "Aye. And bloody unpredictable."

"C'mon, isn't there somebody in charge?" Leo demanded. "I thought there was supposed to be some kind of ruler, like in the bedtime stories my mother told me."

"Oh, aye. The queen has done her very best to keep things fair and peaceful, but when the old king died, much of her influence died with him. Now most of the Tylwyth Teg do what they like and hang the rest," said the ellyll.

"The king *died*? You just told me that faeries live forever."

"Being immortal doesn't mean they can't be killed," said Rhys.

Ranyon folded his spindly arms. "Remember my clan who perished. So, aye, even the king of the Tylwyth Teg was slain. There was treachery behind it, a play for the throne, and the queen narrowly held her power. But hold it she did, for all the good it's done her. No one dares to challenge her openly, but many work behind her back. And so no one is safe, not human nor fae."

"It's just not right," declared Leo and reset his baseball cap on his head as if to emphasize the point. "It's not right at all. No one's unimportant. *No one.*"

Ranyon patted his friend's arm. "Aye, not when they're around Leo Waterson, they're not."

Rhys heartily agreed, but inside he was disquieted. *No one is safe, not human nor fae.* The bleak conversation had served to remind him that the Tylwyth Teg were probably far from finished with him. So far, they'd sent a spy and an assassin. What would be next?

～

After the jousting finished—with Brandan and Boo claiming the title—the remaining events involved humans only. Morgan was free to wander the makeshift streets of the fair, taking in the many displays and demonstrations. It felt strange not to rush back to the clinic, but Grady and Tyler no doubt had the place under control. In fact, Jay and Grady had both *insisted* that Morgan take a few days off after she finished with today's events.

For once, she hadn't argued. After all, she hadn't slept well since her falling-out with Rhys. Most nights she was too miserable to nod off for very long, and when she did, the results were astonishing. She was *still* experiencing blatantly sexy dreams, and they all revolved around Rhys. Was the man an addiction? And, of course, it only added to the difficulty of getting over him.

Part of her was no longer certain that was possible…

She passed a booth with charming felted hats that had a mirror angled in her direction. *Good grief.* It was obvious that all the cover stick in the world could no longer hide the shadows under her eyes—no wonder her partners had told her to take time off.

Maybe some time to herself was just what she needed. *A little rest, a little relaxation, a little recreation…*Morgan imagined that a trip to a shopping mall would have been more therapeutic than an event where Rhys was impossible to avoid. But, as she lectured herself inwardly, she loved the fair and she attended every year. Even if she had hated it, she would have come for the sake of supporting her friends. *No way* was she going to be chased off because Mr. Celtic Warrior was walking around looking better than Brad Pitt on his best day.

She lingered at a booth that was selling handwoven baskets, then watched a woman creating an intricately patterned fabric on an enormous loom. Morgan's stomach reminded her that she'd skipped lunch, so she bought a small chicken pie from a busker carrying a tray of them on his head. The tender pastry was redolent of rosemary, and she savored it to the last crumb as she walked.

It was easy for her to spot her friends here and there in the crowd (and avoid Rhys). They'd elected to adopt a simple costume, dressing all in black with blue tabards—simple sleeveless tunics—that were strikingly edged in white. Jay had originally wanted red, Mike and Brandan had both voted for gold, but all were quick to go with Rhys's suggestion of blue. They'd been enthusiastic too about Starr's suggestion for the group's logo—a Celtic hound in the center of the tabard, front and back, and also on the shields they carried. Starr did all the sewing and needlework, and when she was finished, the hound was the spitting image of the tattoo on Rhys's collarbone and the inlaid design on Rhyswr's broken collar.

The symbol had disturbed Morgan at first—okay, it still disturbed her *plenty* since Rhys hadn't renounced his claim of being an ancient Celt—but there was no denying it was a beautiful design. Morgan made a point of stopping by Starr's booth to compliment her on her craftsmanship.

"I'm really happy with how well it turned out," Starr said as she and another woman worked the booth, taking money, making change, and answering customer questions about the handmade jewelry and herbal remedies on display. "Rhys took his shirt off and let me trace his tattoo, and then I just enlarged the design."

The thought of Starr's hands on Rhys's bare chest gave Morgan a rude jolt. She didn't know which bothered her more: that someone else had touched Rhys's skin or that she personally gave a damn. Starr had done nothing wrong, of course. *How long before I quit caring about the guy?* Morgan asked herself and then was sorry she'd done so.

Yanking her thoughts away from the touchy subject, she turned her attention to the many crystals and handmade jewelry displayed beside neatly labeled jars and packets of healing plants. On impulse, she drew Nainie's necklace from her purse—she hadn't dared wear it while she was working in case it got damaged or dirty, but she seemed to feel better if it was with her—and showed Starr the medallion. "I was wondering if you could tell me what this is made of."

"Omigosh." Her friend looked startled, then recovered herself. "It's *gorgeous*, Morgan! Just look at all the colors in it. And the pattern seems Celtic." Starr touched a finger to the dark stone pendant, then drew back. "Holy cow, it's powerful too—you can really feel the positive energy coming off it. Where did you find this? Who made this?"

"I don't know. Someone in Wales, I imagine. Nainie left it to me." Morgan didn't feel any energy radiating from it herself, just knew that she felt good when she held the necklace. But if there *were* such a thing as good energy associated with it, it had surely come from her grandmother. "I know what some of the surrounding stones are, but this big one—I can't find any information on it."

Starr shook her head, making the tiny bells in her long braids sing out. The carved stone seemed to brighten for a split second, the light playing off hidden depths, but Morgan blinked and the effect was gone.

"It's incredibly beautiful, but honestly, I don't know what it is," said Starr. "Vanessa? Have you ever seen a stone like this?" Her partner came over to look at the pendant.

"It's a bit like labradorite, just the way it's got depth and fire to it. Almost a cross between a black opal and a pearl." The woman shook her head. "But you don't carve pearls or opals, and you certainly don't facet them, so I can't even hazard a guess. Lovely, though." She left to help an elderly woman choose a large piece of rose quartz from a display.

"Your event's been announced, Starr," called someone from the crowd.

"Thanks, Norrie. I'll be right there." Starr ran a finger over the pendant once more and shivered. "Amazing. Just *amazing*. I'll try looking it up in some of my books at home," she said to Morgan. "Even the setting and the chain are a wonder—it looks just like something the elves would make in one of Tolkien's books."

Morgan thanked her and tucked the necklace back in her bag as Starr bounced away. If anyone could find out what the stone was, she knew that her friend could. But Morgan wished she hadn't mentioned elves—they were way too much like faeries, and Morgan had had more than enough of *that* subject.

She dodged a trio of stilt walkers, tossed coins in a minstrel's bowl, and joined Leo in the stands to watch the rest of the events. He had a spot open on either side of him, and she headed for the one on his left, but he put his hand up. "Best to sit on the other side," he said. "Um, my right ear's the good one, you know."

"Sure," she said, although she didn't remember him ever mentioning having trouble with his hearing before. She sat on his right. "Wow, it feels good to get off my feet."

"I've done enough walking for one day too," he said. "And way more than enough eating. After I finished an apple dumpling and a custard tart, I told Rhys he'd have to save himself—it was too late for me. I'm staying right here till the fat lady sings. And I just might sing with her." Chuckling, he patted his waistline.

"I hear you," she laughed. "Either medieval people were very active or they were all very round. I just had a little chicken pie that'll keep me full till next week. I'm sure there was real cream in it. Everything seems really rich."

"Oh, everything *is* rich, believe me. One of the cooks was telling me they use authentic ingredients from medieval times— lard, suet, pork fat, all that good stuff."

Morgan made a face. "I'm not sure I wanted to know that," she said.

"My wife, Tina, would certainly have had a conniption and lectured me on my cholesterol and all that." Leo leaned forward with a conspiratorial whisper. "But I have to admit, it tasted pretty damn good."

They laughed and enjoyed the events. Starr won the women's archery competition handily with a small recurve bow that packed a lot of power despite its delicate appearance. *Just like Starr herself,* thought Morgan.

Jay seemed to surprise himself by placing third in dagger throwing. Rhys had helped him with his technique at the farm, and Morgan had marveled at the strange little knives—they were all metal, the handles being simply blunt extensions of the blades themselves. For balance, Jay had said. She jumped up and cheered loudly when he took second in throwing hatchets. The targets were metal shields and the armor-piercing capability of the small axes was amply demonstrated. It was a little chilling to think of that, but she was excited for her friend and partner just the same.

Mike, Brandan, and Rhys were all entered in the longbow event. Morgan had been trying to ignore Rhys's existence all day, and the fact that he looked good no matter what he was doing didn't help a bit. Nor did the appreciative comments she overheard from the women seated around her in the stands. And especially not the tittering remarks between some of them as to what else might be *long* about the tall, dark warrior besides his bow. Still, Morgan wanted to be supportive of the team, so she wasn't going to miss the event. Leo seemed to be glad she was there, and she had to admit, the old man's enthusiasm was contagious even in her present state of mind.

The ten contestants had drawn numbers to determine their order. Mike was up third and sent three arrows into the straw targets at the end of the field. Two were in the bull's-eye, which put him in first place. Brandan only got one in the center of the target, but he seemed happy with that. Rhys had coached both of them, and they'd improved a lot in the past few weeks. Rhys was last on the roster, and for a moment Morgan considered not watching—but decided that was just too high school. Besides, Leo was intent on sharing the moment.

"Look at that form," he said, patting her arm. "Our boy is rock steady. Do you know how much power it takes to draw a bow like that? It's six feet tall!"

Morgan had no idea, but even from here she could see Rhys's muscles bulge. He didn't draw the wooden bow as much as lean into it, and the great bow yielded accordingly. Three arrows were nocked and sent into the bull's-eye in quick succession.

"He's in first place now," declared Leo. "Let's see if he can stay there."

The next phase involved setting the targets farther back. Mike, Brandan, and Rhys retained their places through three more rounds, although Morgan imagined their arms must be feeling like spaghetti. During the last round, she could see the shine of sweat on Mike's face as he sought to hit a target that was now a daunting two hundred yards away, agreed to be the maximum possible range of an English longbow. All three of his arrows stuck—but not in the bull's-eye. Brandan managed to get two lodged in the outer rings. The other competitors achieved one at the most. All other arrows missed entirely.

It was Rhys's turn, and Morgan found herself holding her breath. It didn't matter that she was at odds with this man, didn't matter if he believed himself a Celtic warrior or a dancing bear. All that mattered in that moment was that there was dead silence in the arena and that every eye was on him as he drew the enormous bow, bending it nearly in half with the effort. The arrow loosed and a great roar went up from the crowd as it not only struck the target but grazed the bull's-eye. The second and third arrows were within the ring surrounding it.

"He's done it!" shouted Leo, but he was all but drowned out in the roar of the crowd. Morgan stood and clapped until her hands were sore. Brandan and Mike slapped Rhys on the back and punched him in the shoulders. Their other teammates emerged from the onlookers and mobbed him, throwing pitchers of beer over him, bouncing their chests against him, and rubbing his head until his hair stood up. *Like watching the winning touchdown in a football game*, thought Morgan.

"This puts the whole team in first place now," Leo explained, as things settled down and they took their seats again.

Rhys and Mike dominated the next few events as well, all with various combinations of swordplay. Brandan, Jay, and the others stood on the sidelines and cheered them on. Morgan was just thankful that the blades were either padded or were substituted with thick rattan staves. Even then, one contestant was knocked out cold and another had an injured arm, probably broken.

"Holy crap, are they *trying* to kill each other?"

"Brandan told me that they don't hold back. Everyone who participates signs a waiver," explained Leo. "Of course, nobody enters unless they're gonna give it their all."

It has to be a guy thing. Morgan shrugged.

Starr came and squeezed in beside her. "Vanessa's got the booth. I promised Jay I'd watch the heavy combat. This is the first year they're putting on a Capture the Castle event," she said. "It took them three weeks to build that castle facade. One of the board members is an engineer, and he designed it to withstand an army. Literally."

"I've got twenty dollars that says Rhys's team will come out on top," said Leo.

Both Starr and Morgan rolled their eyes. "No way am I taking a bet like that!" said Starr. "You'll have to find someone who hasn't watched them practice. The guys have been at the farm almost every night for the past two weeks."

"I'm surprised they're still talking to Rhys," said Morgan. "He's really pushed them hard."

Leo nodded. "He'd have made a great drill sergeant, that's certain. Puts me in mind of the one that made my life hell when I signed up."

"Well, at least he doesn't call them names," said Starr, passing out bottles of cold water from her big straw tote.

"Shit, he doesn't *have* to insult them to motivate them," snorted Leo. "Every one of them wants to *be* him when they grow up."

"I know Jay does," said Starr, rolling her eyes. "It's all he talks about at home."

"He talks about Rhys at work too," said Morgan. What she didn't say was how much she wished Jay *wouldn't*, at least not lately. She turned her attention to the field where the contestants were gathering. It certainly promised to be a colorful spectacle, with many of the dozen or so teams striving to accurately portray a particular era—or in some cases, a particular movie.

"*The Lord of the Rings* has plenty of fans by the looks of things," said Morgan.

Starr nodded. "In order to get enough people, the board decided not to restrict the event to specific historical periods. It's just for fun, really, although there are strict rules for safety."

"Huh. You can't keep that many people totally safe even if you arm them all with feathers," said Leo, as he scanned the teams. So far, they were assembled into fairly tidy groups across the field from a great wooden castle—but there were a lot of them.

"Well, the weapons aren't feathers, but they're not steel either. Not for this. They have to be bamboo or rattan. And all vital parts of the body have to be shielded with armor of some kind."

"I don't see much armor on our team," said Morgan. "Most of them seem to just have helmets."

"It's a rule that all helmets have to be steel. Body armor doesn't have to be," explained Starr. "Our team is wearing chain mail. But under *that*, Jay's got carpet duct-taped around his shins and a Kevlar vest. Some of the guys are using hockey gear under their mail." She pointed. "Brandan and Mike are the only ones who own real armor. It's really expensive."

Morgan could see that Mike's exquisite helmet matched his hand-tooled steel suit. He looked like Lancelot from a King Arthur movie, and she wondered how he moved. Or saw anything. Or even breathed comfortably. A few others in the crowd sported full body armor too, and much of it was very ornate. Many of the participants—including Jay's group—wore very plain helms with a brim and a cage protecting the face. In fact, Morgan thought their team looked outstanding with their blue-and-white hound tabards over their chain mail—and thankfully, they were easy for her to spot in the midst of the crowded field.

A tall figure in blue was standing apart from the others. The wind stirred his dark hair and stirred Morgan's memories at the same time. She'd run her hands through that hair, clutched at it in her ecstasy, nuzzled it in affection—

As if aware of her, Rhys raised his head and met her gaze across the distance. She couldn't see his expression, but she could *feel* him. Then he jammed his helmet on with both hands and turned to the others as loud trumpets blared.

The battle was on.

EIGHTEEN

⌒〴〢⌒

The teams had formed alliances in advance, but if there had been strategy in the beginning, it quickly degenerated into a free-for-all. Combatants engaged one another with rattan swords and maces, and Morgan winced at the sounds of impact. The weapons might not kill anyone, but surely the blows had to hurt.

"There'll be plenty of bruises and bruised egos at the end of this war," Starr said. "I don't know why Jay always wants me to watch this violence. He knows I don't enjoy it."

"He just wants you to see him being manly." Leo laughed.

Morgan grinned. Her attention was then caught and held by a powerful man who was systematically clearing a path through the fighters. It was Rhys, of course. All her wishes to avoid watching him, to keep her views of the man to a minimum, vanished abruptly, and she couldn't pull her gaze away. She'd expected he would be good, but the practices at the farm hadn't begun to prepare her for what the man was like in action. The words *irresistible force* had new meaning as he literally hewed down his competitors and tossed them aside with seeming ease.

Leo thumped her knee. "Lookit him go! Holy moly, our man's like a hot knife through butter!"

He was indeed, and Morgan felt sorry for whoever stood in his way. She didn't know much about battle, but as she watched Rhys make his way forward, she noticed something odd. He wasn't engaging the opposition, at least not in the same way as his teammates. She saw Mike and Brandan struggling with their opponents—each pair forming a separate fight within the overall battle. Rhys, on the other hand, was making extraordinary progress by simply wading through the enemy lines, disarming each foe with one hand and knocking him down with the other.

Morgan wasn't certain that the men were simply falling down on cue either. The rules of heavy combat stated that if you were struck with sufficient force, you counted yourself as wounded or dead and fell accordingly. As far as she could tell, most of Rhys's challengers weren't getting the opportunity to decide for themselves…

"He's pulling his punches," said Leo in wonder.

"What?" Morgan almost took her eyes off the field to stare at her friend. "Are you kidding me? Look at what he's doing to his opponents!"

"Look at what they're doing to *him*."

It was true. Rhys was making his uncanny progress despite a countless number of stabs and slices from the castle defenders' staves. She squinted and discerned that Rhys appeared to be anticipating the blows, turning his body aside at the last moment to shield his vitals and often ripping the weapon from their hands at the same time. There was a rhythm to it like the swing of a pendulum—*twist, bend, seize*, with a follow-through of collected force. The offender was either clubbed with his own bamboo sword or felled with Rhys's fist. One enemy, one blow.

What kind of skill and calculation did that take in the midst of chaos?

Their team's tactic was simple. Rhys was the point of an arrow, with Brandan, Mike, Jay, and the others forming a wedge behind him. Together they drove a path through the defenders to the faux castle, and it wasn't long before they had gained the uppermost tower and claimed its flag. Thunderous applause erupted from the crowd, even from those who had originally been cheering for other teams. Many of the fighters Rhys had knocked down were clapping and cheering and waving as well.

Men, thought Morgan. *Beat the living daylights out of each other, and then they're all pals.*

The humor was lost, however, as cold realization chilled her blood. Medical attendants were on the field, checking everyone over. It didn't look like anyone was too badly hurt. And all of Rhys's opponents were on their feet. *But if he'd been armed with a real blade*, she thought, *none of them would be getting up. Not one. And the body count would be enormous.* Jay's words echoed in her brain: *His style of swordplay isn't play. It's kill or be killed. It's the real thing, Morgan. And you can only get that kind of skill one way.*

From one place...

Leo's voice broke into her thoughts. "Will you *look* at that dog," he said. "I've never seen a hound so big."

Morgan looked in the direction he was pointing. "Where?"

"Right there, down at the bottom of the stands. The big black one."

Rhyswr? She jumped to her feet even as her heart leapt in hope, but she saw nothing but the crowd of people emptying the bleachers and heading out to the field. "I can't see it. Starr, do you see a dog anywhere?"

Her friend had risen to follow the crowd, no doubt to get to Jay, but the frantic note in Morgan's voice made her stop. "Is there a dog? There shouldn't be—the board didn't allow dogs this year because people didn't pick up after them at the last fair." She glanced around, appeared to see nothing, and continued down the steps.

"Where is it?" Morgan asked Leo, and was surprised when he stood and pointed.

"How can you miss it? It's *right there* in front of us. Biggest dog ever. Looks like a goddamn pony and black as sin."

The area directly in front of the bleachers cleared, and for a moment Morgan saw absolutely nothing but bare, hard-packed ground with a few fluttering bits of debris stuck to the brave few blades of grass. She blinked—

And suddenly she *did* see a dog. It wasn't Rhyswr. It wasn't even a mastiff. Rangy and tall, more like a wolfhound from hell, it sat with grinning jaws that seemed too wide for its face and looked directly up at Leo.

"I'll bet it eats a whole bag of dog food in a sitting," he said.

Morgan wasn't sure the animal ate anything so benign. Maybe she was overtired and her imagination was running off with her, but there was something downright creepy about this dog. And how on earth had she missed—

A movement to her left drew her attention back to her friend. His left arm was jerking spasmodically away from his body and back again. "Leo, are you all right?"

The old man appeared to be talking to his disobedient arm. "What in blue blazes is the matter with you?"

Omigod, I think he's having a stroke! "Leo, sit down now. Let me have a look at you."

The giant dog raised its head and howled loud and long, a dismal ululation that vibrated her very bones. At the same moment, Leo's eyes rolled back in his head and he collapsed. Morgan's cell phone tumbled through the bleachers to the ground below as she made a frantic grab for her friend.

On the battlement of the central tower of the castle, Rhys and his teammates had their hands in the air, shouting in triumph. It was a perfect moment, with the entire crowd below hollering and waving at them. Better than anything was the purely male satisfaction of knowing that the woman he loved was in the stands and that she had witnessed his victory.

An unearthly howl sliced through the noise of the crowd like a sword's edge through paper.

No one reacted. In fact, no one seemed to have heard it except him—and that made his blood chill even more. Rhys looked over at the bleachers where Morgan stood beside Leo and Ranyon. Something wasn't right. The ellyll was swinging on Leo's arm as if trying to pull him away from something. Morgan had hold of Leo's other arm, even as he was trying to point down at the field. Rhys's gaze followed to the ground in front of the bleachers where something large and black—

Gods alive, it was a grim.

"No!" he yelled and began pushing his way down the steps. It was impossible with so many people trying to make their way up. He ran back to the balustrade—shouting at his friends: "Leo's in trouble!"—and sprang to a ladder that was leaning against the castle wall. There was a sea of people beneath it, and some were on it. *Damn it!* He couldn't jump—it was a good thirty feet to the ground.

Jay and Mike were at his side at once. "Leo's going down," said Mike, and Rhys snapped his head around in time to see Leo crumple to the floor of the bleachers.

As Jay whipped out a cell phone and dialed 911, Brandan jumped onto the ladder ahead of Rhys and started booting at people and waving them away. "Emergency," he yelled. "Get the fuck out of the way!" He menaced them with his padded sword and swatted a few with the flat of it. For a moment it looked like the crowd wasn't paying attention, but Brandan was nearly as big as Rhys, and finally they began moving back, slowly at first, then quickly. The ladder emptied in front of him, and Rhys came down fast behind him.

Moments later, Rhys was running to the bleachers with everything he had. An ambulance with lights flashing and sirens blaring was racing up the infield toward them. He could see Morgan kneeling over Leo and shouting at him, calling on the old man to hang on, *hang on—*

Everything in Rhys's heart urged him to go to her and to go to his friend, right now. But if he did so, he'd doom Leo for certain. There was only one chance to save the man who had taken him in, mentored and befriended him—and it was a long shot. As he reached the stands, Rhys veered to the left, following the path of the great black grim that only he could see.

If only Morgan hadn't seen *him*...

The EMTs had been fast, thank heavens. In minutes, Leo was on his way to the hospital, with half the team and Morgan following behind in Brandan's truck. She was grateful for the ride, feeling shaken to the core by Leo's sudden collapse. And cut to the quick by Rhys's bizarre disappearing act. Why would he run off like that? Why chase a dog? Didn't he care about Leo? Or her? Surely he couldn't have been that reluctant to come near her—she wasn't exactly scary, even when angry. And if he cared about her as he claimed, wouldn't he have come to her side no matter what?

She put it out of her mind and jumped up as the doctor came into the waiting room. She was relieved to see it was someone she knew, Kate Walmsley. "Is Leo okay? Is it a stroke?"

The doctor put her hands up in a calming gesture. "Technically, I'm supposed to talk to family only, Morgan, but I know you came in with him and his family isn't here. So, strictly professional to professional—meaning, you never heard a thing from me—Mr. Waterson is stable for the moment. We're running some tests, but he doesn't appear to have had a stroke. His heart's okay. We're not sure what the problem is yet. It might be heat exhaustion, even heat-stroke—you mentioned he was outside, and it was a warm day."

"He had a hat, and I saw him drinking water." Thank heavens for Starr passing out the bottles; Morgan wasn't sure she would have thought of it. Still, she disagreed with the heatstroke theory. "Leo was a little excited, but he'd been seated for most of the time, and the bleachers were shaded. I was outside as much as he was, and I'm fine."

"But you're not taking three prescriptions that make you even *more* susceptible to heat exhaustion."

Point. "I didn't even think of that," she said. "I should have."

"There's something else." Kate leaned closer and lowered her voice. "I know he's your friend, Morgan, but Mr. Waterson is eighty-five years old. There might not be anything *wrong* with him per se. We're still doing tests of course, but he just doesn't look good to me. We have to take into consideration that it could just be his time."

Eighty-five? How had she not known that? Morgan would have guessed that Leo was in his seventies. "His time—you mean he might not pull out of this?"

"He might have ten more years to go line dancing, or he might have a week. Things get iffier the older you get. My grand-mother is ninety-four and still going strong, but my dad passed just last year," said Kate. "So if you know how to get ahold of his kids, they really should be notified. Just in case."

Morgan nodded. "He has a son and a daughter in Seattle—I'll make sure they're called. I probably should have done it already. Is Leo awake? Can I see him?"

"Sure. But keep it as short as you can. We don't want to wear him out."

As the doctor disappeared down another hallway, Starr came up and put an arm around Morgan. "I can call Leo's kids for you. I know them both pretty well. You go ahead and check on him— you'll feel a lot better if you see he's okay."

"Thanks," said Morgan. "I appreciate it."

Room 315 was fairly cheerful as hospital rooms went. It had a large window overlooking the trees that covered the grounds, and the walls were a pleasant creamy yellow. But Leo himself looked washed-out—his skin almost gray against the white sheets.

"Forgive me for not standing up in the presence of a pretty girl," he said, without opening his eyes.

"Sage before beauty," she quipped and took his hand.

He chuckled. "Quick as well as pretty. No wonder Rhys is so sweet on you."

Morgan swallowed hard. "He doesn't seem that sweet today. I could have used his help."

"Ranyon said Rhys went after that dog—it's a goddamn grim you know."

"Oh, Leo…" She swallowed hard, a task made harder by the fact that all the moisture seemed to have disappeared from her mouth and throat. She settled for gently rubbing the old man's hand in silence, although she felt like bawling. Either Rhys had talked Leo into believing his crazy story or Leo was in far worse shape than the doctor thought.

And who the hell was *Ranyon*?

≈

He cornered the grim at last behind the blacksmith shop of the temporary medieval town. Rather than a mastiff, as Rhys had once been, the monstrous dog was a tall sight hound. But it was as black as the night itself, just like every other grim created by the Tylwyth Teg. The dog bared enormous teeth, its broad head well above Rhys's waist. It didn't bother to struggle as Rhys seized its silver collar. Instead it made a low chuffing sound as if laughing at him.

"You have no right to be here," snarled Rhys. "This isn't fae land; this isn't under the control of the Fair Ones. Undo what you've done to Leo. It isn't your task."

Unable to form words with canine lips, the creature spoke with its mind, and it was all Rhys could do not to recoil at the dark, oily feel of its voice in his head. *It'll be fae land soon enough if they have their way. There are many seeking new territories to rule, new diversions.*

"And you? You need diversion too that you would dare come here? Grims do not perform their tasks on this side of the waters."

Why not? Pathetic humans die here just as surely. It seems that a grim would find unending satisfaction in this new land, countless delicious deaths to herald. Besides, a barghest goes where he is commanded to go.

"You were mortal once. You had a will of your own."

The great dog made a noise of disgust. *I am powerful now. I am immortal now. What need have I for will? Your will did not make you human again.*

"No, but it was my will that brought me here, because I chose whom I would serve. And it was not the Tylwyth Teg." Rhys looked at the intricate silver links in his grasp, the collar, so similar to the one that he had been forced to wear. He released it in revulsion. The tall black dog made no effort to escape, and it occurred to him that it had *wanted* Rhys to catch up to him. The creature could have simply disappeared in a scattering of vapor—

You'll not walk on two legs for long. The Fair Ones will have you back. Perhaps, they'll make you a mindless bwgan this time. Perhaps they'll send you to visit the woman who unmade your spell—

"I'll die before that happens." In a move almost too fast to follow, he had a knife to the creature's throat. "And you'll die if you don't release Leo. The Fair Ones have no cause to harm him."

The chuffing laugh returned, louder now, but the humor didn't reach its pitiless eyes. *I already do not breathe, or have you forgotten so soon? My heart does not beat, I do not bleed. You cannot injure me. It's* you *the fae wish to injure, by preying on those you are so foolishly attached to.*

The dark creature sat as if relaxed and unconcerned, with Rhys's knife still pressing against its massive neck. The blade hissed as it scorched the skin beneath the fur, as the iron in the steel reacted to the fae elements. Incredibly, the monster leaned forward slightly so that the blade pressed deeper, mocking Rhys's efforts to intimidate it.

And when have the Fair Ones ever needed cause in order to do as they wish? They want you back. But the spell was broken, and you're not in their realm. And so they will offer a trade, one you will not dare to turn down.

Rhys cursed inwardly and sheathed the useless weapon, as a sick feeling settled in his gut. The grim's words were all too true. Rhys was completely mortal and thinking like one. *Of course* he had no power over the grim—nor would it be swayed from its mission. All barghests had been human once, but that didn't mean they retained their humanity. Some lost it quickly, some lost it a little at a time over the centuries. Some, like the black creature before him, discarded it willingly. They came to relish their merciless work, thriving on the fear and chaos they caused, savoring death and suffering in all its forms, as they had once savored food and drink. Rhys repressed a shiver as he realized what could have happened to him if he had remained much longer in the faery realm—what he might have *become*. What he could still become if the Fair Ones dragged him back...

Suddenly a small form flew past Rhys and descended on the dog with a flurry of punches and kicks. "Ya *plentyn gordderch*! Ya great black bastard! I'll tear ya apart with my own hands fer what ya done to him! Ya bloody *llofrudd*!"

Rhys yanked Ranyon out of the way just as long white fangs snapped together where the ellyll had been. The little man continued to swing his strange twiggy arms as Rhys held the back of his blue shirt.

"Ya murderin' *lladdwr*!" Ranyon shouted at the dog, who simply shook his fur out all over as if the ellyll's words were nothing more than annoying flies.

Rhys wondered what the grim *would* care about. "Never mind, Ranyon," he said. "The dog is only a slave. He just told me he has no need of free will."

The creature stilled.

"No mind of his own, so he cannot be held accountable," Rhys continued, taking a few steps back as if trying to drag the ellyll away. "There's no point in calling a puppet names."

Ranyon stopped struggling in Rhys's grasp. "Aye, I see what ya mean," he said, playing along. "I should have realized it's just a foolish toy for the fae to play with."

The big canine's lips curled back to expose its shining teeth, and its eyes glowed red.

"Only a servant," said Rhys, sliding one hand into his pocket. "Good for bowing and scraping and taking orders. More to be pitied than feared."

The monstrous black dog leapt for his throat. Rhys's reflexes were a scant half second faster only because he'd been ready. He dove out of the way—but not before slapping a small white cotton pouch into the creature's gaping maw, hoping it would go straight down the black gullet. The beast spun to savage him where he'd rolled, when it stopped suddenly. It backed up a step, then another. Gnashing its jaws, white foam began to bubble up from its throat and it began clawing at its muzzle and belly. Rhys snatched up Ranyon and dashed behind a row of portable toilets just as a soundless explosion sent shock waves through the air.

When they peered around to look, the grim was gone save for a blackened spot on the dusty ground. Rhys tensed, waiting for the humans to come running.

Nothing happened. A bored-looking shopkeeper walked around the back to empty a bucket of soapy water, looked at the charred spot, and yelled at someone inside the booth, "Those boys have been setting fires again." When he left, Ranyon looked up at Rhys.

"What *cymysgiad* was that ya fed the murderin' beast?"

"No potion at all," said Rhys. He sat Ranyon on his shoulders and jogged back toward the bleachers. "It was just salt from the sea. Starr gave a bag to each of us this morning. For protection, she said, because it was pure."

"I'll wager she meant to keep ya from getting yer head bashed in, not defendin' ya against a grim."

"Aye, well, it worked." Rhys didn't mention that he hadn't been certain that it would. All he'd had to go on was the effects of salt on the bwgan's carcass. "Tell me about Leo."

The ellyll made a choking sound. "It's not his time, yet he's not long fer this world. 'Twas a spell the grim delivered upon him! 'Tis draining Leo's life away by degrees."

Rhys's worst fears were confirmed. Just as he had suspected, his friend was simply one more pawn in the Fair Ones' deadly games. A deep burning anger settled in his gut. The Tylwyth Teg had to be stopped, but damned if he could think of how to do it. And if he failed, Leo was not going to be the only victim. The Fair Ones would never stop trying to take over this land, and more humans would fall prey. Gods alive, had he been the one to open the floodgates? Had the Tylwyth Teg been trying to establish themselves here all along, or had he inadvertently shown them the way?

"I've not got enough magic to counter the spell," sniffled Ranyon. "I have no charm that can ease what's happening to him, and I know no enchantment strong enough."

"Will a bwgan stone help?"

"Aye, 'twould help a great deal, but where ya gonna get something like that in *this* world?"

He smiled without humor. "The Fair Ones gifted me with one."

~

Jay intercepted Rhys at the bleachers. "Hey, where the hell did you go, man? Leo's been taken to the hospital, and Morgan's pissed at you for taking off. Brandan's there with her—he says Leo's stable for the moment, but they don't know what's wrong with him."

"I know what's wrong with him," answered Rhys. He stopped at the first bench and motioned at Jay to take a seat. "And I'm needing to set it right."

"What the—I'm not sitting down at a time like this!"

Rhys ignored him and looked at his left foot. "Ranyon, this man is worthy of trust. He knows what I am and what I've been. We need his help in order to help Leo."

"Aye, well for Leo's sake then." The ellyll revealed himself.

Jay's face lost all color and he sat down. Hard.

Ranyon chuckled and tipped his baseball cap. "Seeing as we're soon to be in a bit of a war together, Jay, ya best be knowing who's on yer side. Pleased to make your acquaintance I am."

It took a couple of tries, but finally Jay stammered out, "Same here." He shook his head hard, then seemed to recover himself and stuck out a hand to the strange little creature.

Ranyon shook it enthusiastically with both of his.

"Jay, we must get to the farm quickly," said Rhys. "I've something there that could help Leo."

"I'm your man," he said and gamely got to his feet. "The clinic truck's still here, and I have keys for it." He led the way, only slightly unsteady for the shock he'd just received. The field events were over for the day, with most of the crowd gathered at the drinking tents. The way to the parking lot for emergency vehicles, the veterinary truck included, was thankfully unimpeded.

Rhys looked down at Ranyon. "There's iron all about the farm, and you don't have your charm from Leo's car—perhaps you should stay here."

The ellyll drew a small acorn from his hair. The nut was carefully wound with fine copper wire and sported a small spotted feather and a miniature copper bell. "Nay, I've made up another one to keep in my pocket. I'm not needing such a powerful charm now."

"But when Leo first brought you to the farm, you couldn't even cross the gateway."

"Aye, it wouldn't shield me from your damnable nails and horseshoes before, because of yer intent."

"That makes perfect sense. Intention always plays a huge role in magic," Jay said over his shoulder, and both Rhys and Ranyon looked at him in surprise. "What? I'm a practicing pagan. Besides, I read."

"The boy's a sharp one," chuckled Ranyon. "And he'd be right."

"You're my friend. I have no desire to keep you from the farm," said Rhys.

"Aye, I'm yer friend *now*. Ya hadn't met me when you nailed up them horseshoes and determined ya were going to keep *all* fae from the farm. It's yer friendship, plus the spells I've put into this new charm, that should keep me safe from yer bloody iron."

"Should?" asked Jay, as he unlocked the truck. "Then you haven't tested it yet?"

The ellyll shrugged. "Fer Leo, I'd test walkin' on coals."

The men nodded in agreement. They all would.

NINETEEN

~~~

Leo was asleep, his condition unchanged. His children had been called, and they were flying in from the coast. Brandan and Mike and the others had gone back to the fair to take care of their horses and load them up. Only Starr remained, talking quietly on her cell by the vending machines in the waiting room. Finally she pocketed the phone and came over to where Morgan was leafing aimlessly through the last of a stack of *Classic & Custom Cars* and *Quilters Monthly* magazines.

"Jay says to tell you he has the clinic truck and he and Rhys are on their way here. I'm going to wait for them, but you can take my van if you want to go home."

"Don't you still have to take down the fair booth? I could help you," said Morgan.

Starr shook her head. "Thanks, but Vanessa has already taken care of it."

"Well, Jay's on call tonight so I guess he might as well keep the truck. And truthfully, I'd just as soon not be here when Rhys shows up."

"I kinda thought so. It looks like you two are going through a rough patch."

"You could say that, I guess." Actually a *rough patch* was something Morgan would use to describe a bump in the road of a long-established couple. She and Rhys barely qualified as a couple at all, despite their feelings. They hardly knew each other, or more accurately, *she* didn't know *him*, and that was the crux of the whole problem. Damn it, her eyes were starting to fill just thinking about it. "I'd love to borrow your van, thanks. You're a lifesaver, Starr."

Grateful for the chance to escape before Mr. Celtic Warrior showed up, she hurried into the elevator with the keys in her hand, trying to remember the location of the van in the neighboring parking garage. *Third floor, west wall, seventh or eighth stall. Third floor, west wall, seventh…*

The door slid open to reveal the hospital lobby. Morgan's getaway was going really well—until she all but crashed into the solid wall that was Rhys. He grabbed her shoulders to steady her but ended up hugging her to him. Part of her wanted to stay in that embrace, take comfort in his strength—but most of her just wanted to punch him. Her anger won and she pushed at him.

He released her reluctantly. "How is Leo?" he asked, as Jay came jogging up behind him.

"Stable so far, no thanks to you," she said. "I don't know where the hell you took off to, but I could have used some help with him. I needed you; *he* needed you."

"I *was* helping him."

"By running in the other direction? What the hell were you afraid of?" Morgan knew she'd hit a nerve then. Rhys's face darkened, and his golden eyes fairly sparked with temper. In her peripheral vision, Jay was giving her some sort of sign language, but her attention was firmly fastened on the big man in front of her. She'd tried to avoid him, tried to just go home and relax for a while before tackling the issue, but maybe a head-to-head confrontation *now* was just what was needed—

"I fear nothing, except that I cannot persuade you to listen."

"Listen to what? All I've heard so far is this warrior crap and how you're older than a hundred human lifetimes."

With uncanny speed, he snared her hand and held it against his chest. "You hear nothing else? My heart reaches for yours as do my arms. You hear not how I feel? What I would gladly do for you, give to you?" His gaze was fierce. "My desires are to you, my every thought flies to you. I see in your eyes that you feel the same. And yet you are determined to hold yourself apart from me."

"Well, excuse me. I can't just say, 'Oh, well, he's crazy but he loves me so that makes everything all right.' What planet are you from?—" Morgan put her free hand to her head. "Don't answer that, please. I can only handle one wild story at a time."

"You're the most kindhearted woman I've ever seen draw breath. And yet your heart is closed and locked."

She yanked her hand out of his grip. "Like hell it is! I wouldn't be suffering like this if it was, because you wouldn't have gotten into it." That was a lot more than she planned to say, but maybe he damn well ought to know that she was in a world of pain.

Rhys was silent for a long moment, and when he spoke again, his voice was gentler. "Aye, well, you've let me into your heart then, but not the truth that comes with me."

"So it's a package deal, you and your insanity?"

"Nothing can be built without truth."

"And so far, you and I can't agree on what that is," she said, folding her arms tightly over her chest. "You don't understand what this is like for me. It's as if I'm under some kind of stupid curse that nothing I love will *stay* in my life. I loved my parents and they vanished. I was close to Nainie and she died. I thought I'd made a dear friend with Gwen in Wales, but I've never heard from her since. I loved my big, beautiful dog and then he disappeared. Then I developed feelings for you, but you keep leaving as well."

"I'm here, right before you."

"No. No, you're not. Oh, sure, you're here physically, but every time we get close, you leave *reality*. What am I supposed to do with that?"

"Have faith in me. Have faith in *us*."

She had no answer to that, no comeback, no question. Something about the way he'd said it had resonated in her. And for no reason, Nainie's words about the necklace echoed in her head. *It'll help you to have faith...*

What exactly did it mean to have faith in someone? Surely it didn't mean to believe the unbelievable? Damn it, she wasn't falling for this crap. "You say you'll do anything for me? Fine. See a doctor. Get help. Better yet, get some medication and some therapy. Because until you do, I want you to stay as far away from me as possible. We have nothing to say to each other."

Rhys shook his head. "Nay, we have much to say to each other yet, anwylyd. But we've no time right now. Leo needs me." He entered the elevator and Jay followed. The last thing she saw as the doors slid shut was the expression on Jay's face.

If she didn't know better, she'd say he felt sorry for her. *Well, that's what I get for arguing in front of friends.* Still, it stung a bit to see her *friend* apparently on Rhys's side.

"Men," she muttered as she marched out to the parking lot. The sun had set, but there were still streamers of orange and purple in the sky. She didn't relish the thought of going home to an empty house. What she really wanted was someone to talk to—and she knew where to find the perfect listener.

Even if he *was* male.

∾

As Ranyon sat on the bed next to his pillow, Leo's eyes fluttered open. "Hey, buddy," he whispered and held up a shaky hand, which the ellyll immediately wrapped his twiggy fingers around.

"Sorry I am to wake you, but these fellows brought you something that might put some spring back in your step," Ranyon said.

"You brought me a naked woman?"

Rhys grinned, hiding his concern at the weakness of Leo's voice and the pallor of his skin. "We'll bring one for you next time. Right now you need your strength, and I'm hoping this will help." He pulled a wadded sock from his pocket and dumped out a palm-size stone on the bed.

The old man glanced down. "I'm not swallowing that," he rasped. "Not even for *two* naked gals."

Just then, Jay slipped inside the door. "Starr's in the hall. Is it okay to let her in, or shall I go wait with her?"

Rhys exchanged glances with Ranyon, who nodded. "We may need all of our allies. Aye, bring her in."

"No screaming," said Ranyon quickly. "I can't abide a woman's screams. Like cat's claws on slate, it is."

To her credit, Starr didn't make a sound when Jay first ushered her in. She simply stared at the tiny man sitting by Leo's pillow, her eyes wide and wondering. Jay squeezed her shoulder and she seemed to pull herself together. As her husband had done, she extended her hand to the ellyll. "I'm very pleased to meet you, Mr. Ranyon. My name is Starr."

"And surely yer a light in the darkness," said the ellyll, inclining his head, and she laughed.

"No one warned me you were charming."

"No one suspected," muttered Leo.

Jay leaned over the smooth, dark stone gleaming against the stark white sheets. "What is this? It almost looks like a pearl." Despite his fascination, he didn't make any move to touch it. "Kinda looks like a crystal too—never seen anything quite like it."

"There's nothing in my collection that resembles it," said Starr. She seemed about to say something else but fell silent.

"It's from the skull of a bwgan I killed. It grows in its forehead." Rhys touched a spot on his own to indicate the spot.

Jay pulled back. "What the hell is a *boogun*?"

"It's a monstrous fae creature that's fond of human flesh."

Leo snorted. "And you put that nasty thing on my *bed*?" he rasped.

"Is it magic?" asked Starr.

"Well, not to the creature that grows it during its life—a bwgan has too little of brain and too big of teeth to need magic for anything," explained Rhys. "But legend says when the creature dies, all its fae essence goes into its stone. That's why druids and magi prized these."

"So it stores energy then," Starr held her palm several inches above the dark pearlescent surface. "Omigosh, I can feel it from here!"

"Aye. The older the bwgan, the stronger the magic. This stone is very powerful." Rhys picked it up and tucked it into the old man's left hand, gently closing his gnarled fingers around it. "Keep it with you, my friend. I'm hoping it may shield you from the worst of the Fair Ones' spell."

"Feels warm," murmured Leo. "Kinda nice for a monster's rock." He paused to take a couple of breaths. "If I get nightmares though, I'm kicking your ass."

Rhys squeezed his hand gently. "Aye, well, I'll present my arse to be kicked as long as you stay with us."

"Ain't going nowhere." The old man sighed and closed his eyes. The ellyll moved closer to him and patted his shoulder.

"The stone's got to be close to ya all the time," instructed Ranyon. "Ya can't be putting it down and leaving it about. A pocket'll do."

"Damn hospital gown doesn't have one," muttered Leo without opening his eyes. "But I promise I'll keep it with me, bud. I'll shove it in my underwear if I have to."

The ellyll waved everyone else back, then folded his long fingers around Leo's fist that cupped the stone. He muttered an incantation in an odd blend of Gaelic, Welsh, and something else that Rhys recognized as an ancient fae language that even the Tylwyth Teg no longer used. The lights in the room flickered out for a brief moment, just long enough for a bright greenish glow to escape from between Leo's fingers. When the lights came on, the glow was gone. And Leo was sound asleep, his worn face relaxed, and his color much better than it had been.

"That was awesome," said Jay. "Is he cured?"

Ranyon sat back and shook his head. "Nay. I know much magic and many incantations, but this cursed spell is too strong. All I was able to do was bind the bwgan stone to him so he cannot lose it nor can it be taken from him. It's got a glamour on it now, so it can't be seen by anyone who hasn't seen it afore."

"And I sent him off to dream—the dear old *hen ddyn* needs his rest, or he'll not have the strength for this battle." The ellyll sniffled a little and accepted a handful of tissues from Starr. "I fear fer him greatly. The bwgan stone will keep him alive, and thanks be that we have it, but it cannot heal him."

"So it gives us *time* but little else," growled Rhys. He wanted badly to punch something, and only the fact that Leo might need what little was in the room kept him from giving in to the impulse.

"What do we do now?" asked Jay.

The ellyll jumped to his feet. "I'm fer givin' the Tylwyth Teg a black eye for what they've done to Leo, that's what. Those that have wrought the spell have to be made to undo it."

"Agreed," said Rhys. "But someone needs to watch over him, and Ranyon, you would be best."

"You'll be needing someone to watch yer back too, ya know. The Fair Ones are crafty as well as cruel, and who can know what they're planning to spring on ya next? They won't be happy till yer back in their realm with a collar on ya."

"If the faeries have it in for you, Rhys, then is Morgan in danger too?" asked Jay.

He was already thinking that. "I had hoped not, but the attack on Leo changes my thinking. I shouldn't have let her leave alone." If the Tylwyth Teg had attacked Leo because he was Rhys's friend, then Morgan could very well be their next target. She might have been declared eithriedig by the queen of the Tylwyth Teg herself, but it now appeared unwise to rely on that status. The monarch had many enemies—why would they hesitate to breach the immunity she'd granted to Morgan?

"Leo and Morgan are our friends, so this is our battle too," said Starr. "We'd like to help."

Rhys shook his head. He had vowed to protect Morgan, and he would continue to do so—however, he knew he couldn't protect Jay and Starr as well. "My thanks to you for the offer, but we can't risk the Fair Ones getting their hands on you," he said firmly. "They'd like nothing better than to have extra human captives to bargain with." Or play with.

Jay was about to protest when Ranyon added. "'Tis true. Yer like to disappear without a trace, both of ya. We dare not reveal ya to the Tylwyth Teg. For sure they'll have Rhys trading his freedom to pay for yer lives. We need ya to be our help in secret."

"Okay," Jay sighed. "I don't like it, but I see your point. So we'll be *covertly* helpful instead. That means we should look after Leo, and Ranyon, you should be going with Rhys. After all, you've got some magic, and you're familiar with the fae."

Starr put her hand on the little ellyll's shoulder. "I can't cure Leo either, but I have healing skills and I can make sure he's comfortable. At least until his family gets here in the morning." She bent and whispered, "I'll stop by and feed Spike too."

In answer, Ranyon pulled off his new blue T-shirt and spoke a few words over it, then handed it to her. "Spike's a fearful little beast because he can't hear or see, and it makes him testy. Give 'em the shirt—it'll soothe him as soon as he puts his nose to it." He sighed. "I'll trust him and Leo to ya then. Leo would be telling me to go and help Rhys anyway."

She gave him a hug and gently patted his leafy back. "I know he would."

"I'll take first watch with Leo," said Jay. "Starr can drive you guys out to the farm, but I have a feeling there's going to be a stop at our house first."

Starr grinned and squeezed her husband's hand, then turned her attention to Rhys and Ranyon. "I don't have any magical monster's rocks," she said. "But I do have some other things that might be useful to you in this kind of fight."

~

Ellen didn't seem surprised in the least when Morgan turned up at Gentle Giant Rescue. "I didn't mean to come so late—" was as much as she got out before she was wrapped in an enthusiastic hug.

"You're welcome here anytime, girl," said Ellen. "If you're here to see Fred, it's getting dark, but I've got some of those solar lights along the path that'll help."

Morgan made her way to Fred's enclosure without a hitch. The dog was in the same position as always, tail hanging listlessly out the door and onto the ground. "Hey, Fred," she called out as she sat with her back against the enormous doghouse. "Ellen told me a secret. She said you came out for a little while today. She said you ate half your food too. You're doing good, buddy."

She sighed and wished she could say as much. The emotional events of the day had piled up, and her plans to simply talk them out were hijacked by tears. First a trickle, then a full-blown cloudburst. She rubbed her face on her sleeve, thinking how mortifying it was going to be to have to carry a box of Kleenex in each hand everywhere she went—when her entire face came under attack from a giant tongue. And there was an unbelievably *massive* dog behind it.

"Fred, you big old softie." Sitting down, she was at a definite disadvantage against two hundred pounds of affectionate mastiff. She struggled to her knees, as Fred enthusiastically continued his ministrations. When she turned her face away, he licked her hair into a wet tangle. Finally she managed to squirm under his chin and throw her arms around his ginormous neck. It was like wrestling a lion, especially when it took a few minutes for Fred to give up trying to lick her. But it felt *good* to hug this big canine, and she rested her face on the soft dark coat. Maybe her love life was a total mess, but she could feel a measure of closure over her missing dog, Rhyswr. She had loved him. She could love this dog too.

It wasn't long before the two of them were in an untidy pile of arms and legs and more legs, and she was rubbing his belly.

"Are you all right in there?" Ellen called out from the gate.

Morgan sniffled and laughed. "Better than all right. Are there some papers I can sign? Because this guy says he's coming home with me tonight."

TWENTY

⌒⟅⟆⌒

I t was full dark but unusually warm as Rhys and Ranyon walked up the long driveway of the farm. Although the stars were visible in the black velvet sky directly above, the horizon was obscured with darker clouds that blotted out the rising moon. The occasional flash of heat lightning illuminated the trees in the distance.

Starr and Jay had armed them both, each in their own way. At Jay's instruction, Starr produced weapons from his collection—two swords that were real, not padded wood or rattan. The blades were truly beautiful, with breathtaking dragons and exquisite lions worked into their hilts and ornamented with gemstones. Such swords must have been costly, but Rhys turned them down.

Instead, he had chosen a very plain sword crafted by a friend of Jay's. It was short like a Roman sword, and Rhys knew from experience that the length was excellent for close-quarter fighting, for both cutting and stabbing. The sword had no decoration, but its heft and balance felt good in Rhys's hands. The natural patterns in the blade told him that the iron had been meticulously hammered and folded on a blacksmith's anvil just as blades had been made centuries ago, tempered and blended with just enough carbon to make strong steel.

He considered taking a round metal shield. It would be a natural choice for the arena against a human or animal opponent, but his battle with the fae was unlikely to last long enough to use it. His only hope was to make a quick decisive assault, and for that, he'd need a weapon in both hands. The sword would be in his right. For his left, he chose a long iron dagger with blades that sprang out at the sides, giving it a trident appearance. The design was highly functional—it could catch the downstroke of a sword blade and perhaps even break it.

Maybe the Fair Ones couldn't be repelled by the presence of iron, but the touch of it could still wound and even kill them. Rhys was counting on that.

Ranyon was apparently thinking the same. Starr found a length of thick cotton rope that he could tie around his tiny waist. The narrow dagger he stuck in it hung like a great sword against his small frame. The ellyll added first one, then two, of Jay's small throwing axes to his makeshift belt. "All I need now is a fine great horse like Brandan's Boo," he declared.

"A horse like that would mistake you for a thistle in its coat and roll on you," said Rhys.

Ranyon sniffed. "I've a charm fer that."

Starr's offerings had been different. She produced small pouches of dried flowers—primroses, Saint-John's-wort, and marsh marigolds—all offering a measure of protection against faery magic. In the yard behind the house, Rhys and Ranyon helped her cut a fat bundle of ash and rowan branches, with their bright fall berries still attached. Rhys remembered his mother tying bunches of them over the doorframes of the house each year. *Perhaps they'd be useful against the lesser fae*, he thought. He doubted that any plant was strong enough to shield him from the Tylwyth Teg's spells.

Starr's final gift was a pair of small pouches containing several gemstones—hematite, garnet, amber, tiger's-eye, and obsidian—which she directed them to stuff into their pockets.

After she drove away, Rhys asked the ellyll about the stones. "They're pretty, but I don't feel magic in them, not like the bwgan stone. Do I throw them at the fae or use them to bargain with?" He was only half joking.

"No, ya *twpsyn*." Ranyon squinted at Rhys from beneath his Blue Jays cap. "Ya keep 'em close to ya fer strength and protection. And they'll give you a clear head too, so ya can think what to do."

Rhys snorted at that. "Then they're not working at all. I don't yet know what to do." *Not about the fae and not about anything else*, he thought, as they passed Morgan's dark house. The woman he loved thought he was either a liar or crazy, and his best friend was dying of a malicious spell. Things couldn't be worse.

"Aye, well, it's like a battle. Ya lay yer plans, then when they go wrong, ya make things up as ya go."

"I remember my mother saying that *life* was like that."

"A wise woman then," said Ranyon. "Life is naught but battles big and small, and most of them unexpected." The truth of his words became starkly apparent as soon as they found the stable door wide open.

The horse was gone.

～

Morgan had her own battle going on as she tried to drive with an enormous mastiff stuffed into the backseat—and part of the front seat—of her little red car. She'd thought at first about going back to the clinic and getting the van, which she'd once used to transport Rhyswr. But she hadn't counted on Fred's determination. Having finally made up his mind to accept her, he wasn't about to let her out of his sight. Rather than stress him, she decided to make the best of it.

Which meant her car's interior was about seven-eighths occupied with dog.

"You need a breath mint, bud," she said as she kept trying to shove his massive drooling muzzle aside so she could center herself behind the steering wheel. *Thank heavens for power windows.* She opened the front passenger one all the way despite the coolness of the night and was relieved when Fred automatically stuck his head out of it. It helped alleviate the thick doggy odor in the vehicle too. Morgan mentally put *bath* at the top of her list of *Things to Do with Fred.* Then relegated that chore to second place. Job one was going to have to be finding a bigger vehicle if she was going to have a canine companion of such size.

They thankfully made it to her farm without incident. She got out of the car, planning to go around and open the door for Fred. Instead, he bolted out of the driver's side behind her and Morgan landed on her butt in the driveway. Of course he thought she was playing...

Morgan decided that letting Fred in the house right away would be a big mistake. While Rhyswr had been dignified and careful—not to mention recuperating from a life-threatening wound—Fred was far too excited at the moment to curb his enthusiasm. Plus, she was willing to bet he had a lot of pent-up energy to spend.

It was dark and moonless, with a distant storm on the horizon, but she had strings of colored lights around the backyard, leftovers from the previous owner. Some of the vintage plastic shades looked like giant flowers, some looked like Japanese lanterns, and many looked like grimacing tiki gods. All were faded by countless summers. The light they cast was more than pleasant, however, even magical. Or maybe the magic was in the simple joy of playing with a dog that so resembled the one she had loved. Morgan pulled a small bin of brand-new pet toys out of the shed, things she'd collected to share with Rhyswr. Now she tossed tennis balls and Frisbees for Fred, played tug-of-war with big chew ropes. A heavy-duty rubber toy shaped like a tire quickly became his favorite, and when he'd had enough chasing, he settled at her feet with it between his massive front paws.

"You look like one of the stone lions on the steps of the library," she laughed. *Wrong color, though.* While Fred's expressive face had the typical black mask associated with his breed, his dark coat wasn't completely black. Instead, stripes of rich coffee brown and tufts of sandy gray were woven through it to create an engaging brindle color. "Come on, handsome boy," she said. "Let's get you a drink, and then we'll get you settled." Morgan glanced at the barn, but all was dark. It was getting late enough that if Rhys was there, he was probably asleep.

Or he might have taken her at her word and left.

She grabbed her chest as a pain that was very nearly physical lanced her heart. *Crap.* She expected that thinking about Rhys would hurt, but not this much. At least not this much *still*. And for some perverse reason, the man's words came back to her: *It's not the number of days that decides the strength of the bond.*

Her rational mind insisted that Rhys had simply lingered at Leo's bedside or perhaps even gone home with Jay and Starr so he could be closer to the hospital. Most of all, her mind told her she shouldn't care so much where the hell Rhys was. Her heart didn't seem to be buying it, but *damned* if she was going out to the barn to look for him.

"Come on, Fred," she repeated and headed for the house. She probably wasn't going to get much sleep again tonight, but at least she wouldn't be alone. In fact, she might have more company than she really wanted—Fred probably wasn't going to be receptive to sleeping in the laundry room.

∾

Lucy's stall was empty—its gate flung wide as the stable door had been. A quick search of the corral and immediate fields turned up nothing. The horse's coat was pale dapple-gray, her mane and tail white. With that coloring, she should stand out like a ghost against the night landscape no matter how dark it was. And the faint rumble of faraway thunder on the horizon warned that it would grow darker yet before the night was over. Yet Rhys could not see a hint of the horse anywhere, and worse, neither could Ranyon even with the natural night vision of his kind. There were no tracks to be seen, not even so much as a bent grass stem to indicate which way the big mare had gone.

Rhys whistled for Lucy as they walked past the silent fields. The horse would surely come if she could hear him. *If she was able to.* He already had his suspicions. It was certain that Lucy didn't open the stall or the barn doors on her own—and it wasn't that she couldn't have. At full strength, a big draft horse like her could easily kick the barn door to splinters if she was of a mind to. Instead, the latches and hinges of the stall gate and the barn door were perfectly intact. They'd been deliberately opened by *hands*.

Rhys noticed that Ranyon was having trouble keeping up with his long stride. He scooped him up and sat him on his wide shoulder.

"A fine seat this is and a better view, but I see no horse. Could be that Morgan gave the beast back to her owners."

Rhys shook his head. "The timid woman who owns Lucy is too nervous to have the mare back until she's completely healed. And Morgan would put the good of the horse first, always. Lucy's wounds are still being dressed daily, and two of those cuts are fair deep. They must heal from the inside out and infection is still a worry." They crossed the rise and got their first clear view of the line between Morgan's farmland and the forest beyond.

Three fence posts were down, broken wires limp and flattening the tall grass. Many things could have caused it, Rhys told himself as he approached the tangle. Rotted wood. Moose or elk. Even humans on their damned noisy ATVs. He appealed to the gods. *Let it be anything but what I think it is.*

But the gods didn't appear to be listening as he spied a pale tangle of long white horsehairs caught in the wire. "Gods alive," hissed Rhys, as rage threatened to choke him. "She tried to jump the fence." Ugly pictures ran through his mind of the already injured horse failing to clear the fence and crashing through it instead. The thought of all those deep and ragged cuts, so painstakingly sutured by Morgan and now torn asunder, sickened him.

Ranyon slid from his shoulder and studied the ground. "A horse with her injuries would never try this fence on her own. And no human could drive her to run at it either."

Rhys had thought the same, but hearing it was like a blow to the heart. "The Fair Ones have her," he murmured. *And they'll ride her into the ground.* His people had always employed a variety of methods to keep faery beings from getting to their horses in the night. The tiny *pisgies* would only tease, and in the morning, an owner would find his animals' manes cleverly braided or their tails tied into knots. Ranyon's people, the ellyllon, dearly loved to play tricks, often putting the bridles and blankets on the cattle or the sheep. But other faeries, like the *gwyllion*, were inclined to ride the horses over the countryside until dawn. In the morning, a farmer would find his beasts in their enclosures—exhausted, lathered, and wild-eyed.

It was exactly the kind of thing that the horseshoes mounted over the doorways of the barn were supposed to prevent. But Rhys had known as he was placing them that only lesser fae could be so easily repelled.

"The Tylwyth Teg themselves have had a hand in this," he declared, as white-hot anger flooded his gut. He drew the Roman-like sword from its sheath—he could use it one-handed, and its shorter blade path would afford him better maneuverability in the forest beyond. With his other hand, he drew his dagger.

Ranyon seized the hem of Rhys's shirt with a twiggy hand. "Ya can't be thinking of going in there."

"I'll not have another chance to track them so surely—I can see from here they've left a path through the brush that a child could follow."

"Aye, and 'tis no mistake. They'll be expecting ya to follow them. You'll be a grim or you'll be dead before ya reach the end of that path. And for naught, because Lucy is surely miles from here. *Look.*" The ellyll pointed to the north where black clouds piled up along the horizon, far darker than the night sky and simmering with lightning.

Rhys's knuckles were white around the hilt of his sword, and the muscles in his jaws jumped with the tension. He felt like a tightly coiled spring, keen to deliver justice to the cruel and callous beings who had bespelled his friend's life and now drove a good horse to its doom. But Ranyon was right. What Rhys sought was not at the end of this path.

"I'd follow those murdering lladdwyr to hell if it'd help Leo," said Ranyon. He adjusted his Blue Jays hat and pulled one of the throwing hatchets from the rope around his waist. His small hands brandished it like a battle-ax, and Rhys had no doubt he would wield it like one. "But we're up against a crafty and powerful foe. Tell me, if the fae were Romans seeking to take over yer land, would ya go after them in this manner?"

It was another cold slap of reality. Rhys's father and older brothers had been among the many brave Celts who had died in battle against the troops of Rome. By the time Rhys had reached his full growth, it was obvious to all that the conquerors could not be defeated directly. While many of the remnants of his clan and the surrounding tribes accepted their new rulers, Rhys and others devoted themselves to building bands of resistance fighters. If the occupiers could be harried enough, they might decide the misty forests and hills of his people weren't worth the inconvenience of holding them.

"No," he admitted. The Romans were many and mighty. It would have been foolish to launch an assault head-on. The fae were no less numerous than they, and far more powerful.

A new thought came to him swiftly and painfully, like a kick to the gut. *The fae are like the Romans in more ways than one.* Were there wagers being made on what he would choose to do? Rhys made a noise of disgust and spat on the ground, cursing his own stupidity. Had he truly thought he was free? What was this but Isca Silurum all over again? He was merely entertaining a different set of captors.

He'd never left the damned arena.

Rhys wanted to scream out his rage and frustration, hack and gouge at a flesh and blood opponent. Tear the forest down with his bare hands. Anything to channel the fury that roared through him. Anything to wreak vengeance and retribution upon his former captors. Taking a deep cleansing breath and then another, he fought to get control of his temper. *Anger leads to folly.* He paced back and forth along the fence line, calling on all the disciplines he'd ever learned in battle and in the ring. *There can be no revenge without a plan.* He needed a clear head; he needed to think.

Always do the unexpected.

Surprise had been Rhys's greatest weapon when he fought the Romans. He had survived in the arena by utilizing the element of surprise there too. So if the Tylwyth Teg expected him to follow the path they'd made into the forest, then the best tactic was to do precisely the opposite. It rankled to leave Lucy in the hands of the fae—the steadfast mare deserved better—but Ranyon was right. The poor ceffyl was out of his reach and likely to be already dead or dying. As in battle, he ordered himself to feel the pain of her loss later, to focus on the demands of the present. Deep inside, however, he vowed that the Fair Ones would pay dearly for their cruelty.

Slowly, carefully, he sheathed his sword and dagger as he sheathed his smoldering anger, and addressed the ellyll. "Will the Tylwyth Teg bring Lucy back to her stall? Is the Law of Benthyg yet great enough that even they will honor it?"

"The Fair Ones are as prideful as ever. The mare will be returned by dawn—if the lesser fae don't feast on her first."

Rhys cursed again. The idea of the big gray horse, lame and bleeding, being trailed by a motley collection of hungry creatures from the faery realm was horrifying. By all the gods, he should have dispatched the leering, hissing misfits that snarled at him as he'd hammered iron nails into the fence posts. Instead, he'd pitied them. They'd been used and then betrayed by the Tylwyth Teg, just as he had. But he should have considered that, though the creatures were small, they still needed to eat, and the gods alone knew what they might prey upon. "We need to close this fence against the unnatural beasts."

The two of them walked back and forth along the break in the fence line, sprinkling Starr's dried primroses and marsh marigolds over the ground where the fallen wire lay. Rhys dared not blunt the edges of his weapons trying to cut the coils, but Ranyon donated one of the throwing axes to the cause. Used as a hatchet, it quickly freed the wire from the fallen posts, and Rhys threw the tangled mess safely aside. The way was clear through the trampled grass if Lucy came this way again—and was brave enough to cross it. She had to be terrified of wire by now. But if she made it back to Morgan's land, any lesser fae would be unable to pursue her farther.

"That's all we can do for poor Lucy," Rhys said at last and began jogging back the way they'd come. He caught hold of Ranyon's twiggy hand and swung him up to his shoulder once more. "We need to hurry and prepare a fit welcome for the Fair Ones."

"Aye," said the ellyll, setting his hat low over his eyes. "Ya can wager I've a charm fer that."

TWENTY-ONE

⌒ᔆᔓ

Morgan lay on her bed, staring at the ceiling. She'd expected to have trouble sleeping, but it wasn't the massive dog's snores that were keeping her awake. Fred hadn't tried to climb in with her either, thank heavens. Instead, he seemed perfectly comfortable at the foot of her bed, on the giant dog pillow that had once been Rhyswr's. Perfectly content too. At bedtime, he'd laid down immediately with what sounded like a happy sigh, and was snoring moments later.

A big day for a big dog, she thought, especially after so little activity for over a month. Traveling to what Ellen had charmingly called his forever home, and then exploring it, had tired him. Not to mention playing for an hour in the yard and then inhaling dog food as if he'd never seen it before. *If he has his appetite back, he's feeling pretty good.*

She felt good too, at least about Fred. Everything else, however, was weighing heavily on her. Morgan was worried about Leo. And seeing Rhys at the Ren fair had bothered her more than she thought. As had that last encounter at the hospital.

Have faith in me, he'd said. *Have faith in us…We have much to say to each other yet, anwylyd.*

Tears started in her eyes, and she scrubbed them away angrily on the sleeve of her pajamas. She was so done with crying. Hoping for a distraction, she got up as quietly as she could and padded down the hallway in the dark. She'd barely reached the kitchen before Fred was at her side, an enormous shadow in more ways than one. He was quiet, however, and simply lay at her feet as she sat at the table.

Nainie's photo in its oversize frame was illuminated by the kitchen night-light. It lent the picture a rich golden glow and highlighted parts not usually apparent in the daytime. Morgan turned her head slowly from side to side, studying the photo from different angles. The camera had reflected on a narrow glimmering line just inside the neck of Nainie's dress. That had to be the chain of her necklace—the one that Morgan was now wearing beneath her pajama top. She patted the medallion beneath the flannel, chuckling a little at the silly cartoon cats and dogs that adorned the fabric. It was an irreverent setting for such exquisite jewelry. Yet Nainie had never spoken of the value of the necklace, at least not in monetary terms. She'd never cautioned her granddaughter to be careful of the priceless item, or to wear it only on special occasions, or to even hide it. It was clearly a tool and meant to be used. But for what?

Her eyes still on the photograph, Morgan drew the medallion from its resting place against her skin. *It'll help you to have faith...and show you truth...*

Faith in what? The truth of what, exactly?

Rhys's words came unbidden. *Have faith in me. Have faith in us.*

She studied the medallion in her hand, its glittering silver chain draped over her fingers. The mysterious central stone gleamed in the soft light. "Nainie, what am I supposed to do?

What on earth is the truth in all of this?" she asked aloud. "I'm so darn confused." Morgan knew, when all was said and done, that what she felt for Rhys was far more than just physical attraction. Though that itself was powerful, it wasn't why she thought about him constantly. Why she was both furious with him and lapsing into crying jags at the drop of a hat.

"I love him. I want to be with him, even if he *is* crazy. And— *even if he isn't.*"

There. She'd finally said it out loud. Confessed it before her grandmother's photo that looked down from the wall like a kindly icon. Spoken the words before the great dog that lay at her feet with his guileless soul in his eyes as he looked up at her. The medallion, naturally cool, felt warm in her hand as she considered what she'd just said.

For the first time, she allowed herself to freely examine the strange events that had unfolded ever since she first visited Wales, and all the evidence she'd insisted on dismissing and denying. The mysterious arrival of her beloved black dog, Rhyswr, and his equally strange disappearance. The dog's unique collar, created from soft silver made impossibly strong by unknown methods. The timing of Rhys's appearance in her laundry room—not to mention his lack of clothing. Rhys's uncanny proficiency with both animals and ancient weapons. And *of course* Morgan recognized her own work on Rhys's body. It was as unique as a signature. Her instructors at veterinary college had always been able to pinpoint her tiny careful sutures, teasing her that she could have a successful backup career as a tailor. That the incision was now on a man's body rather than a dog's didn't negate the fact that it was her handiwork.

She murmured Jay's favorite quote, one from Sherlock Holmes that normally would have irritated her: "When you have eliminated the impossible, whatever remains, however improbable, must be the truth..."

Must be.

Which meant she'd been a complete and total idiot.

"Rhys. I have to tell Rhys!" A chill ran through her as she remembered she'd ordered him to leave—what if he were already gone? *No. He wouldn't leave the horse. Not without making sure I knew.* So was he still with Leo, or was he right over there in the barn, sound asleep?

Hell, with Leo in the hospital, Rhys probably wasn't getting much more sleep than she was. And maybe, just maybe, he was thinking about Morgan too. She hoped so. Damned if she wanted to be the only person in this relationship who was totally miserable...

Damned if she wanted to be the only person in this relationship, period.

She got up and found Fred at the window. She hadn't even heard him move, but his body language clearly spoke of high alert. His muzzle was pressed against the glass, but she couldn't see much outside herself. The yard light was on the pitiful side, with barely enough wattage to cast a faint greenish glow on the buildings. "Whatcha looking at, bud?" she asked and rested her hand on his broad back, but Fred didn't move. The faint rumble of thunder told her that a storm was moving in, and Morgan wondered if the dog was afraid of it. He didn't look very fearful, however—beneath her hand, the fur along his spine bristled up into a thick ridge. A deep growl resonated from his throat, but he didn't bark.

"Did you hear some coyotes out there?" Although she'd never seen one on her own land, bears wandered the area too. Only last month, she'd been called in to help examine an enormous black bear that had been tranked by wildlife officials in the middle of a Spokane Valley neighborhood. There was no hint of movement in the farmyard, though—at least not anywhere the light shone.

Maybe Fred had sensed Lucy moving around in the barn? Or perhaps even Rhys.

"Shall we go check it out?" she asked the dog. Truthfully, she wasn't the least bit concerned if local wildlife was paying a visit to the farm. What she really wanted was to talk to Rhys, even if it was the middle of the night—or well into the wee hours, as her nainie would say. Morgan sighed as she got dressed. *Didn't feel like sleeping anyway.* Thank heavens she had a couple more days off. Maybe she could grab a nap on the porch swing later…

Fred followed her readily to the kitchen and watched as she tied her shoes. He seemed keen to go yet wasn't frantic to get out the door as many dogs would be. Morgan talked to him about the importance of staying with her as she snapped on his thick leather leash, yet all the while she had a mental picture of being dragged into the forest at high speed if the two hundred–plus pounds of dog decided to chase something.

She needn't have worried. Fred didn't launch himself out the door like a rocket, nor did he even tug at the leash in her hand. Instead, he walked beside her. He was still on high alert, and he swung his great head back and forth, watching, watching…It was like having a lion as an escort, decided Morgan. Fortified by Fred's giant presence, she elected to do a quick sweep of the yard around the buildings, just in case. Behind the barn, she was stopped in her tracks—literally. Fred stood sideways, blocking her in the same way she'd seen seeing-eye dogs use their bodies to prevent their blind owners from making a dangerous misstep. He looked up at her, then looked away to growl at the storm approaching from the north. And gazed back at her again. Morgan frowned as she tried to make sense of the dog's actions. Clearly he was trying to communicate something. Was it the storm that had been bothering him all along? If so, this was strange behavior. Most dogs bothered by thunder and lightning hid under the bed or in the basement—they didn't venture outside to deliberately challenge it. But then she thought about the great black dog in Wales that had seemingly followed the tour bus wherever it went. Come to think of it, that dog—Rhyswr—had sat outside in a tremendous storm without so much as a tremble. Were all mastiffs a little on the odd side?

"Okay, *storm bad*, I get it." And the dog might be right. The night was already dark due to the hidden moon, but the rapidly approaching clouds seemed blacker than black. Near-continuous lightning illumed the roiling mass with strange colors. She wasn't usually afraid of storms, but something in the pit of her stomach was repelled by this one. Quickly, Morgan headed for the back door of the barn with Fred in tow. Thankfully the big dog didn't try to go through the small entrance at the same time, but followed close behind her. She closed the door after him and stood for a few minutes until her eyes adjusted. The yard light's pale, greenish rays barely penetrated the windows. Beside her, Fred was alert, but calm and quiet. Morgan was relieved by that—she hadn't even thought of what might happen if he barked and startled Lucy. Finally she could see well enough to make her way to the mare's box stall. It was empty.

Morgan went from stall to stall, expecting that Rhys had simply moved the horse to another spot. Dim as it was, it wouldn't be possible to hide the pale-coated mare. The horse simply wasn't in the stable anywhere.

"Rhys!" she yelled. "Rhys, where are you?" She ran to the stacked bales where the man had made his bed. A part of her reacted viscerally to the spot where passion had once rocked them both and bonded them. The rest of her was all too furious that he was sleeping peacefully under the quilts while her patient was MIA. She lunged forward to shake him awake—

Powerful arms grabbed her from behind. A hand the size of her whole face covered her mouth before she could yell for Fred, and she was yanked back against a hard, muscled body. She did her best to fight and managed to get in a couple of solid elbow jabs before his arms clamped down so hard her upper body could no longer move. She settled for kicking backward at her assailant's shins and trying to get a leg between his and trip him as she was dragged inside the small dark tack room. Where was her dog? Why wasn't he chewing this guy's ass off?

"Be calm," ordered a familiar voice in her ear. "You've no reason to fear, anwylyd. But you must be quiet. Gods alive, why are you here at this time?"

He released her and she whirled, slapping for the light switch on the wall. The forty-watt bulb was like high noon in the tiny windowless room, and she had to squint to focus. She didn't need to see Rhys to yell at him, however. "Where is Lucy? And what have you done to my dog? And who the hell is *that* in your bed?"

In a heartbeat, he had his hand over her mouth again, and she was backed against the wall. "Your dog is unharmed, and there's naught but straw and clothes in my bed made to look like me." He paused and seemed to take a deep breath. "You must keep your voice low. The Fair Ones are coming, and there may be advance guards. You would be in danger if they learn of your presence here with me."

She stilled and he removed his hand. "The Tylwyth Teg are coming *here*?" she whispered.

"Aye. They've taken the horse, and fae law says they must return her by dawn." He looked expectant, and his palm was open and at the ready, no doubt anticipating that he would have to muffle a flurry of angry protests.

Instead she was quiet for a long moment. "What can we do?" she asked finally.

The simple question caught him off guard. Wonder and hope crossed his features even as the harsh light made his face look just as battle hardened as he claimed to be. Morgan looked down and saw the sheathed sword and the dagger in his belt. "You're going to fight them, aren't you?"

He recovered himself. "Aye, I am. But not with you here. Go back to the house and stay there. The fae cannot cross the threshold of a dwelling without an invitation. You'll be safe."

"And you'll be out here, one against how many?" She gestured at his sword. "Is this all you have to defend yourself with?"

"Iron is the only thing that harms them."

She nodded, remembering Nainie's stories. Iron was like kryptonite to the Fair Ones. But you had to get close enough to use it. "I know you're amazing with those weapons, but even you can't do this by yourself."

"He's not alone, good lady," said a voice behind her. Morgan jumped sideways and was caught by Rhys's muscled arm as she looked down in amazement. "And we've more than a few tricks up our sleeves."

A small character barely taller than her knees waved at her. Bright-blue eyes looked out from under a brighter-blue baseball cap. Wild brown braids of hair escaped from the hat, tangled with oak leaves. A thick layer of leaves sheathed the stocky little body, and with skin that looked like tree bark, the thin arms and legs bore a strange resemblance to the branches of saplings.

Beside him, Fred lay on the floor snoring. The little man winked at her. "Yer fine great dog is not harmed."

She knelt in wonder, some unknown instinct leading her to make herself of equal height. It was more than simply trying not to frighten the amazing creature. Her brain whirled with numberless thoughts and images, all unintelligible save for Nainie's long-ago words: *There are many things all around us that are old and powerful…They're not to be feared but to be respected, and it's long been a gift in our family to know them.*

"Are you—are you of the Tylwyth Teg?" she asked. Her voice sounded faint, even to her, and she drew back against Rhys's legs as the little creature frowned.

Rhys knelt at once and put a reassuring arm around her. "No, anwylyd, Ranyon is fae but he's an ellyll. The Fair Ones are his enemies too, and he is my friend."

"Aye. And I've thrown my lot in with his," Ranyon said, extending a hand to her.

She grasped the long twiggy fingers gently, surprised to find they were warm. "I'm Morgan. Leo spoke of you. And I'm throwing my lot in here too," she declared. The words had barely left her lips before she was seized by the shoulders and lifted bodily to her feet—and then some. She was standing on empty air as she stared eye to eye with Rhys. "Put me down!"

"Go to the house at once. I cannot fight them if you're not safe." He gave her a shake before setting her on the ground. "They will *kill* you or take you for their own."

"And they won't kill *you*? Won't take you back or turn you into a dog again? Listen, mister, you don't tell me what to do. If you think I'm just going to hide in the house while you're out here—"

Thunder drowned out the rest of her words, rending the air and shaking the floor beneath her. Rhys held her tightly in his powerful arms, and *still* the vibrations rocked her. When the noise died away, Morgan's ears were ringing hard enough to hurt.

The ellyll cursed soundly. "They're coming," he said. Fred, now wide awake, shook himself.

"Wait a minute, *they* did that?" asked Morgan, trying to wriggle free of Rhys's arms.

He released her. "Aye. The Tylwyth Teg are riding the storm."

Terrifying illustrations from some of the old Welsh story-books flashed into Morgan's mind. Rhys grasped her by the wrist and cautiously opened the tack room door. "Come on," he said, then jogged through the barn to its front door with her in tow. Ranyon and Fred followed close behind.

Rhys slid the door open a crack, and they studied the yard between the barn and the house. Nothing moved. No rain had fallen yet, and the air seemed charged with expectancy. Morgan made a mental note to call an electrician to change the yard light fixture as soon as possible—its weak light seemed more greenish than ever, giving the whole area a ghostly feel. Like she needed to feel more frightened than she already did.

Ranyon slipped a strange object into her hand. "If you have this, they cannot see you. 'Tis a charm and a good one."

She was about to ask questions when Rhys opened the door farther and pushed her toward it. "It has to be now, and fast."

"I don't want to—"

His mouth was hot on hers, hard, urgent, and just a little desperate. And then he pulled back. "If you love me, you'll go. If you stay, you'll give them leverage against me, and they will win."

"Run, good lady," urged Ranyon. "Run like the hounds of hell are after ya, because they surely will be if ya stay."

"Crap," said Morgan and bolted from the barn.

TWENTY-TWO

In grade school, she'd never collected more than the white participant ribbon for the hundred-yard dash. Tonight Morgan knew she would have taken first place. Heart thumping hard in her chest as if trying to escape from the cage of her ribs, she ran straight across the terrifyingly open area, as exposed as a rabbit flushed from its thicket. Fred kept pace with her, and if her mind hadn't been completely blank with terror, she might have drawn courage from his big steady presence. What surely should only take a few seconds seemed to stretch on and on—

She collapsed inside her door, forcing Fred to leap over her. With the last of her adrenaline, Morgan spun on her knees and slammed the door behind her, just as another roll of thunder shattered the silence. Fred nosed her, and she threw her arms around the dog's enormous neck, holding on until the echoes died away and the house stopped vibrating. Or maybe *she* was the source of the vibration—when silence finally returned, she discovered she was shaking. The mastiff, on the other hand, seemed concerned about her but otherwise steady as ever. "Fred, you've got nerves of steel," she said, rubbing behind his ears. "I'm not afraid of thunder, but that's the loudest I've ever—"

No, it's not the loudest I've heard. Morgan thought back to the night in the Welsh hotel when she'd been awakened by deafening thunder directly overhead—and discovered the black dog outside. Had the Tylwyth Teg been riding that night too? She shivered at the thought. Nainie's stories had warned that mortals in the path of the Wild Hunt could disappear, spirited away to the faery realm or forced to follow the hunt forever—dead or alive. According to her grandmother's tales, most of the riders in the hunting party were captives, and many of the horses were "borrowed" from mortals. Is that where poor Lucy was?

"Goddamn it, they'll kill her," she said aloud. That horse was in no condition to be running around, much less pushed to her limit. If she remembered right, the stories said that only a few of the hunters were actually of the Tylwyth Teg—but those were without pity. They whipped and drove both horses and captives equally. And their quarry had no hope.

In some of the tales, the Wild Hunt's purpose was to capture a particular individual who had been greedy or unjust, but the Fair Ones were whimsical by nature. Unless appeased or amused, they were as likely to seize the innocent as they were to ride down the guilty.

Did Rhys and Ranyon actually stand a chance against such beings?

The palm of her hand hurt, and she realized she still had Ranyon's charm clutched tightly in her fist. She opened her stiff fingers and studied the strange thing he'd given her. It seemed to be a lump of clear quartz wrapped with copper wire and a few bright glass beads. It was kind of pretty, she thought. She had no idea if it actually worked—but she was going to find out. There was no way she was going to just sit here in the house and do nothing.

If iron was the Achilles' heel of the Tylwyth Teg, then she was going to damn well look for some. And then she was going back to the barn.

~

There was no need to turn the lights on—there was no darkness. The storm was still over the fields, but its lightning strobed strange hues of blue and green and pink through the windows. With it, guttural thunder pounded the senses as if with physical blows.

Shielding his eyes as best as he could, Rhys risked looking out the small window in the back door. He could see the leading edge of the storm clearly, like a great roiling black wall of cloud that nearly brushed the ground as it approached. There had been late grain in the fields, but in the morning, it would be flattened and impossible to harvest.

For a split second, he wondered if he would be around to see it, then shoved that thought away. He was preparing for a battle that was mere minutes away, and doubts were a weakness he couldn't afford. He turned back to the tasks at hand. Looking longer at the encroaching storm would only lead to discerning the horrors within it. He'd seen the Wild Hunt before, when he had been an emotionless grim and unaffected by their terrible appearance. By all the gods, he was glad that Morgan was safely in her house.

"You gave her your charm," he said to Ranyon. They had only to put the finishing touches on their preparations. The ellyll scrambled up the loft ladder and tossed down a rope.

"Aye, well, she needed to be safe or you'd be distracted."

"My thanks to you."

The rope went through a pulley in the ridge beam. Rhys hauled the load upward until Ranyon gave him a signal. "Just hold it there for a wink," he said and busied himself around it. "'Tis solid now."

Rhys released the rope slowly. Nothing fell. "Do you have another charm to hide yourself with?"

"I have many charms, but not another like that. It takes time to make such a thing. But I can burrow in the straw up here like a mouse."

"A strange and spindly mouse, for sure."

Ranyon huffed in mock offense. "Aye, well, it's not me that the Fair Ones are looking for, now is it?" He disappeared into the dark loft.

No, thought Rhys. *It's me they want.* He felt the pommel of the sheathed sword beneath his palm. The strange icy calm that came before a battle settled over him like a cloak. Muscles in his arms twitched, snake-ready as adrenaline began to surge through his system. With the eerie lightning flashing all around him and thunder hammering at his brain, he reached for his anger as a man might reach for a weapon. This time, he was no collared dog for the Fair Ones to play with. And he wasn't a wounded and dying man who couldn't defend himself.

Rhys melted into the deep shadows between the bales and the wall, one of the few spots where even the lightning couldn't reach. He hefted a sword in one hand and a dagger in the other. Iron had been forged into steel to create them, as he had once been forged into the Bringer of Death.

This was no arena match, however. This time he had to win, not to save his own life, but Leo's. Morgan's life was on the line as well, although she didn't know it. Like Leo, the Tylwyth Teg had her singled out and marked for their malicious mischief—all because of him.

It ended here.

～

Iron. What the hell did she have that was made of *iron*? Her kitchen knives were ceramic. She didn't own a gun. As quickly as she could, Morgan searched the house and piled things on the kitchen table as she found them. Finally she stopped and surveyed the motley collection. A pair of iron bookends in the shape of kittens. A rooster doorstop. An old set of fireplace tools. A cast-iron Dutch oven. And a large skillet with a frustratingly short handle. She glanced up at the photo of Nainie. *What am I going to do with this?*

Anything remotely weapon-like was out in the machine shed or the garage—hammers, axes, and other tools. There was even a rusted scythe in the old workshop, although it was probably too clumsy for her to use effectively. But she didn't dare risk trying to reach any of those buildings. She'd be lucky to get to the barn.

A sudden thought had her yanking out the junk drawer on the end of the counter near the door. In the hail of debris that tumbled to the floor, Morgan was able to secure an enormous screwdriver. The vintage tool looked big enough to tune up a tractor, but it had been on the kitchen counter when she moved in. The blade was rusted, and she hoped that meant it was iron. The handle had a few inches of baling wire threaded through it, and she twisted it to a loop on her jeans. It was goofy looking, but she could tear it free in a heartbeat if she had to use it. And she fervently hoped that she had whatever it took to use it.

Morgan looked up at Nainie's picture again. "I can't let Rhys face them alone. I can't. They'll kill him or they'll take him away. I won't let that happen." Somehow she knew that her grandmother would understand. Hell, she'd probably even approve—after all, Nainie had been no shrinking violet. Glad to be wearing the treasured necklace, Morgan grasped the cool stone pendant through the fabric of her shirt. It reminded her of a favor given to a knight to carry into battle, and there was a satisfying sense of *rightness* in having it next to her skin.

Thinking of Nainie shook loose more memories of the old stories. Morgan added a shaker of salt to her arsenal, tucking it in her jeans pocket. A loaf of bread was often useful when dealing with the fae. A fast search yielded three stale slices and a heel in a rumpled bag. Goddamn it, why hadn't she gone shopping? Desperately, she dug through the freezer and finally came up with a leftover cinnamon roll. It was large for a roll, but pretty damn small for a loaf of bread. *It's probably stale enough to use as a weapon.* She took it with her anyway.

Morgan decided the skillet might be a good shield and tied a loop of stout twine through its handle. If she lost her grip, she hoped the loop would stay around her arm and the frying pan wouldn't fly away from her. The poker looked promising. She threw on a vivid red ski vest with very large pockets and stuck a bookend in each one. She wasn't sure how she was going to use them, but she felt better having them—even if they weighed a *ton*. She had a healthy new respect for the knights in armor at the Renaissance fair.

Another length of twine helped her hang Ranyon's strange charm around her neck—and then she looked at Fred. What did *he* have to protect himself? She could leave him behind, safe in the house, but the truth was, she might need him. Nainie had said that when she was growing up, people carried iron nails in their pockets to ward off faery interference or sewed nails into the hems of their clothing. Morgan ran to her office and dumped the magnifying glass out of its small leather pouch, then raced to the cellar to fill the pouch from an old jar of nails in the otherwise empty pantry. A few moments later, the pouch hung against Fred's dark brindle chest, tied and duct-taped to his collar.

Having armed herself and her companion as best as she could, all she had to do now was cross the huge open space that was her yard. Again. Only this time, she had enough metal on her to attract all that lightning that was currently hammering the fields in the distance. *If you can see the cloud, you can be struck.* If that adage was true, then she could have been toasted during the dash to the house. It was completely insane to go outside again. The lightning was near continuous now, and she'd be much smarter to hide in the basement till morning. But that wasn't going to help Rhys.

The power flickered and went out.

Morgan peered out the kitchen window toward the barn. Nothing moved in the yard—although, it was hard to be certain with the strobing effect of the lightning. She squinted her eyes and grabbed a pair of sunglasses from the shelf over the coatrack. Who'd have thought she'd ever need them in the middle of the frickin' night? She studied the farmyard and the area around the barn, but nothing appeared to be lurking there. The field behind the far side of the barn was another story.

The thunderstorm appeared to be hovering low just beyond the fence line. Inky black clouds roiled continuously as if the storm were alive somehow, and the lightning illuminated it from within with strange unnatural colors. Morgan was about to look away from the bright spectacle when she spotted something within the storm. Several somethings. She stared, letting the poker and the skillet slide to the floor unheeded, as the images became clear to her.

A flurry of horses and riders circled the field in the very midst of the storm, a furious and dreadful host: riders in faded finery and tarnished saddlery, riders in rags riding bareback. Riders with the appearance of flesh and blood on wild-eyed steeds. Skeletons astride ivory-boned mounts. Ghostly riders on phantom horses. All were subject to the shining figures on red-eyed horses that drove both riders and mounts with crackling whips of light. The furious host circled round and round in the field, the pounding hooves creating the thunder that even now shook the floor beneath Morgan's feet. Massive hounds, some blackest black, some white, some red as blood, bayed at the heels of the captives.

The Wild Hunt was here.

Both fascinated and terrified, Morgan watched as the spectral figures dashed at the fence and away again, over and over, as if the simple wire were a barrier they couldn't cross. It wasn't until Fred nudged her repeatedly with his nose that she was able to shake free of the vision. She turned and slid down the door until she was cross-legged with her back against it, breathing hard. *Omigod, omigod.* What was she going to do? What made her think that she could go up against something like that? She was no warrior.

But Rhys thought she was. *The best of healers are warriors at heart.* She wasn't sure about the best of healers part, but she did know she was a fighter. She didn't quit. Not on her patients in the clinic, and not now on the man who held her heart. She fingered the charm that Ranyon had given her and hoped like hell it would work. She swallowed hard, gathered up the poker and the skillet, nodded at Fred, and charged outside.

Nothing threatened her as she jogged across the open yard. The thunder and lightning seemed to let up somewhat—a relief when she was carrying so much metal. Her biggest danger was being beaten to death by the iron bookends in her vest pockets, and she clamped her elbows against them to stop them from swinging. It slowed her down not to be able to move her arms, and her collection of iron implements felt as heavy as cannonballs as she headed for the dark barn.

She was two-thirds of the way there when she stopped so abruptly that she had to flail her arms to keep her balance, and both skillet and poker tumbled to the ground. There were only two incandescent light fixtures in the stable that worked, and the power was currently out. So why was brilliant white light suddenly pouring from the open doorway of the stable and spilling out the windows? The powerful light radiated outward in all directions from every crack and crevice in the entire building. There were even tiny beams and rays shooting skyward through what she had assumed was a solid roof.

Rhys and Ranyon might be in the stable, but so was something else.

$\sim$

Without warning, the big double doors at the rear of the barn slammed open, and the entire building shook with the impact. A large pale horse appeared at the threshold, its head hung low, and its nose nearly touching the ground. White froth bubbled at its mouth and nostrils, and its coat was lathered with sweat. The exhausted creature swayed as it shuffled forward on three legs, lame and limping. Blood ran from fresh stripes and gouges on its flanks as well as from the all-too-familiar wounds on its limbs.

Lucy. It was all Rhys could do not to break from his hiding place. The door of her stall swung open as if by unseen hands, and he gritted his teeth as the mare took halting painful steps to it. She could barely lift her head, but managed at last to bury her nose in her water bucket and drain it. There was ample grain and hay, but she was too spent to eat. With a heartrending groan, she simply collapsed in the straw. It sickened Rhys to know that the ill-used mare would likely never get up again.

Still he held his position, knuckles white on the grip of the sword, certain that the horse hadn't come alone. Waiting. Waiting.

And then they were simply *there.* Seven shining figures stood just inside the threshold. The living light that emanated from the flawless skin of the Tylwyth Teg was the same as it had always been. Their flowing white hair was bound back for the hunt, however, and their bright clothing had been traded for dark riding leathers studded with many daggers. In their beautiful hands were copper weapons of war. Rhys recognized Tyne and Daeria from the visitation in Morgan's laundry room on his last night as a dog. Daeria was clearly leading this party, and it was plain by the way she hefted her sword that this was no friendly visit.

Which suited Rhys just fine. He didn't plan to be a gracious host.

In silence, the Fair Ones glided forward, their booted feet not deigning to touch the floor of the barn. The broad walkway along the stalls compressed the party into a loose diamond formation, and Rhys held his breath as the fae crossed each straw-strewn floorboard. Until the leader passed an innocuous fist-size lump of blue livestock salt—

With a war cry that had chilled the blood of many a Roman, Rhys leapt from his hiding place and slashed a taut rope in two with his sword, then took a battle stance. With their eyes on him, the Fair Ones failed to see the harrow swinging swiftly down from the loft behind them, its heavy iron frame covered with ten-inch iron teeth, until it was too late. The farming implement proved as effective at breaking up a faery formation as it was in breaking up clods of dirt in a field. Four of the center fae were impaled outright, their copper weapons clattering to the floor as they died. A fifth stayed on his feet, his unearthly beauty marred by a swipe from an iron spike along the side of his face. Half blinded by his own pale-blue blood, he still sighted Rhys with his bow and released a gleaming silver arrow that curved in midair after its quarry, revealing its enchantment.

Rhys dropped and rolled, barely in time. The projectile looped and dove back on him, and he leapt straight up this time, bringing the sword down upon the arrow's shaft as it passed. The pieces clattered to the floor, the spell broken. Rhys was still in motion, however, and hit the floor running. Three more arrows followed and met the same fate as the first.

"Such sport you give us!" said Daeria, clapping her hands as if in delight. "You see why we simply *must* have you back."

Rhys didn't miss the deadly overtones in the seductive voice. "You have no claim here," he said. "I am sworn to protect Morgan Edwards, and I am hers by your queen's own decree."

Daeria simply laughed, a cascade of tiny bells in a tomb. "The agreement was that you were hers only until she relinquished her claim. We clearly heard the mortal woman tell you to leave."

"A lovers' spat hardly qualifies as a lawful disavowal."

"Perhaps, perhaps not, and so we have bided our time until the mortal woman tried to send you from her on three occasions. With the power of three, our claim is restored."

Rhys kept his face impassive, but he was thinking frantically. Three? Once, certainly, when he awoke in his human body, and Morgan had him taken to jail. Two, probably when she stormed from his bed, because he wouldn't recant his story. But three? Dear gods alive, she'd said it *again* when he met her at the hospital. He cursed in several languages in his head. On the outside, Rhys remained crouched in his fighter's stance, sword and dagger at the ready. "I'm not going with you."

"But we miss our faithful dog so. Think how happy the entire court will be to see you!"

"The court keeps many unwilling humans in the guise of dogs. One more or less hardly matters to you. What about the other grims? Like the one you deliberately sent to Leo Waterson when it's not yet his time, in a place where the Fair Ones have no dominion. That goes against your own laws. What would your queen say if she knew?"

"Do not quote the laws to me, mortal," Daeria hissed.

"Do not consider yourself to be above them," he snarled back.

The fae with the wounded face ran at him with an upraised sword and from beneath the straw, an army of iron nails stood upon their heads, points up, courtesy of one of Ranyon's charms. The faery's momentum carried him forward two steps too far... Cursing as the poison metal penetrated both his boots and his feet, he hurled his sword. The copper blade buried itself to the hilt in a bale next to Rhys's head—but not before Rhys's thrown dagger caught the fae full in the throat.

Daeria screamed in rage at the loss of another of her soldiers, and Tyne was swift to throw one of his many knives. Rhys's instincts sent him diving to the left barely in time. The move saved his heart from the dagger's point, but not his shoulder.

The blade pierced it through and lodged solidly in the bone. He yanked it out before it could spill its aggressive magic into his system, but it took a couple of tries and cost him precious seconds. Just enough time for Daeria to fly across the space and seize him by the throat. His sword tumbled to the floor as his head spun, as skin and bone and tendon suddenly tore away from their moorings and distorted...

TWENTY-THREE

⟨⟩

Despite the strangeness of the night and the terrifying proximity of the Wild Hunt, Fred neither barked nor whined. Alert and watchful, the great dog stuck to Morgan's side as if he were a presidential bodyguard. Perhaps she should get him some dark glasses too so he could look the part...

She led her canine companion to the small side door of the hired man's quarters and slipped inside. There was less of the blindingly white light here, meaning that its source was in the stable area. She clutched Fred's collar for balance and crossed the little apartment in a low crouching walk, made more difficult by all the metal she was carrying. Partway there, she stopped and slung her vest over Fred's broad back, hoping he wouldn't mind being a pack mule for a while. Her own back was relieved without the weight of the iron bookends to carry.

Immediately she could hear Rhys's voice somewhere on the far side of the door. She could hear other voices too, but there was something odd about them, a crystalline quality, like broken glass beneath the rippling surface of a stream. The unnatural sound sent a shiver through her.

Taking a deep breath, she sat with her back to the wall and reached over and turned the doorknob slowly, slowly, until the latch was free of the strike plate. She allowed the door to fall open a crack. Brilliant light blazed through the slender opening immediately. Her eyes could no more adjust to it than they could adjust to staring directly at the sun. She patted the upper pockets of the vest and thanked all the stars that her sunglasses were in one. Donning them with relief, she waited until she was sure the strange voices she heard weren't immediately near the door. The entrance into the stable led first into the half-walled section where the feed and grain was kept. Praying that no one was looking squarely in her direction, she made her way through the door on her hands and knees. It was harder than she thought it would be—she still had a skillet and a poker to carry. Fred padded patiently behind her, apparently unaffected by the weight he carried and looking as if he wore quilted red vests every day of his life. She pulled the door to, so it would appear closed to any casual observers, then continued her awkward way over to that half wall that separated her from the open stable.

Morgan edged along until she found a vantage point—a place where a large knot in the rough wood had split and fallen away. Here she could see and still remain hidden. But she was not prepared for what she saw and clapped her hands over her mouth to keep from making a sound.

The light was coming directly from *them*—three tall, slender beings who were arguing with Rhys. They were breathtaking to look at, with fine, pale features and iridescent eyes that were blue one moment, then green, then violet. Shimmering white hair flowed over their shoulders, and their clothes were exquisitely made. There was no question who they were.

The Fair Ones.

Omigod.

As she watched, the sword-wielding fae fell to the floor. The unearthly shriek of the female fae was as sharp and violent as a flood bursting through plate glass windows. It hurt Morgan's ears but wasn't nearly as horrifying as the sight of a faery dagger appearing in Rhys's shoulder.

As the female lunged for the wounded warrior, Morgan was over the wall. The male fae had glinting copper daggers in each shining white hand, ready to attack again if need be. Anger surged through Morgan's system, coupled with stark fear for Rhys. Silently, she ran up behind the tall male and swung the iron skillet with all her strength. It smashed him in the back of the head and he fell to his knees. She drew the heavy pan back like a baseball bat, ready for another swing, but the luminous being swayed and fell forward onto his face. Morgan didn't know if he was unconscious or dead—she'd never hit anyone before, much less a fae—and the surprise made her hesitate for a split second.

Fred didn't hesitate, however. He leapt onto her back, knocking her flat just as a pair of copper daggers struck the stable door above them. The dog's momentum sent the red vest sliding off with a heavy clunk. Morgan jumped up into a crouch with one of the bookends cradled in her hand like a shot put. It was another middle school event in which she'd never excelled, but fury and adrenaline were giving her a massive boost—and the mocking fae was less than twenty feet away. The otherworldly creature was looking right at her, however, and Morgan automatically felt at her throat. Ranyon's charm was gone, twine and all. It had probably fallen off after she crossed the yard. *Great, just great.*

"You're far too late, useless mortal," laughed the fae. "I've already changed him."

The writhing form at the faery's feet slowly blackened with an eruption of glossy fur even as his limbs flailed and altered before

Morgan's eyes. "No!" she screamed and threw the kitten-shaped bookend with all her strength. Her aim was true enough—but the female simply sidestepped it, and the iron thudded dully to the floor alongside the black shape that lay upon the wooden floor. The dog's sides heaved hard as if from immense exertion, but otherwise, the massive canine didn't move. His familiar golden eyes were open but unfocused.

"He's mine now." The fae shoved at the mastiff with a finely made boot.

Not even in your dreams, you bitch. Morgan could barely keep her hands from forming fists, and she fought to keep her rage and horror from her expression. *Think, damn it, think. What would Nainie tell me to do?* Every faery story she had ever read or heard indicated that she had to step carefully with these powerful beings. However, Nainie had said there were a few things that the Tylwyth Teg respected, and one of them was mortal generosity. Morgan hoped like hell it was true…

"Well fought, my lady. Your cleverness is exceeded only by your beauty," said Morgan, bowing slightly, her words deliberately courteous and deferential although she felt neither. She'd rather be pulling every glossy white hair from that creature's skull than waste time being polite. "This man belongs to me, but perhaps I could make you a gift of something else. Please come inside, and we'll discuss it over tea. You've had such a long journey. Allow me to offer you hospitality."

The fae's glittering smile turned hesitant, a mixture of curiosity and confusion behind it. "You would invite me into your home?" she asked.

A small figure suddenly dropped from the loft in a shower of straw. "They're not deserving of hospitality," Ranyon shouted. "The Tylwyth Teg don't understand kindness or courtesy or even decency."

The fae sniffed. "What would an ugly little ellyll know of such lofty things?"

"There was a time when the Wild Hunt would mete out justice upon the greedy, the slothful, and the heartless," continued Ranyon, standing beside Morgan and pointing a twiggy finger at the fae. His Blue Jays cap had a cocky tilt to it, as if it too defied the Fair Ones. "And now you're naught but bullies."

Morgan made a subtle shushing motion with her hand at Rhys's eye level. "My offer stands," she said to the fae. "It's the least I can do. This rough stable is not a fit place for the Fair Ones. My house is humble, but it is clean, and you are welcome within its walls."

"There is still a matter of balance, of payment and satisfaction," declared the female, and her otherworldly gaze sharpened on Morgan. "Surely, you are not disputing my right to this man?" The fae snapped a length of silvery rope from a hidden pocket and dropped it on the black furry heap beside her. Of its own accord, the rope slid around the neck of the inert black mastiff and dragged him to his feet. The enormous dog shook off his grogginess and erupted into blood-chilling snarls, baring his long fangs and lunging at his luminous captor. She didn't move an inch. A cruel smile quirked her perfect lips as the silver rope yanked the animal back and forced him up on his hind legs, up and up, until the snarling jaws were level with her flawless face— yet neither teeth nor claws could reach her. "I think he looks better like this," remarked the fae. "Don't you?"

Morgan's heart squeezed hard enough to hurt as her eyes witnessed what her heart had finally been willing to believe. Rhys had indeed been Rhyswr, the dog who saved her life and whose disappearance she had mourned. The knowledge did her little good now, however. All of them were in imminent danger, and she had to choose her words carefully. "I desire to show respect to the Tylwyth Teg, yet as a healer, I cannot violate my sacred oath to protect mortal life, be it animal or human. Therefore, I cannot allow this man to be taken. In his place, I offer any and all of my belongings freely. My truck, my house, my farm…whatever possession you want."

"No!" Ranyon stood squarely in front of Morgan. "Have the Tylwyth Teg grown so poor that they must need rob mortals? Are ya thieves now as well as tyrants?"

"Shut up, Ranyon!" she whispered through clenched teeth. To offend the Fair Ones could get both of them changed into dogs, or worse. *Far worse*, if Nainie's stories were any indication. Morgan studied the shining being before her, unable to discern her mood. Was she truly angry or just enjoying the drama? Nainie had once said the Tylwyth Teg suffered from eternal boredom, and mortals were one of their few sources of entertainment.

"What need have we of your silly possessions?" The fae gave a dismissive wave. "Your little house? Your tiny piece of land? Shall we leave the splendor of our kingdom beneath the hills to till the soil above it?"

"It is all I have to offer," said Morgan, and bowed again for good measure.

The female laughed, a cold slurry of crystal shards in arctic waters. "My dear foolish mortal, there are much better things to barter with. What will you give up for this man? Your beauty perhaps? Your youth?"

In a move too fast to follow, Ranyon leapt astride Fred and charged the fae with Morgan's poker in his hands like a lance. His target leapt aside, laughing, but the sound was abruptly cut short. The ellyll must have worked some magic upon the iron tool because it had sliced open the female's upper thigh as he passed. Glistening droplets of pale-blue blood flew as the fae threw out her hand toward Ranyon. The hapless ellyll was hurled from Fred's back and slammed against a wall with such force that the thick wooden planks cracked from the impact of the tiny body. He slid to the floor in a boneless heap, and Morgan was certain he was dead. Rhys, still bound by the silver rope to an upright position that strained his canine form, howled long and loud.

Damn it. She held the tears inside—it wasn't the time for them. Nothing was working, and the situation didn't seem to be following any of the stories. Now she was facing a truly pissed-off fae, alone, with no idea of what to do. She could see the female's smirk of triumph, knew the creature believed she had won. Morgan tried to keep her own face impassive even as her thoughts whirled frantically. She rested a shaking hand on Fred's broad head, grateful he had returned to sit in front of her. Grateful he'd been *able* to do so, unlike Rhys or poor Ranyon. How long would it be before the fae tired of playing and simply destroyed them all with a flick of her elegant fingers?

What would Nainie do? Morgan grasped the pendant through the material of her shirt for comfort—and suddenly she knew she had one more card to play.

"I would offer a gift to Queen Gwenhidw," she declared loudly, hoping not only that the faery queen of Nainie's stories was still on the throne, but that she was pronouncing the name right.

The female snorted. "What dirty little trinket could she *possibly* want from you?"

"In exchange for Rhys's freedom, for a promise that the Tylwyth Teg will consider all debts satisfied, I would give the queen *this*."

Morgan drew the pendant from its hiding place. She kept the long chain around her neck, but held the carved stone medallion up in front of her. In the living light of the fae, it began to glow. In moments, its fiery blue light had eclipsed hers utterly.

"The Sigil!" hissed the female as she slowly sank to her knees, her gaze riveted on the medallion. The mocking smile had completely disappeared from her beautiful face. The silver rope she had used to bind the black dog slackened, and the great creature shook itself free. For a split second, Morgan thought he was going to savage his adversary, but instead, he bounded over to Morgan and planted himself squarely in front of her, alongside Fred.

"I see you recognize this," said Morgan, pretending she knew what the hell it was, although she hadn't the faintest notion.

A gasp came from her left, and she saw that the fae she had hit with the skillet had half risen from the straw. He too was staring at the medallion as if hypnotized by it. "Good lady, the Sigil has been lost to the royal house for many mortal lifetimes." His voice was weak but full of wonder. "It is the symbol of their power, the seal of the realm itself. How came you by it?"

"It has been guarded by my family for generations. My grandmother gave it into my keeping."

"It has been *stolen* by your family!" The female pointed a long delicate finger at Morgan, and her words fairly dripped with venom. "It is obvious now that your ancestor used her friendship with the queen in order to rob us of our greatest treasure! You have brought certain death upon yourself and a curse upon—"

"I think not."

The new voice startled them all. Morgan glanced around until she spotted a pulsing bead of silver light hovering in midair. The light grew rapidly until a glittering being appeared in the midst of it. Both of the faeries quickly pressed their faces to the floor.

Instinctively, Morgan knelt too. "Your Majesty," she breathed. She had thought the faeries beautiful, but their appearance did not compare with the unearthly splendor of the queen of the Tylwyth Teg. Her flowing robes were both iridescent and luminous. They changed color so rapidly that to human sight, they were all colors at once. It was her face, however, framed by intricate braids and loops of silvery hair, which captured the eye and held it. It might have been made of exquisite porcelain, lit from within. She glowed, and her exotic eyes were unexpectedly kind as they turned to the mortal kneeling in the stable.

"How lovely to meet a descendant of my dear friend Aylwen. We used to have such fun together. I am very pleased that you have taken good care of the Sigil, Morgan Edwards. I had given it to Aylwen for safekeeping."

"Why would you give something so important to a human?" Morgan blurted.

The queen laughed prettily, with surprising warmth. "You are as curious as she was. There was an intrigue designed to usurp the throne. Had the traitors gained the Sigil, they might have succeeded. Aylwen smuggled it out of the kingdom for me, and while many searched for the Sigil, none of the fae suspected it might be in mortal hands. Your family has performed a valuable service to me, and I am in your debt."

There was a gasp from the female, who was still pressing her forehead to the floor. Queen Gwenhidw didn't spare her a glance although her mouth quirked. "Yes, Daeria, you heard correctly. I am indebted to a mortal."

"But she is *nothing*!" hissed the fae, glancing up. "Humans are beneath us."

The royal smile disappeared. "In that, you are quite wrong. You defy me, as always, Daeria, and worse, you now defy our laws. You have summoned the Wild Hunt and taken them outside of our dominion, upsetting the balance between realms and causing chaos among innocents. Since you favor the Hunt so much, I decree that you shall join it."

A look of horror crossed Daeria's face. She tried to speak, but her words were choked off as her body began to writhe and spasm, as limbs reshaped and reformed. In a matter of seconds, the beautiful fae's perfect features were gone, and a lean white hound stood where she had been.

From outside, a mournful horn sounded, as long and low as a winter wolf's howl. The thunder and lightning ceased and the wind fell away until all was still and silent.

"The Hunt returns to its rightful place," said the queen. "And *your* place henceforth is wherever it goes." The white dog fled the barn as if pursued by demons. Queen Gwenhidw turned her gaze to the other faery, who visibly trembled, without looking up from his prostrate position. "I see that you yet respect my authority, Tyne. To date, you have chosen your companions poorly, but perhaps without Daeria's influence, you could learn to do better. I will have more to say to you later. For now, take the bodies of the fallen back to our realm, and do not return to this place again."

"As you command," he said and vanished. The dead fae disappeared as well.

Morgan removed the necklace at once and held it out to the queen. "I'm sorry. I didn't know this belonged to you. I had only known it as my grandmother's necklace."

Instead of taking it, the queen grasped Morgan's hand and drew her to her feet. Rhys immediately placed his canine body in front of Morgan protectively, his eyes wary and watchful. Fred was at the ready as well.

"I will take the Sigil after accounts are balanced," said the queen. "What may I give you in return, Morgan Edwards?"

"Rhys's freedom."

"This is all you ask?"

Morgan nodded, hoping against hope that the queen would agree. The faery ruler appeared benevolent, but appearances could be deceiving, particularly when dealing with the Tylwyth Teg. And Morgan had no doubt that this being was far more dangerous than those who had threatened her earlier and the entire Wild Hunt combined.

"I could fill this building with wealth until gold and silver poured from the loft overhead. All for you. You could be famous on every continent, beautiful and sought after until the end of an extended life."

"Thanks, but Rhys is worth far more to me."

Queen Gwenhidw smiled. "True love always is. You shall have what you seek."

The monarch placed a hand on Fred's head and scratched his ears. "You're a handsome fellow, but I think Morgan has already made you happier than anything I can do for you." Her hand then rested on Rhys's broad black head.

"We have not treated you well, have we?" the queen asked Rhys. "I cannot change that, but I can release you."

In an instant, the black dog was gone, and Rhys stood, tall and strong, in its place. The wound in his shoulder had vanished as well.

"Thank you, your Majesty," said Morgan and bowed. Rhys inclined his head slightly as well but said nothing.

"You have no thanks for me?" asked Queen Gwenhidw.

"Two millennia of service seems gratitude enough," he replied.

Morgan was horrified, but the queen simply laughed. "Well said, and so it is."

The ruler put out her hand—the long, slender fingers were adorned with many rings that chimed together—and Morgan placed the necklace in it. There was a pang in her heart as she did so. It was still Nainie's necklace to her, but her grandmother would no doubt have approved of the transaction.

TWENTY-FOUR

～⁊Ｍ🙞

The necklace vanished from the queen's palm and reappeared around her willowy neck. Every jewel glowed vibrantly in its silver setting, and the medallion shone as brightly as Queen Gwenhidw herself. "No one from our realm will trouble either of you again," she said. "And I will do my utmost to set to rights all that has been disrupted by Daeria. However, I will reserve the right to send gifts to you whenever I please, in remembrance of Aylwen. I have missed her sorely these long years."

The monarch still smiled, but there was wistfulness behind it. "You look so very much like her, my dear Morgan. I felt your presence the moment you set foot on our island soil, and I so hope you will forgive my little deception during your stay. It was a great pleasure to pretend I was with Aylwen again, and a comfort to my heart."

For a moment, Morgan saw not the queen's face but that of the older woman who had been her delightful traveling companion in Wales. Her mouth fell open. "Gwen? Omigosh, it was *you* all along!" No wonder Morgan had been unable to contact her after the trip. "I missed you. I tried and tried to phone. I—we— well, we just *have* to do a road trip together the next time I'm in Wales."

"I shall look forward to it, my dear." The queen gave a long, slow wink and a girlish grin, then assumed her own perfect features before vanishing completely.

Darkness rushed back into the stable as if it had been a tide held back, and Rhys held Morgan tightly. She clung in return, until she could stop the sudden shaking that had overtaken her. "I'm sorry," she stammered. "I don't know what's wrong with me!"

"It happens to some after battle. You've nothing to be sorry about. You were brave as a lioness and clever as well." He put a finger under her chin, tipped her face up, and kissed her tenderly. "I'd sworn to protect you. But I think 'twas you who did most of the protecting tonight. You've freed me twice: first from the collar and now from the Fair Ones themselves."

"But we lost Ranyon," she said. "He took on Daeria all by himself."

Rhys rested his forehead on hers. "He was a brave friend and a wise one. I'll not relish telling Leo what became of him."

"You'll not be telling Leo anything of the sort," came an indignant voice from behind them. "And I'll thank ya not to bury me afore I'm dead!"

Morgan felt her way to the wall switches and flipped on the overhead fixtures. After all the light that had bathed the barn's interior in the last hour, it was as if she'd struck a match, not turned on a pair of one-hundred-watt bulbs. She blinked in the yellowed light that seemed both bright and dim at the same time, and persuaded her eyes to focus just as the ellyll emerged from one of the stalls.

Morgan and Rhys rushed over to him. Miraculously, he seemed none the worse for wear, but he was much more concerned with the state of his prized Blue Jays cap than with answering their questions. Several shards of wood impaled the bright logo. The bill was cracked and half torn from the crown. He cradled the sorry remains in his twiggy hands, shaking his head over it.

"We'll get you another hat," said Morgan, patting the ellyll gently on the shoulder as much to reassure herself that he was all right as to comfort him. *Gwenhidw must have healed him.* She glanced over at the wall, the cracked and broken planks marking where Ranyon had impacted it, and shuddered. There was no other explanation for the ellyll's condition. By rights, his little body should have looked far worse than the hat.

The ellyll sniffed loudly. "That's kind of ya, good lady, but this is the one that dear Leo gave me."

"Then we'll give it a place of honor," she said softly.

"Morgan! Come over here!" Rhys was in Lucy's stall, and Morgan's heart sank. She would never forget the terrifying sight of the Wild Hunt amid the unnatural storm. If Lucy had been forced to run with it, what condition was she in now?

Morgan leaned in to look where Rhys was pointing, her heart in her throat. And then her knees gave way, and she was sitting in the straw, staring.

There was nothing wrong with the horse. Nothing at all.

Rhys brought her the big flashlight from the toolbox on the wall, and she examined the horse's legs closely, running her hands over what used to be dozens of ghastly, deep gashes held together only by her own sutures. Instead, there was nothing but silvery gray hair over smooth, unbroken skin.

"Gwenhidw did this," said Morgan in awe. "That's—" She nearly jumped out of her skin as her long-forgotten cell phone rang in her front jeans pocket. Fishing it out hurriedly, she thumbed it open, and two things struck her at once. One, that it was barely 5:30 in the morning. And two, it was Jay. Hoping it was a clinic emergency and not worse news, she put the phone to her ear as Rhys put his hands on her shoulders.

"Good morning," said Jay.

"Don't *good morning* me—is Leo okay?"

"Better than okay. Walking around, visiting with his kids, and complaining about the food." There was a pause. "He wants to know if—never mind, just put Ranyon or Rhys on the phone. He won't be happy till he talks to one of them in person."

Morgan grinned and handed the phone to Ranyon. She wasn't sure he could hold it, but his twiggy fingers were far more flexible than they looked. In fact, the ellyll settled himself on the grain bin as if getting comfortable for a lengthy conversation.

"Leo's all right," she said to Rhys.

"By all the gods, the queen has indeed set things to rights." The mare stamped impatiently and whickered. "And now Lucy wants to try out her legs." Rhys led the horse to the yard with Morgan and Fred at his side.

The couple stood with arms around each other watching the great horse prance and trot, buck and caper, as the big dog ran playfully beside her. The moonlight turned the mare's dapple-gray coat to silver, and for a moment, Morgan thought Lucy looked like a faery horse. Perhaps she was.

Rhys took a deep breath and released it. "I'll not be looking over my shoulder for the fae anymore. 'Tis a good feeling. A very good feeling." He nuzzled Morgan's hair, his deep voice rumbling pleasantly in her ear. "I've a mind to sample you here under the stars."

"I've a mind to let you. But Lludd of the Silver Hand is watching and so is his dog." She pointed up at the sky and grinned.

"I'm certain they would approve."

"And *our* dog and our horse and our friend are here as well."

"I'm certain they would also approve."

"Probably, but let's go see Leo first."

Rhys kissed the back of her neck, making her shiver and her breasts tighten. "Aye, well, we can tell him our news then," he said.

"That we defeated the fae?"

"That we're going to marry."

Morgan's mouth fell open. "What? When did we decide this?"

"I decided it a long time ago. And you decided it when you left the safety of the house to face down the Wild Hunt and return to the barn, my brave anwylyd."

"It seemed like a good idea at the time?"

"'Twas not a sensible idea. You could have been killed."

"Maybe, but someone once told me that 'instinct often reveals the greater truth.' My instincts told me to do it, that we belonged together, no matter what."

"Aye, and that's why we're marrying."

Morgan opened her mouth and closed it again. The man had a point. So she acted on instinct again and simply kissed him with everything she had.

∾

THE END

Read on for a sneak peek of
Storm Bound

CHAPTER ONE

~⁊⁊~

Black Mountains, Wales
AD 1124

Heavy muscles bulged as the tall man strained repeatedly against the fine silver chains that bound him, wrist and ankle, to the stone.

"Such an ungrateful mortal you are, Aidan ap Llanfor," she chided. "Is it not an honor to be a guest of the *Tylwyth Teg*?"

He lunged at her, but though she stood within an arm's length of him, she neither recoiled nor shrank. Aidan's chains had been forged with faery magic, and as such they would not break, not even for the largest *bwgan*, much less a human. The man's iron-gray eyes, however—were they daggers, she thought, she would be pierced and her sapphire blood would be poisoned and pooling around her delicate silk slippers.

For the briefest of moments, she felt something, and thrilled to it, eager for more. But Aidan immediately stilled, bridling his anger and reining it back as if he could sense her craving for emotion—any emotion—and refused to give it to her.

"I have not sought to visit your land," he gritted out between his teeth. "Nor have I trespassed upon it. I have given thee no cause to bring me here against my will."

"Are you so certain of that? I seem to remember a bold and comely child playing on the faery mound beyond the village. Such a dear little wooden sword he had, hacking at bushes and slicing at trees as if they were dreadful monsters." It was satisfying that she'd succeeded in surprising him, yet puzzling to her. How was it that mortals remembered so little when their lives were so short? Years had passed for him, but for her? It was scarcely a day ago that Aidan had traded his wooden sword for the business of adults. Mere hours since he'd apprenticed to the village blacksmith. Moments since he inherited the forge and took over the business. She had observed it all, fascinated, in the way that a cat is fascinated by a bird.

"I could have spirited you away that first time," she continued, "Simply for setting foot on fae territory. But it was much more fun to watch you. You played often at the mound, though you saw me not. I was witness to not one but *many* trespasses, Aidan ap Llanfor. You've lived your life thus far in your tiny mortal world only because I permitted it."

"A child is not held accountable for things he knows not of."

"Human rules," she sniffed. "Why do you waste so much time making them when you have such fleeting lives? You're like the mayflies that dance above the water for less than a day. The Tylwyth Teg are ancient beyond your ability to count and our laws are ancient too—made once, to stand for all time. And by those laws, you are mine to do with as I like."

"Release me, Faery," he said in a dangerous tone. It was not a request.

"Think you to make demands?" She laughed and shook back her waist-length hair, well aware of her unearthly beauty and its near-hypnotic effects on most mortals. "Know to whom you speak. I am Celynnen of the Thorn House of the Tylwyth Teg, and my blood is pure."

"You are a *tywysoges* then, a princess of the Fair Ones." He gave her the slightest of nods, a scant acknowledgement of her station—and not one mote of reverence more.

Others had died for less, and Celynnen could have killed him herself if she'd been so inclined. Still, for the sake of the entertainment he afforded her, she could forgive him much—for a time. She had often watched him hammer hot metals into clever shapes, particularly that most fearful of all elements, iron. Years of striking sparks amid the glow of flames had not bent his tall frame, only added strength. Even clad in his dull-brown tunic and scarred leather apron, his face streaked with soot and sweat, she had to admit that the comely child had grown into a very attractive man. Her people often took human lovers, and she had begun to consider the delicious possibilities—

Until this morning, when Aiden had not gone to his forge as usual. He had not donned blacksmith's clothing either. Instead, he had bathed at length and dressed in what passed for finery among these common mortals. His blue woolen tunic was open at the neck to reveal a pale linen *pais* beneath. His dark cloak was newly made and clasped with an artful brooch of silver and amber that she had not seen before. It was a gift that a woman would give, a human woman.

Annwyl.

The raven-haired Annwyl of the village of Aberhonddu was the woman that Aidan ap Llanfor planned to marry. Today. And that's when Celynnen made her decision to spirit him away to the kingdom far below the Black Mountains.

"Release me, *Your Grace*," he said.

The significance of the royal title was not lost on her. It was hardly filled with admiration and awe, but it *was* devoid of sarcasm. This was not a man who would beg, ever—but she had just won a major concession from him. *What else can I win?* The thought of such a challenge excited her. She would enjoy playing games with Aidan ap Llanfor just as much as lying with him, perhaps even more. "Nay, I believe I will keep you."

"Do not do this, *Your Eminence*. For the sake of my bride that I will wed this day, for the sake of the promises I have made to her and her family. Make me not an oathbreaker, for ye yourselves do despise such."

It was an eloquent argument. Once given, the word of any of the Tylwyth Teg was unbreakable. In fact, humans who did not keep their promises to each other often suffered justice at the hands of the fae. Celynnen brushed her fingers over the brilliant scarlet of her dress and traced the birds and flowers embroidered there in silver thread and seed pearls. "A man of his word *is* a rare commodity, so it seems fitting that such be rewarded. You may put your mind at ease on that point. No oath will be broken."

From her sleeve, she drew a solid cluster of brilliant yellow-green crystals—mortals would call it peridot—and cupped it in her hand, where the stone's many facets gleamed and flashed. Bringing it close to her lips, she whispered the words of the ancient language, then blew gently over it. A wisp of pale-green light, like an emerald spirit, spiraled from the crystals and floated toward Aidan.

He drew back, suspicious but unable to avoid the approaching wraith. "What are you doing?" He jerked as it touched him and enveloped his entire body in a caul of green light.

"I have simply granted you what you wanted." The green light flared suddenly, then disappeared, and she turned toward the high-arched doorway. "I must make an appearance at the court for a time."

"Wait," he called. "Release me! My wedding—Anwyll will be waiting for me!" He rattled the fine silver chains until they pealed like tiny silver bells.

Celynnen turned and arched a delicate eyebrow. "You did not wish to be an oathbreaker, and so you will not be. Your intended is *not* waiting for you."

The look of horror on his face was immediately eclipsed by rage. "What have you done to her?" he roared, straining so mightily against his bonds that for a brief instant she thought they might actually give way. Instead, blood ran down his wrists and spattered on the floor around him. A droplet struck her hand and she backed out of range, blotting the spot away hastily with her sleeve as it began to burn her skin. Human blood got its curious red color from the iron it contained—and iron was deadly poison to all fae creatures, including the Tylwyth Teg.

The precious fabric failed to clean the spot well enough, however. Her hand *hurt*, and pain was not something she was acquainted with. She snapped at him. "You foolish mortal. Did you think I was going to *let you go*? You were concerned for your honor, and I have graciously protected it. Even more merciful, your precious Annwyl will suffer no broken heart over you because *she does not remember you*. Her family does not know who you are, and in fact, even your own family will not recall they ever had a son.

"In short, you have ceased to exist outside of this kingdom. You. Are. Mine."

On that note she swept from the room to find a healer before the tiny mark upon her hand became an abhorrent scar. Halfway down the vast hallway, the last thing she heard from Aidan was a full-fledged snarl: *"I'll not be your pet!"*

A laugh burst from her lips then. "Oh, I think you will."

Here ends Chapter One of *Storm Bound.*

ACKNOWLEDGMENTS

What would I do without my fearless team of beta readers? These are the people who let me know if the story's continuity has run off the rails or that I've run afoul of Canadian versus American phraseology again—and thank goodness, they're sworn to secrecy! My betas are also the ones who talk me off the ledge when I'm discouraged, hand me fresh coffee, and tell me to keep writing. On this particular project, a very special thank-you goes out to Ron Silvester, Samantha Craig, and Sharon Stogner.

I'd also like to express my appreciation to my agent, Stephany Evans of FinePrint Literary Management (who talks me off the ledge when my beta readers are busy), and to my new editor, Eleni Caminis of Montlake Romance, plus the entire Montlake and Amazon team. I feel very fortunate to work with such enthusiastic and talented people.

Most of all, I'd like to thank my readers. You are the reason I write. There is nothing like that moment of connection when the story becomes a cocreation between us. I might pen the words, but my story doesn't LIVE until it is read. I thank you for this shared joy.

ABOUT THE AUTHOR

Dani Harper is a former newspaper editor whose passion for all things supernatural led her to a second career writing paranormal fiction. A longtime resident of the Canadian north and southeastern Alaska, Dani recently ventured south with her husband to rural Washington to be closer to their grown children. She is also the author of *Changeling Moon*, *Changeling Dream*, and *Changeling Dawn*.